PRAISE FOR
The Thing with Feathers

"Filled with poignancy, sparkling wit, and Southern charm, *The Thing with Feathers* made my heart absolutely soar! It's everything I love in a YA contemporary."

"The inspiring story of one girl's struggle not to be defined by her illness, *The Thing with Feathers* soars as it explores what it means to live—and love—without fear,"

"Heartfelt and affecting. Hoyle tells a familiar story, but does so in a voice that is rarely heard, and that makes all the difference."

"Epilepsy is a quiet but serious disorder that needs more awareness, and I'm so very excited to see that McCall Hoyle is bringing it to the YA community in this stunning debut. *The Thing with Feathers* is a gorgeous, hope-filled novel!"

"A refreshing, quality debut—meaningfully woven and beautifully engaging, from the first page to the last."

"*The Thing with Feathers* is a story of hope and acceptance. Emilie's struggle will remind us all of the courage it takes to show the world who we are—flaws included."

"Poetic and raw, *The Thing with Feathers* portrays the reality for many teens with epilepsy. But more importantly, Emilie's story articulates the desire we all have to be known and loved just as we are."

"Very highly recommended for personal reading lists, *The Thing with Feathers* will prove to be an ideal and enduringly popular addition to school and community YA fiction collections."

"A heart-warming debut that will leave readers filled with hope."

"AMAZING. The writing is so good, the characters are real and relatable, and the story is sweet and swoony and everything you want in a YA romance."

The thing
with feathers

The thing with feathers

McCALL HOYLE

BLINK

*To girls past, present, and future—especially
Frances McCall Haynsworth, Emilie Beattie
Hildebrand, and Emilie Beattie Hoyle.*

I'm Nobody! Who are you?

EMILY DICKINSON

My mother lost her mind today, and I'm going to prison.

Some people call it North Ridge High School, but believe me: it's this girl's worst punishment. I drive past it every week on the way home from my counselor's office. Sparkly girls with sun-kissed cheeks spill out its front doors. Boys with shaggy haircuts surround them, toting lacrosse sticks, backpacks, and the occasional band instrument. They look comfortable in their skin, like they walked off the cover of *Seventeen* or like they're ready to burst into a peppy musical number at a moment's notice.

"Emilie." My mother's voice interrupts my thoughts, and I jump, cracking my knuckles on the passenger-side window. Shaking off the pain in my hand, I glance over at her in the driver's seat without speaking. Her white fists clench the steering wheel. A muscle twitches in her jaw. Good. She's on edge. She should be. She and Dr. Wellesley are ruining my life.

"Honey, please try to keep an open mind." She studies my face. "Public school won't be that bad."

"The light's green." I point to the stoplight swaying in the breeze. Someone behind us honks, and we lurch forward. I've lived in Crystal Cove on the coast of North Carolina for sixteen years, and I'm still not used to sharing my home with tourists like the one behind us in the expensive convertible. Apparently, neither is my mother.

Mom readjusts her death grip, exhaling through gritted teeth. "And stop biting your fingernails. They look awful."

Like I care about appearances when my life is crumbling around me. I chew another hangnail, wincing when a drop of blood forms at the cuticle. When Hitch paws at my seat, I unbuckle and crawl into the backseat with him. His tail swishes the sandy floor mat.

"You're going to cause an accident," Mom snaps.

Biting my tongue, I run a hand through the thick fur behind Hitch's right ear. My shoulders relax a tiny bit. When he rests his blocky head on my thigh and flashes his toothy golden retriever grin, a smile tugs at the corner of my mouth.

"Dr. Wellesley has your best interests at heart. He doesn't think homeschooling is meeting your social and emotional needs." She sounds like a recording, repeating word for word what my therapist said less than an hour ago.

"I don't care what he thinks." I enunciate each word, careful not to let the emotions rising in my throat escape my mouth. I don't mean to be difficult. Really. It's just sometimes I feel like I'm about to explode. And with no dad, no siblings, no real friends, there's no one else to explode on.

Hitch raises concerned eyes to my face while I rub tiny circles on his floppy ear. "I'm not going to North Ridge next Monday." My voice cracks on the last word. So much for sounding tough.

"Yes, you are." Mom pauses—the scary pause, reserved for when she's reached emotional meltdown. Now she'll either cry to make me feel guilty or switch to her serious-mom voice to pressure me into doing whatever she wants.

"Emilie, please. I only want what's best for you." Her eyes glisten in the rearview mirror.

Here we go. All aboard for a ride on the guilt train.

Seventy-two hours' worth of crying, bargaining, and promising I'll go to Harvard accomplish almost nothing. All I can do is convince Mom to send me to school on a trial basis—three months and then we'll reevaluate. In three months she'll probably just force me to go back, so it's not exactly a win. But it's a speck of light at the end of the tunnel. I'll endure ninety days without forming attachments and prove to her that my social and emotional needs are just fine. At least that's what I'm telling myself.

We're back in the Honda this morning, heading south on the beach road. I study the teetering cottages to my left. Their lives are like mine. They've survived countless hurricanes, but no one knows if they'll survive the next big storm. They could make it another hundred years, hunched like gnomes on the dunes with nothing to protect them but sea oats, or the next big wind gust could wash them into oblivion.

But unlike the cedar-sided shacks, I've got a mom to protect me. A mom who cares a little too much about my well-being sometimes. A mom who's sending me to school today for my own good. No matter what.

"It's going to be all right." She nods and tucks a wisp of hair

11

behind her ear with a shaky hand. "And we agreed to give it three months."

Easy for her to say. She's not the one with epilepsy. She's not the one with grand mal seizures. She's not the one at risk of convulsing in front of a bunch of strangers, of puking all over herself with her eyes rolled back in her head . . . or worse. For me, three months might as well be a lifetime sentence in Alcatraz.

I don't answer. She squeezes my arm as I stare out the passenger window.

Less than twenty minutes later, she hugs me and abandons me in the guidance office. I'm like half of Hansel and Gretel, except I forgot to drop the breadcrumbs and there's no way out. The hum of air from the ceiling vent is the only distraction in the dimly lit room as I wait for the secretary to return with a student ambassador to show me around the building.

As I pick at the cuticle on my index finger, the door bangs open. A boy with blue eyes and dimples barges in.

"You must be Emilie." He scoops my backpack off the floor, slinging it over his shoulder as he offers me his hand. "Chatham York, at your service."

His eyes and T-shirt match the color of the Atlantic Ocean on a cloudless day. He's tall—really tall. I'm eye level with his chest and a shirt that reads *Keep Calm. We've got this.* It's pretty much the exact opposite of what I feel.

"So what brings you to the Ridge?" His hand brushes my arm as he reaches for the door.

"I, uh . . ." My voice trails off. I blink, reminding myself he's just a boy and I have bigger concerns today than melting into a puddle of goo at the feet of the first cute guy to cross my path.

He flashes me a bright smile that could be totally genuine

or totally practiced. I have no idea which. The counselors probably chose him to give tours specifically because of that smile. If this were one of my favorite movies, there'd be clues to his intentions in the sound effects or the lighting or the background music or something. Here, I'm on my own—a fish out of water with no clues to guide me.

"I was tired of homeschool," I say, because of course the first thing you should do when you meet a cute boy is lay a foundation of half-truths. I'm not about to tell Prince Charming that I'd gladly stay holed up in the safety of my own home for the rest of my life. That I'd rather hang out with my dog than my peers. That I'd rather be isolated than risk being humiliated.

He pushes open the door leading out to the rotunda. "Oh, man. I hear you." He pauses, waiting for me to walk out ahead of him. "My mom and I would kill each other. I don't see how people do that."

"It's not that bad." I force a smile, avoiding the eyes of two perky girls hanging a banner for a canned-food drive. They watch us as we head up the right hall. The place is eerily quiet, but in less than half an hour it will swarm with hundreds of kids.

I hand over my schedule when Chatham asks for it, praying he doesn't notice the moisture from my palm on the paper.

"Oh, cool." He points at the second block.

The adjective *cool* hasn't applied to anything in my life since my diagnosis.

I glance at the schedule clasped in his hand. He has nice hands. My stomach twists. The last real memory I have of my dad is holding his hand in the hospital before he died. Dad had good hands too—gentle but firm, with a few calluses to prove he wasn't afraid of hard work.

Hands tell a lot about a person.

"We have second period together." Chatham pauses, waiting for me to look up. "You'll like Ms. Ringgold. She's awesome."

"Yeah?" I force what I hope resembles a smile. This guy is nice. Too nice—not at all like the guys on the mean-girl movies I binge watch.

The few students and teachers we pass greet Chatham by name. As we walk up the first hall, a girl in a strapless dress that has to be breaking every dress code known to public education stops to greet him. She glances at my face, then down at my bland T-shirt and shorts, sizing me up.

"Maddie, this is Emilie. She's new," Chatham explains.

"Cool. Where did you move from?" Maddie asks, her attention drifting to Chatham before I've ever answered.

"Nowhere," I say to the side of her face.

Her head swivels in my direction. Now she seems intrigued. "Nowhere?"

"What I mean is, I've lived here all my life."

Her perfectly tweezed eyebrows lift in a question. I answer it. "I've been homeschooled for a while."

"Oh, that's . . . interesting," she says, clearly *losing* interest as she turns back to Chatham. I've been dismissed in a millisecond, which might be some kind of record. Obviously, I'm unworthy of her attention—not good enough to make friends and not threatening enough to be competition. Maybe the mean-girl movies were right after all. This place could be brutal.

She flips her hair, smiling up at Chatham. "Don't forget you promised to help me set up for the debate tomorrow."

"Got it." He smiles back. It's like he's the sun. He's this bright ball of light at the center of his own universe, and everyone's drawn to his energy. I just met him, but somehow I know that if I'm not careful, I'll be sucked into orbit too. As tempting as it feels right this second, I know better than to let it happen. If Chatham, or anyone else here, gets too close, they'll learn my secret, and I'd just as soon keep my skeleton locked securely in her closet.

Maddie's agenda settled, we head farther away from the counseling office. Chatham points out my second- and third-period classrooms, which are still dark. Then we double back to the next hall.

"Swimming's not on your schedule, but we have the best indoor pool in eastern North Carolina," he explains, pointing to two sets of double doors at the end of the hallway.

"Really?" I say, trying to sound casual. I want to run. Me and water don't mix.

"You've got to see it." He swings open one of the heavy metal doors, waits for me to pass, then points toward the pool. "I'd swim every day if I could."

I should keep my mouth shut, but I don't. "Why can't you?"

"It's complicated." His smile flickers. "I'm focusing on basketball. It's a time thing." He shakes his sandy-brown hair out of his eyes, his lips pushed together in what I think is supposed to be a smile.

A wave of chlorine fumes invades my nostrils, and I bite my lower lip. I know I'm supposed to be impressed by the high ceiling and the wall of glass spanning one end of the pool. But I can't focus with the humid air filling my lungs. I'm suffocating.

"Nice," I say, rubbing the back of my neck, trying to listen to what he's saying about the locker rooms to our right. When I glance in that direction, I spy the high-dive platform and shiver. In addition to my phobia of drowning, I have a pretty serious fear of heights.

He glances at his watch, stepping away from the pool. "The first bell's going to ring in a few minutes." He opens the heavy door, and we step back into the hallway. "We better hurry."

Cool, dry air brushes my cheek, and I remember to breathe as we move back toward the main hall, where he shows me the cafeteria and media center. The library is a bright spot on the tour, with floor-to-ceiling wood shelves and leather-like armchairs. It's not Starbucks, but someone's gone to a lot of trouble to give it that feel, and I'm thankful.

"What time does it open?" I ask, formulating a hideout plan for the time between drop-off and first bell.

"Seven thirty, I think." He leads me back to the counseling office where we started, pointing to my first-period class on the way. "So that's the grand tour." He pauses, handing me my backpack. "You know where you're headed, right?"

From what I've seen, the high school is easy to navigate. Four long hallways branch off at angles from the center of the building—one for English and history, one for science and math, one for elective classes, and the one I most hope to avoid that leads back to the gym, weight room, and pool.

"Yep, I think I've got it." I reach for my schedule. When our hands touch, I pull back and look away. "Thanks."

With a quick good-bye, I scurry toward the room marked on my sheet, thankful for a minute to myself. I'm pretty sure I won't be getting many of those around here.

First period is a blur. My math teacher butchers my name. I pretend to take notes for a few minutes until the intercom on the phone interrupts his droning voice. When he points at me, my cheeks heat up.

"You. Clinic." He hangs up, turning back to the equation on

his fancy Smart Board without further direction. I decide then and there that the man's got the personality of a cranky turnip.

I close my notebook, letting my dark side bangs fall over my face. Twenty-something sets of eyes bore into my back as I exit the room.

By the time the nurse finishes interrogating me about my meds and medical history, the bell is ringing for second period. I hurry toward Ms. Ringgold's class on the English hall, praying for a seat in the back of the room. I need a minute to decompress; I'm on sensory overload. Everything moves so fast around here. At home, it was math, coffee, pj's, and the occasional visit from the little girl next door who likes to play with Hitch when she's not at school. Here, herds of students stampede from one location to another on a strict schedule.

Steadying myself, I take a deep breath and cross the threshold with my pink binder clutched to my chest. When I step into the room, my world tilts on its axis. This classroom is nothing like the military-style math class I just left. Here, clumps of people stand around everywhere. Guys in skinny jeans talk to a girl with purple hair by the whiteboard. Two girls sit in the corner, their noses in books. A group of girls with the whitest teeth and straightest hair I've ever seen chatter in back, and Chatham sits off to the side, surrounded by laughing friends.

My heart races as I veer toward an empty seat near the teacher's desk.

I am clump-less. Alone.

And conflicted. I don't know whether to be ecstatic or devastated that no one seems to notice me.

CHAPTER TWO

I hide myself within my flower . . .

EMILY DICKINSON

I somehow survived round one at North Ridge yesterday. Today, Mom shoves me back in the ring for round two. We have a horrible meeting with the guidance counselor in the morning, but thankfully first period whizzes by in a blur of formulas and numbers. My math teacher gets my name right today and is a wee bit less turnip-y.

Chatham sits beside me in second period. I appreciate he's trying to be nice and make me feel welcome, but I hope he's not sitting beside me out of pity.

"Do you like North Ridge?" he asks just as the bell rings.

"Better than Shermer High School and Principal Rooney." I smile, trying to sound witty but having a hard time concentrating. My mind's still back in the counselor's office.

He studies my face a second, then grins. "Nice. *Ferris Bueller.* You know the classics."

I relax a little. This conversation seems safe enough. I can hold my own when it comes to all things movie related. I just don't want him—or anyone else—to start asking a lot of questions about me that might lead them to my disability.

I never really thought of myself as disabled. Sick, maybe, but not disabled. But when Mom and I met with the guidance counselor again this morning, he said something about scheduling a meeting to discuss my Individualized Education Plan. As if I don't have enough problems to deal with, apparently I'm also special ed.

It's just one more reason I'm furious Mom betrayed me and sent me here. She used to be on my side, until Dr. Wellesley started fussing about me being isolated and disconnected. He wasn't worried about homeschool so much as the fact I'm an only child and not involved in any activities or anything. I should have made more of an effort to get out of the house. I should've known better than to spend a whole week in my pj's. That was some sort of last straw. I crossed an invisible line that resulted in more therapy sessions and then . . . this.

"*Ferris Bueller's Day Off* isn't as intelligent as *Dead Poets Society*. But still . . ." Chatham interrupts my thinking.

I can't focus on my anger any longer because he just spoke three of the most mesmerizing words in the English language: *Dead Poets Society*. Now that's a modern cinematic classic.

I'm about to comment on *his* good taste when the girl with purple hair interrupts us. "Hey, Big Chat."

"What's up, Jules?" he asks.

"I need a quote for journalism about the game Friday." She nods at me.

"I'll come up with something after class. Okay?"

"Yeah. Sure." She gives me another nod before she strolls back toward her skinny-jeaned friends near the whiteboard.

When Chatham turns back to me, the *Dead Poets Society* moment has passed. He fidgets with his mechanical pencil. "You shouldn't have had to take the quiz yesterday."

I shrug. It wasn't a big deal. "Ms. Ringgold said it wouldn't count. She'll just use it like a pretest."

He clicks lead in and out of his pencil, over and over, like some kind of nervous tic. What could be making him anxious? "Cool. How do you think you did?"

"Okay, I guess." I study an old pair of initials carved into the desktop. The multiple-choice part of the test was easy, and the written section required only minimal thought, but I'm not advertising that fact. Smart kids don't usually fare well in movies. It seems safer to blend in for a while than to draw attention to my IQ.

"Really?" He sits up when Ms. Ringgold enters the room with a stack of papers cradled in her arm. "How do you know all those authors and what they wrote?"

"I like to read," I answer, which is true. It's also the safest pastime in the universe, second only to watching paint dry.

But he's not listening. He's tracking Ms. Ringgold with his eyes.

She walks to the front of the room, turning to face us. Frizzy red hair frames her cheeks. "Guys, you know I love you, but these grades are horrific."

A chorus of groans erupts. I glance at Chatham, who's wiping his hands on his cargo shorts.

"If you made lower than a seventy and if you come in for morning tutoring, I'll replace this quiz grade with your next one."

A couple of people sigh. Chatham was right about Ms. Ringgold. I like her. Other than my dad, I've never known adults who talk to kids like we're real people.

She hands a paper to Maddie, the girl Chatham introduced

me to yesterday in the hall. "Who made the highest grade?" Maddie leans forward expectantly.

Ms. Ringgold remains silent as she slides a paper facedown onto Chatham's desk. He lifts one corner, and I see a flash of red ink that looks like the number twenty-seven. Do teachers give grades that low? From the look on his face, they must. His jaw tightens, a tendon popping on the side of his neck as he crumples his quiz. Well, that kind of tarnishes my vision of his shiny life . . . and means several of my favorite movies got the charmed-athlete stereotype all wrong.

She returns another paper before making her way toward me. She beams and pauses dramatically. "Our new student made a ninety-nine, the highest grade in the class."

And there goes my invisibility cloak. Crap. Every head in the room turns to check me out. Out of my peripheral vision, I see Chatham's eyes bulging. I stare down at my paper, hiding behind my hair.

"We're so happy to have you, Emilie," Ms. Ringgold gushes before moving on to the next person.

I don't hear anything anyone says for the rest of the class period as I wait for the bell to ring. For forty-three minutes, I study the floor, the ceiling, my pencil, anything but faces. Instead, I read some of the quotes Ms. Ringgold has posted around the room. They match her personality and the violets blooming on her windowsill—all upbeat and inspiring.

I pause at the oversized words of Henry David Thoreau written in calligraphy above her head: *Go confidently in the direction of your dreams. Live the life you have imagined.* This guy left all his worldly concerns behind to live alone in nature for two years, which sounds kind of appealing, if you ask me. I'd gladly trade the unknowns of public school for a tent and swarms of mosquitoes as long as I could have Hitch and my books.

Ms. Ringgold's voice rises, interrupting my visions of s'mores and roasted hot dogs. Her hands flutter excitedly when she starts talking about poetry. I try to imagine what she was like as a teenager. Like me, she probably lived at the library with her nose stuck in a book.

When the bell interrupts her lecture, I grab my binder and sling my backpack over my shoulder, ready to bolt. But Chatham stops me before I can escape.

"Emilie, wait." He touches my elbow with his hand. "It looks like you survived your first quiz." He flashes me a smile, seemingly recovered from the shock of his failing grade.

"Yeah." For one second, I lose myself in that smile. My heart floats like the hang gliders over the dunes behind my house. If anyone looks at my chest, they'll see my heart swelling beneath my black T-shirt.

"Hey, listen. I could use a little help. I'm . . . failing Ms. Ringgold's class." He looks away for a second. "If I don't bring up my grade, Coach Carnes is going to put me on probation."

That sucks, but I don't see where I come into the equation.

Then he raises his eyebrows, his expression hopeful. "You want to be my tutor?"

Ugh. I rack my brain for a quick excuse, but my mind is blank. As I stand there panicking, an artsy-looking girl with platinum hair walks up behind Chatham. She's Tinker Bell without the fairy costume. Instead, she wears flip-flops and a soft button-down with paint splattered on the sleeves tied at her waist.

Thank goodness—a distraction.

"Hey, Ayla." Chatham glances over his shoulder. "Have you met Emilie?"

"I have now." She offers a fine-boned hand, perfect for painting or pottery or whatever creative hobby she enjoys. "So you're some kind of literary prodigy, huh?"

"H-h-hardly," I stutter, eyes darting, looking for an escape.

"Yeah, and she's my tutor." Chatham grins at me, blue eyes twinkling. I open my mouth to say no, I'm not, but nothing happens. My voice fails me. My big brain fails me too.

"That's nice." Ayla nods, transferring her binders from one arm to the other. "So you're nice *and* smart. Be sure to count tutoring Chatham here as your community service for the year." She winks at me encouragingly.

That's the problem with never speaking up. A voice is like a muscle, and mine must be all flab, because I don't have the strength to tell Chatham no, especially not in front of this girl who thinks I'm kind *and* intelligent.

So I just smile and say nothing at all.

CHAPTER THREE

. . . I tasted life. It was a vast morsel.

EMILY DICKINSON

After school, all I really want to do is curl up on the couch and watch a movie, to lose myself in Narnia or Middle Earth or even a galaxy far, far away. But Hitch nudges my hand with his wet nose, and I can't ignore him. He's my best friend, and the whole public school thing is getting to him too. His ears have been droopy all week.

"You want to go for a walk, handsome?" I tickle the golden hair under his chin. He grins at me, his bushy tail thumping the coffee table.

With a sigh, I drag myself the ten steps to the kitchen bar to leave Mom a note. She'll freak if she comes home from her part-time job at the library and can't find me. That done, I grab my faded "I Got Crabs at the Crab Shack" hoodie and a tennis ball for Hitch and head toward the back deck. The screen door thumps behind us as Hitch tears off ahead of me, his earlier funk forgotten.

That's one of the things I love about Hitch: He lives in the moment. He doesn't worry about the fact that he was home alone all day or the fact that he'll probably be home alone again tomorrow. All he cares about is right now. And right now he's with me. It's low tide, and the ocean is calling his name.

By the time I scramble down the weathered steps of the boardwalk, he's down at the water's edge, tongue hanging out, waiting for me. I toss the ball out past the low-breaking waves, and he charges into the surf to retrieve it.

We've been at it for a while when Cindy, the eight-year-old who lives next door in the Malibu McMansion, joins me at the edge of the wet sand. Her shoulders relax when she turns to Hitch playing in the water, and the freckles on her nose and cheeks come alive as she twirls her ponytail around her index finger.

"Hey, Cindy. What's up?" I smile at her.

"I'm bored," she says without taking her eyes off Hitch. "I don't have anyone to play with when I get off the bus."

Ouch. Her innocent comment hits me in the gut. I should have realized she would miss me and Hitch in the afternoon. We used to take our afternoon walk at two thirty, so we could meet her getting off the bus. Now I don't get home till almost four thirty. This is a perfect stretch of beach for someone who wants to be left alone. It's not so great for bubbly elementary kids who need after-school playmates.

"I'm sorry, Cindy. This whole school thing . . ." The guilt in my belly expands. "I've missed you too. We should play Monopoly this weekend."

She looks up at me. "If you promise not to buy Boardwalk."

I cross my arms and frown, pretending to think. I'm kind of competitive when it comes to board games. Cindy's the only person I would ever let break the rules. "Just this once. Okay?"

She grins mischievously and places her little hand on her hip. "And . . . I get to be the Scottie dog."

I narrow my eyes. That's my lucky piece. "How about we roll for it?"

"Please?" When she folds her hands beneath her chin, she's too stinking adorable to resist.

"Oh, okay," I say as Hitch races toward us to show Cindy his tennis ball.

"You're the smartest dog ever." Dropping to the ground, she wraps her arms around his wet neck. He blinks at me over her shoulder, eyes rolling back in his head, and sighs like he's in doggy heaven. Cindy nuzzles her face in the patch of dry fur near his ear. "I love you too," she coos.

I study the two of them, lost in a second of sheer joy. But it doesn't last. Cindy stiffens when a high-pitched voice screeches from the steel-and-glass structure that serves as her home. The perfect moment recedes like the waves.

My stomach twists. Something about that family and her home puts me on edge. Maybe I watch too many scary movies, but that big, cold mansion reminds me of the house in that movie where the main character fakes her own death to get away from her psycho husband.

I shake off the gloomy thoughts. At least they're a family— a real family, with a mom *and* a dad. Granted, the dad isn't around much. But even that must be better than knowing he's gone forever.

Hitch watches Cindy go. After a minute, he drops the ball at my feet, plopping down on his butt, staring up at me with hopeful eyes. He wants me to join him in the water, but . . .

I don't swim.

I know: it's ridiculous. A twenty-first-century teenager who lives on the barrier islands of North Carolina and doesn't swim.

Dad took me to swimming lessons at the YMCA when I was seven, convinced I'd grow up and have a normal life. He said I'd be fine as long as someone was in the water with me. Not true. About the time I mastered the art of doggie paddling, I had a bad seizure and puked in the pool. Before the adolescent instructor or Dad could get me out of the water, I'd humiliated myself and almost drowned. Mom made Dad swear he'd keep me out of the water. She's been trying to protect me from the dangers of my epilepsy ever since.

※

A long walk later, Hitch and I reach the rickety boardwalk that leads to our cottage on stilts. I inspect it as we cross over. Everything around this place needs work, but after Mom pays the bills there's never anything left at the end of the month to fix loose boards, leaky pipes, or weathered shingles. Dad's life insurance was just enough to pay off the mortgage and cover the first couple years of my college education, so that's something, at least. But I'm pretty sure some of the kids at the Ridge have larger allowances than Mom's part-time library income.

The only reason I go to North Ridge with the preps is because Mom and Dad bought this tiny house on the water when they first married. Crystal Cove was desolate back then, with sand dunes taller than my head and a herd of wild ponies roaming the beaches. The mustangs are long gone, relocated for their own protection when the millionaires moved north to get away from the fast-food restaurants and strip malls taking over the southern end of the island. Now gigantic beach homes dwarf our house on both sides.

Every light in the house is on when I open the back door. I spot my frowning mother and two sad frozen dinners waiting at the table. Forcing a smile, I drag myself across the bare wood floor.

"You're late." Mom pushes some rice around with her fork.

Sensing her aggravation with us, Hitch plops his head on her feet in apology.

"Sorry." I slide into my seat. "Hitch needed exercise. He's going stir crazy without me." Ha! Good one. Finally, the mouth and brain *both* fire when I need them.

She smiles.

Uh-oh.

"Well, then, I think I have some good news."

Lately, Mom and I don't agree on what constitutes *good news*. My chest tightens.

She puts her fork down. "I've spoken with Principal Brown about Hitch going to school with you." Hitch cocks his head at the sound of his name, and Mom rubs the top of his head with her bare foot. "He said now that your Individualized Education Plan is in effect, he'd get back to me in a week or so with the school board's decision about Hitch—that a seizure response dog might fall under the same disability rules as assistant dogs."

I try to swallow, but a pea lodges in my throat. Gagging, I reach for my water glass.

I should be thrilled at the idea of Hitch going to the Ridge. He almost always knows when I'm about to seize. He's been trained to tug on my pants or shirt before an attack, and he knows how to break my fall if I black out. Plus, he's my best friend.

But it's going to be hard to explain a seizure response dog to Chatham and everyone else when I haven't told anyone I have epilepsy.

CHAPTER FOUR

The Sky is low—the Clouds are mean.

EMILY DICKINSON

The next morning I tell Mom I'm sick and need to stay home. She says to take my meds and go straight to jail, not to pass Go, not to collect two hundred dollars. I glance at the handful of colorful pills she has laid out for me on the counter. They're a blessing and a curse, a new regimen from the good doctor. They seem to finally be controlling my seizures, but they also make me really tired and really moody. And, according to my mom, those are the last two qualities any teenager needs amplified.

As I wash down the prescriptions with a swig of water, the morning sun bounces off the dunes. It shines through the kitchen window and reflects off Dad's sea glass collection on the sill. But even that string of beautiful colors can't distract me from the fact I have to face another day at school. Living in fear sucks. I could seize at any moment, lose control in front of a bunch of strangers, convulse, pee in my pants. And my mother no longer seems to care.

This woman—the one who won't let me ride a bike or swim or even shower with the bathroom door locked for fear I might injure myself—is oblivious to the emotional dangers of North Ridge.

I keep my mouth shut until we're in the car and almost to school. "Dr. Wellesley said stress can aggravate my seizures," I blurt, tossing out another reason why I should be learning at home, not enrolled in public school.

"We've already discussed this, Emilie. We're going to try it for three months and then decide about the rest of the year." She flicks her turn signal.

Three *days* have felt like forever. I can't wrap my brain around three months.

We're seconds from the drop-off line. My heart races in my tight chest. Grasping the door handle, I concentrate on my breathing.

"You haven't had a seizure in over two months. Dr. Wellesley said it's time to branch out and try new things." Her jaw twitches, and I know she doesn't completely believe Dr. Wellesley herself. "He said it's time to start focusing on your social and emotional well-being. You can't do that if you never leave the house."

I grunt like old Ms. Potts, who shelves books at the library when she's not at home with her throng of cats. I wish I had her life.

"You'll feel better when Hitch can come with you." Mom brakes our Honda Civic to a stop at the front entrance. We're the only compact vehicle in a long line of luxury sedans and SUVs.

She used to know everything about me. Now, we're total strangers. We've been growing apart ever since she joined the support group for people who have lost a spouse. She talks to her support-group friends instead of me, which I know helps. But it's like we don't know how to be around each other anymore, like everything good and normal about our family started to fall apart when Dad left us. We toss words around, but we're not really communicating.

When Mom leans over to kiss me on the cheek, I push open the door and jump out. I know it's wrong. Dad wouldn't be happy. But she's hurting me. Even if she thinks what she's doing is for the best, it hurts. And sometimes, I want to hurt her too.

I don't look back.

Ms. Ringgold is fired up. She's babbling a hundred miles an hour about our upcoming American author research project while I try not to be distracted by Chatham. Today, he's classic surfer dude without trying in his faded Vans and tie-dyed T-shirt.

"So in just a minute, I'm going to start assigning partners." Ms. Ringgold's red curls dance around her face when she talks.

I tear my eyes away from Chatham, my stomach sinking at the word *partners*. I don't know what I'll do if she pairs me with Maddie or one of her friends. Based on the length of their hair and their perfectly coordinated outfits, they appear to have more in common with Barbie than they do me. Though for all I know, they may be really nice. In my few days at the Ridge, I've realized the stereotypes in books and movies aren't always accurate in real life. But enough of those labels seem grounded in reality to make me cautious.

"I'll pull an author's name from the green cup"—Ms. Ringgold jiggles the cup in front of our faces like it's the Holy Grail or something—"then I'll pull two student names from the blue cup."

We all watch as she draws a white square of paper. "The father of the macabre—Edgar Allen Poe." Ms. Ringgold beams.

"Cool." A boy in the back mumbles something about drugs and alcohol. The guys seated near him lean forward, hopeful. But Poe goes to two bubbly girls near the front.

Ayla and her partner, a serious guy in wire-rimmed glasses, are assigned Jack London, who's pretty cool. He was crazy adventurous and loved dogs. A guy who loves dogs can't be all bad, right? I make a mental note to reread *Call of the Wild* as Ms. Ringgold bounces around the room on the balls of her feet.

She waves another little slip of paper in front of the class. "Emily Dickinson. My favorite poet." After a dramatic pause, she reaches into the blue cup and pulls another name. "Emilie Day."

I slink down in my seat.

"Ironic." Ayla smiles from across the room. "Two Emilys."

A couple of the smarter kids chuckle.

My Emilie's not spelled the same as Dickinson's, but I don't correct her. I can't—I'm too nervous waiting to learn my fate. Maddie turns and narrows her eyes, like I'm some kind of competition. She doesn't seem to like Ms. Ringgold—or Chatham, for that matter—paying attention to me. Yesterday, I could have sworn she was intentionally blocking the row with her tan legs. When I said "Excuse me," she acted surprised, like she hadn't seen me trying to get by. I could have misread her body language; I'm a bit rusty when it comes to inferring social cues. But something about the interaction just felt . . . tense.

"And *du-du-du-dum* . . ." Ms. Ringgold's chubby hand disappears inside the cup again.

I hold my breath. Time slows.

"Derek Champion."

A couple of people laugh. Ayla speaks over them, "Ms. Ringgold, don't do that to her."

"Yeah." Jules, the girl with the purple hair, jumps in. "She'll end up doing all the work."

My eyes ping-pong around the room, trying to keep up with their conversation. I remember enough names to know Derek is the enormous football player who hangs out with Chatham before class.

He throws his hands up in the air. "I'm not totally useless, people." His voice sounds serious, but he looks like he's trying hard not to laugh.

Ms. Ringgold rests her hand on her hip. "Okay, Jules, Ayla. Who, pray tell, would you pair our new student with?"

They glance at each other. Jules shrugs as Ayla surveys the room. My life hangs in the balance.

"Chatham," Ayla says.

Ms. Ringgold looks from Derek to Chatham, then at me. "Okay. That could work. In fact, yes, Chatham, you and Emilie work together."

I can't tell whether this is better or worse. Maybe the slacker with the sense of humor would have been better. Or even one of the life-sized Barbies. I could've done the work for both of us and turned it in without much interaction. But Chatham's so nice. We'll be forced to get to know each other, which goes against my number one goal here: keeping my distance.

Chatham leans toward me. When he smiles, little lines form at the corner of his eyes. It's like his whole face wants in on the action, not just his lips. "Cool. My tutor and now my partner."

I bite the inside of my cheek. "Yeah, cool." I manage to move the muscles in my face, but I'm not sure if I'm grinning or grimacing. My escape plan disintegrates.

Ms. Ringgold and Emily Dickinson are complicating my life. I had this whole elaborate excuse about Mom's schedule planned out and was going to tell Chatham this afternoon while in the media center that I couldn't be his tutor. But there's no way to get out of the Dickinson thing.

Ms. Ringgold jabbers about one of her favorite Dickinson quotes—the one about not living in vain if you can stop at least one heart from breaking. Which is pretty funny considering her research project is causing a pain in my chest right this second.

I doodle in the margin of my paper, trying to brainstorm a getaway strategy. Surely, if I think hard enough, something will come to me.

CHAPTER FIVE

Come slowly—Eden!

EMILY DICKINSON

At lunch, I use a limp pickle to poke at the ham sandwich on my Styrofoam plate.

"That bad?" Ayla asks, sliding into the seat beside me.

It was nice of her to ask me to sit at the lit-mag table, so I dig down deep and force a half smile. As I drop my soggy spear, she reaches inside her metal Wonder Woman lunchbox.

"At least you're sitting with the coolest kids in the building." She raises one eyebrow.

I can't help but laugh. I know she's totally joking. But from what I've seen, the student literary magazine crew is actually pretty cool. Jules sits at this table. Katsu, a Japanese guy with glossy black hair and eyes to match, sits here too. He's always glancing at Ayla, unless he's immersed in his sketchbook. Or maybe not. Maybe his interest in Ayla is another instance of my social antennae misinterpreting a frequency.

"Yeah." I smile. I owe her one. She invited me into her group, which is more than anyone else in this lunch period has done, and it's way better than hiding in the bathroom. Which I may or may not have done earlier this week.

Ayla smears hummus on a stalk of celery. "You might even start coming to the meetings. You seem like the writer type," she says, then tilts her head to look at the clock.

I turn as well. When I do, I notice Chatham two tables over. Maddie sits beside him, sipping a bottle of water and talking with such enthusiasm that the massive bow in her hair bounces up and down, punctuating her sentences. The North Ridge Cheer logo plastered on her chest screams "Look at me!" Apparently, she's on the debate team *and* the cheerleading squad. That's actually kind of impressive.

Chatham nods at me. I sit frozen, mesmerized by his genuine smile and . . . full lips. When Maddie jiggles his arm with a French-manicured hand, he looks away, and I remember to exhale.

Ayla crunches a carrot stick. I try to swallow, but a bit of rubbery pickle catches in my throat. Ayla pounds me on the back until a tiny chunk of green shoots out my mouth, landing near the tray of the girl seated across from me. Thankfully, the girl doesn't notice. She's deep in conversation with a guy in glasses about the layout for the next edition of *Over the Ridge*.

"Sorry," I cough. "I don't know what that was all about."

Ayla raises that flawless brow again. Without a stitch of makeup, she is beautiful. She's got this whole artsy, natural thing going that I could never pull off. Maybe Mom and I should substitute the TV dinners with more of Ayla's crisp veggies.

"It's just— I'm supposed to tutor Chatham after school. And I know it's going to be . . . awkward." I push my tray away. My stomach is no longer inside the cafeteria with me. It's moved ahead to this afternoon's study session in the media center. There's no way I can eat the food on my plate, even if it was actually digestible.

Two minutes before the bell, Chatham pushes back his chair and heads toward the trash can with his tray. I see this because I've been unsuccessfully trying not to watch him out of the corner of my eye for the entire twenty-seven-minute period.

I focus on Ayla as she delivers another sales pitch on the benefits of being a part of the lit mag. Ever since Ms. Ringgold read part of my first essay to the class, Ayla's been after me to join. I love to write, but I'm not so sure I want to share my private thoughts. I've never written for anyone but myself, and I don't know what I'd have to say that the rest of the school would want to read.

When Ayla pauses in the middle of a sentence about creative writing, the hair on the back of my neck tingles. Without looking, I know someone is standing behind me. I don't move—until Ayla nudges me under the table and a lightbulb flickers in my dense head. It must be Chatham.

I turn around. He smiles down at me. "Hey, tutor."

"Um, hi." The tables on either side of us hush as if they're trying to overhear our conversation. Maybe they're curious what the golden boy has to say to the quiet new girl.

"Can I have your number?" he asks, ignoring their prying eyes.

"My number?" I glance at Ayla and back at Chatham, confused by the request.

He nods. "Your phone number."

Someone at the table behind us snickers.

"Oh, uh, yeah. My phone number." Flustered, I jumble the first three numbers and have to correct myself.

He adds me to his contacts. "I'll text you."

I try to nod, but the muscles in my neck don't work. Ayla pinches my thigh, and I snap out of it. "Yeah. Right. Text—"

The bell interrupts me. Hundreds of kids push back their chairs, ready for the mad dash to fourth period. When I stand to join the masses, a huge upperclassman bumps me with his overloaded backpack, pushing me chest-first into Chatham.

I gasp.

My. Boobs. Are. Touching. Chatham. York.

"S-sorry." I apologize, tilting my head back to meet his eyes. He's so tall, the room spins when I lean back to look up at him.

He places a steadying hand on my waist, the left side of his mouth turning up in a half smile. "Please. Don't apologize."

With a wave, he turns to go. I suck down a lungful of air in an attempt to steady myself, unsure whether he's flirting or teasing or both. He only wants my number because of the tutoring thing this afternoon, but I have a flock of seagulls flapping in my belly—a flock of very unruly seagulls who must be restrained before I reach fourth period.

I search for Ayla's steadying face in the masses. When I can't find her, I head out to the main hall completely on my own.

CHAPTER SIX

It's such a little thing to weep—

EMILY DICKINSON

Mom's Honda is not in the pickup line after school.

All I want to do is go home, take a hot shower, and lay on the bed with Hitch. If I can muster the energy, I might read some of the Dickinson poems Chatham and I printed in the library. If not, I'll crawl under the covers and sleep. My seizure meds make me tired and moody enough as it is. Sometimes they make my face break out—because that's really the kind of thing I need. And today's emotional rollercoaster is bound to magnify all the negative side effects.

My first tutoring session with Chatham was both amazing and horrifying—the way I imagine parasailing would be if I ever had the nerve to try it. I don't remember much of anything after our hands touched when I offered him a pencil. Somehow I filled thirty minutes talking about poetry, theme, and mood, because it was four thirty when the librarian ran us out of the media center.

I zone out like that sometimes. It's not as serious as a fullblown, muscle-contracting, loss-of-consciousness seizure. It's not even as bad as an absence seizure, where I lose bits of time without convulsing. It's more like when you're sitting in class aware that the teacher's talking, but you're not really comprehending what's being said—kind of like daydreaming. In fact, my neurologist says it's not even a real seizure. It's more like a warning. He calls it an aura.

Thankfully, since he switched my meds again, I haven't experienced anything beyond that weird out-of-body feeling. I still don't like it, though. It's a reminder of what could happen if my meds fail and the auras progress to the real deal.

The breeze rushing in from the Atlantic is a perfect mid-October temperature only experienced on the Outer Banks. It's not hot or cold. It's not damp or dry. It's more like the movement of music across your skin than actual molecules of air. My hair flutters around my face as I pull out my phone to text Mom. I told her I'd be finished at four thirty, and she's not here. Something's up. My mother is never late. Never.

My finger is hovering over the Send button when a spot of green catches my eye. Mom's Honda whips around a curve and into the parking lot. The woman flying into the lane cannot be my mother, though, because my mother never speeds. And yet it looks like her, and she's smiling. So I slide into the passenger seat and pray I'm not being abducted by aliens.

"I'm sorry I'm late." She wipes her palm on her tan linen pants.

"No problem." I watch the woman who looks like my mom out of the corner of my eye in case she morphs into some kind of mutant being.

We drive north on the beach road with the windows rolled down a few inches. I count the fifty-year-old shacks dotting the shore, struggling to maintain their perches on the narrow strips of sand that haven't been eroded by wind and waves. I've been studying them most of my life. If I've learned one thing from their precarious situation, it's that Mother Nature is in control. She'll take what she wants when she wants.

That's what happened with Dad. One day he was there for me, rubbing my back during the night after a nasty seizure. Before I could comprehend what was happening, he'd been ripped out of my life by forces outside my control, leaving me with an ache in my chest that never seems to subside.

When Mom's phone vibrates in the cup holder between our seats, I reach for it. An unfamiliar number blinks on the screen, which is weird, because nobody calls Mom. She doesn't socialize much anymore.

Before Dad died, my parents had people over all the time for their famous seafood shish kebabs. Mom would stake tiki torches out around the deck and serve frosty drinks with little umbrellas in them. I'd stay up way past my bedtime listening to the waves, Jimmy Buffet blaring on a portable CD player, and the sound of voices on the wind.

But most of their friends were married with kids, and I think it got awkward for Mom being the third wheel. And it got awkward for me because my body was changing thanks to the joys of puberty. The doctors were having a hard time stabilizing my meds and seizures. No matter how kind the parents, their kids were scared by my seizures. And I couldn't blame them. I was scared by my seizures.

The last time Mom tried hanging out with a friend she met at the library, it didn't go well. We went to eat dinner at the woman's house. The two of them were going to organize a book club, but I seized before dessert and bumped my eyebrow on the woman's kitchen table. My head bled like crazy.

Mom's friend was fine, but her husband said something about their homeowner's insurance policy. He made both of us feel uncomfortable, like he thought we were going to sue them or something. After that, it just seemed easier to stay home than to venture out.

"Who is that?" I ask, handing her the phone.

"Oh. Probably a wrong number." She rejects the call, sliding the phone under her thigh and pressing the power button on the radio. While she tunes the station to the talk show she likes, I blink to clear my vision, certain my eyes are playing tricks on me. Mom's nails are painted a cheery shade of pink.

My head spins. She hasn't manicured her nails since before Dad died.

Something is wrong—very wrong. My head swivels from side to side as I survey my surroundings, making sure we're on the beach road leading to our house and not sliding down the rabbit hole into Wonderland.

When we turn into the driveway, Cindy sits cross-legged on the deck. She and Hitch are communicating through the front window.

"Hey, squirt!" I say as I climb the steps, trying not to think about Mom's fingernails. "What are y'all talking about?"

Cindy turns back to Hitch, wagging her finger at him. "We can't tell. It's a secret."

"What if I give you cookies?"

"I'll take cookies, but I can't tell. I promised."

Mom shuffles past us to unlock the door. "I made snicker-doodles," she says, holding the door open for us.

Cindy's eyes light up. "Lucky! Snickerdoodles."

They're store-bought refrigerated cookie dough, so I'm not sure how lucky that makes me. But I keep my mouth shut.

We play several hands of Old Maid, drink lemonade, and eat cookies while Mom pulls a couple of microwavable lasagnas out of the freezer. Hitch sits on high alert beside Cindy in case she drops a crumb. Finally, an ocean breeze rattles the chimes out back, and Cindy glances out the window toward her house.

"I guess I better go," she says, grabbing three cookies for the road.

"Do you want me and Hitch to walk you home?"

She turns to look in the direction of her house and shakes her head. "No. You know how Dad feels about dog hair."

Yes, I do. That's another reason to steer clear of their house. That and the fact that it's kind of cold and unfriendly. Oh, and pretty much every time Mom and I speak to Cindy's parents, they offer to buy our house. If Mom would sell, they'd tear down our house in two-point-seven seconds flat for a "more uninterrupted view of the ocean." What they mean is our old cottage is an eyesore.

"'Bye, squirt," I say.

She waves and heads to the door, dropping a few crumbs along the way, much to Hitch's delight.

After she leaves, Mom and I eat microwavable lasagna in silence. Mom's fork scrapes her plate, and I flinch.

"Do you want to watch a movie?" she asks, poking at the

tasteless red stuff on her plate. When I don't respond, she notices me staring at her nails again. "I got a manicure."

Uh, yeah. I remain quiet, hoping my silence will force her to explain.

"Dr. Wellesley says I should set an example for you by working on my emotional well-being." She picks at the polish on her index finger.

I want to ask how her getting a manicure is going to improve *my* emotional well-being, but I bite my tongue. The muscles in my shoulders tense the way they do when I fall asleep propped up in front of the TV. Hitch nuzzles my hand, worming his nose under my fingers so I'll pet him.

"You didn't answer my question. About the movie." She's not going to let it go. Clearly, she wants to distract me from the paint on her nails.

I swallow, avoiding her eyes.

"We haven't done Movie Monday in a while." She reaches over to squeeze my hand.

I start to pull away but stop myself. She's right. When Dad was sick, we started this movie thing. Each week we'd draw straws. Whoever won got to choose a theme. Dad always chose something slapstick like a Looney Toons marathon. Mom and I preferred chick flicks and Disney classics. Dad liked Goobers and popcorn. We liked Twizzlers and gummy bears. We kept it up after Dad died, until a few months ago when Dr. Wellesley started talking about "moving forward" and pressured Mom to put me in school. Now, we've just kind of quit.

She studies my face. I swallow again and look away.

"I have too much homework." It's not a total lie. I do need

to find a picture of myself for a genetics project in biology, and Ms. Ringgold told us to find at least five important quotes for our author research assignment. I could do both in about ten minutes, but I'm not telling my mom that.

Hitch stares back and forth between our serious faces. I force a smile. He doesn't deserve the additional stress of our strained relationship.

Mom apparently decides not to force the issue. So I clear the table while she wipes down the counters. When she's situated on the couch in front of our ancient TV, I head to my room to fake study. Hitch pads along behind me, plopping on the cool hardwood floor in front of my nightstand. I clear a spot on the quilt my grandmother made for my parents on their first wedding anniversary and pat the bed, inviting him to join me. When he takes me up on it, I lie down beside him, sinking my face into his thick fur, inhaling his smell—saltwater and sand with a tinge of wet dog.

I should do my homework, but I need a few minutes to decompress. So I cuddle Hitch and close my eyes for just a second.

When I open my eyes, the room is dark, the moon high in the sky. Hitch's fur glows in the silver light. I brush tangled hair off my face, blinking in confusion. He stares at me, his ears droopy. I ruffle his fur. Sometimes I wish he wouldn't take his job of protecting me so seriously.

He jumps to the floor, glancing back and forth from me to the door, and I remember I didn't take him outside for his bedtime potty break. Plus, I need to wash my face and change into my pajamas. So I drag myself off the warm quilt and down the hallway toward the living room and the back door.

Mom's asleep on the couch, her cell phone clutched to her chest. The TV casts a warm glow on her face. She must be dreaming, because she's smiling. I watch her for a minute, trying to remember the last time I saw her look happy. I honestly can't remember. In fact, I'd forgotten that she's pretty—in a middle-aged mom kind of way—when she smiles.

Hitch pushes the screen door open with his nose, letting himself out onto the deck, and I follow. He heads out into the dunes. I sit in Dad's old Adirondack chair, drawing my knees to my chest. The night breeze rustles the sea oats, muffling the sound of the waves. Out here, near the ocean, life is simple. Earth. Wind. Water. The sea moves in its own slow dance with the moon.

I tilt my head back, closing my eyes, sucking the fresh air in through my nose and holding it for a second before exhaling through my mouth. My muscles unwind. For a minute, I forget about school, about epilepsy, about how much I miss Dad. For one second, I live in the present like Hitch—until the sound of breaking glass shatters the night.

My eyes shoot open.

"Please! Just shut up," a woman shouts.

Hitch barks from the beach. I scramble toward him, calling his name under my breath. In an instant he's at my side, seated, on high alert as he's been trained to do any time there's a hint of danger.

The lights come on in Cindy's kitchen next door, illuminating a wall of glass. The house is attractive in a sleek, modern kind of way, but entirely out of place in Crystal Cove. It hovers over our cottage like a nuclear reactor beside a wilderness cabin. Bright lights reflect off glossy white paint and stainless steel appliances.

Inside, Cindy's mom grips her head, and I'm reminded of the harsh reality of life—for every positive, there's a negative. For every slow-receding tide, there's a forceful rising tide ready to drown and erode everything in its path. For every teenage girl drinking in the glory of the night, there's some sad, lost soul bobbing in choppy water.

I know it's rude to watch. Plus, I promised Mom I'd steer clear of Cindy's parents. As I turn away, I remind myself it's perfectly normal for husbands and wives to argue. Mom and Dad argued. There were tears and raised voices involved, but they always told me that was normal. Families argue. That doesn't mean they don't love each other.

I turn toward the door, patting my thigh, signaling Hitch to come with me and sidestepping the turbulent water of my neighbors' lives.

CHAPTER SEVEN

Saying nothing ... sometimes says the Most.

EMILY DICKINSON

I n English, we're supposed to work on our research projects, but Ms. Ringgold is absent. Maybe she's sick, but I'm guessing she probably needed a break. She expends an enormous amount of energy teaching. I've never seen anyone so jacked up about Frost and Longfellow. She's determined eleventh graders will be interested in a bunch of dead white men and their flowery poems.

Most of the class goofs off on their phones. After the sub reads Ms. Ringgold's instructions to the class to work on our project, she plops down behind the desk and loses herself in an outdated issue of *People* magazine. The guy sitting behind Ayla snores even though she turns around and huffs at him every few minutes. Chatham scoots his desk next to mine, oblivious to the curious stares of Maddie and her Hawaiian Tropic buddies.

"So let's do this." He opens his binder, pulling out the stapled packet Ms. Ringgold gave us last week. "I have to get an A to stay off the bench." He leans forward, ready to attack this project, determination etched on his tan face. "My dad will blow a gasket if I don't start."

I'd hate to run up against Chatham on the basketball court. He's about the tallest, fittest guy in school. Plus, he seems really driven to succeed. From what I can remember of our poetry discussion the other day in the media center, he seemed focused and smart. So I don't get why he has such a hard time with this class. Our project shouldn't be that difficult: read and annotate a few Dickinson poems, research some biographical information, write an analysis essay—done.

"So what else do you know about Dickinson?" I ask, already thinking about how quickly we can finish our assignment. I have a plan: make sure Chatham earns an A on this Dickinson thing and tutor him a couple of times before the next test. By that time I will have convinced Mom to let me go back to homeschooling or at least to take virtual classes online. I will have repaid Chatham for his kindness. And I can go back to hanging around the house with Hitch without worrying about seizing in front of a bunch of strangers. Back to my neutral little world without the worries of being dragged out to sea by Chatham's blue eyes or drowning in sorrow when he learns how weird I am and bails on our friendship.

"Not much. She wrote a ton of poems that nobody read until after she died." He shrugs, twirling his pencil around his index finger.

Okay, so he did a little research.

I thumb the pages of my binder, looking for my notes, and a piece of paper slides from the pocket folder in the back. We both lean down to grab it, and our hands touch, his fingers brushing the back of my wrist. I yank my hand back. "A few of them were read, but you're right. She went mostly unrecognized until after her death."

"That's sad." He cocks his head, studying my face like he's seeing me for the first time. "Don't you think if you have a gift like that, you need to share it with the world?"

Well, first of all, I don't have any gifts—at least ones that are that big and important. But if I did, I could totally relate to Emily Dickinson keeping her writing to herself. A person's private life should be exactly that: private. And she was the queen of keeping to herself. I totally respect that.

I realize I haven't answered Chatham's question, so I nod. "Yeah, you're right."

He chuckles.

"What's funny?" I pick at a hangnail, fidgeting under his stare.

He playfully bumps my arm with his fist.

I look away. How can a fist bump to the bicep feel scary *and* intimate? Is it possible to want to melt into Chatham's arms and into the floor, both at the same time?

"Nothing." He smiles. "I'm just not sure if you'd say anything if you disagreed."

I swallow the humongous lump lodged in my throat. "I would. Well . . . I might. It depends." I blink, looking away again. Maybe he's right. I don't like to speak up, especially in front of strangers. But I'm not the only person who feels that way. Lots of wise, artsy types like Thoreau chose nature and solitude over social lives and noise. I'd like to think I could grow up to be a wise, artsy type too.

He smiles. "You like movies?"

"Yeah." He knows I do. We've talked about that before. I have no idea why he changed the subject so suddenly, but I'm thankful nonetheless.

"Best teen movie of all time?"

I roll my pencil on the desk. "Easy. *The Breakfast Club.*"

"Agreed." He leans forward, resting his hands on top of the desk. "Most popular movie you wish you'd never seen."

This is stupid, but at least his attention has moved to something less personal. "*Jaws.* Definitely *Jaws.*" There's no need to explain this one to anyone who lives on a barrier island.

"Wrong. Not *Jaws.*"

"Excuse me? How can I be wrong? It's an opinion."

"Your opinion is wrong. There are worse movies." He drums his fingers on the desk like he's enjoying this.

I open my mouth to argue, but the sub peers at us over the top of her magazine. I glance over at Ayla, but she's lost in her own world, drawing on the back of a spiral notebook with her earbuds in.

I wipe a moist palm on my denim shorts. "Yeah, okay. About Dickinson. Did you find any quotes you like?" I ask loud enough for the sub to hear. My posture relaxes when she goes back to her reading.

"'Beauty—be not caused—It *Is.*'" When he smiles, his eyes light up. "I like that one."

I'm pretty sure he's flirting with me. And if he is, I'm flattered—really flattered. But I have no idea how to respond. I haven't had a substantial conversation with a guy since before Dad died. And that was back when I was thirteen and my substantial conversations consisted of arguing with Austin, the geeky son of one of my parents' friends, over who was going to eat the last s'more.

"Okay. That's good." I start to write the word *beauty*, pressing down so hard the lead in my pencil breaks. He hands me a pen.

I'm studying my paper in an effort to avoid his eyes, so I don't see Maddie approaching until it's too late.

A shadow falls across my desk. When I look up, I'm blinded by her bleached hair and teeth and the halo of fluorescent light encircling her face.

She smiles at Chatham. "So, Chatham." She drags his name out into three long syllables instead of two. "How's the project going?"

She smiles down at me.

I can't help noticing what polar opposites we are. She's what Granddaddy Day, who was born and raised in North Carolina tobacco fields, would've called a cool drink of water—tall, thin, and attractive. I'm more lukewarm lemonade. There's no catchy southern saying for that one.

"Maddie, you remember my friend, Emilie Day." He winks at me encouragingly.

"How could I forget?" She smirks and holds out a hand. There's an awkward pause while she waits for me to put down the pen and hold out my nail-bitten fingers. We shake.

The substitute glances at us again, sizing us up, deciding whether it's worth the effort of getting up out of her seat. She settles for a firm "Shush."

"She's also my tutor," Chatham whispers, flashing his sunniest smile and propping an elbow on my desk.

"Really? I thought you said you could take care of your grades on your own." Maddie arches a waxed brow.

"I know, but I changed my mind," he says without explanation.

Her eyebrow threatens to lift off her face. "Well . . . if she's your friend *and* your tutor, you must bring her to Daddy's shrimp boil next weekend." She manages to make the invitation sound scary, like drawing a switchblade across someone's throat. "We should show our appreciation for the girl who's going to keep our starting point guard on the court."

I cringe. I thought she was chilly, but I was wrong. She's dry ice and frostbite, and my self-preservation instinct tells me there's no way I'm going to her daddy's shrimp boil or anywhere within a five-mile radius of her house.

After school, I swing by the lit-mag teacher's room like I promised Ayla I would. I stand in the doorway, observing the people inside. A balding teacher sits behind his desk reading from a fat stack of papers. He occasionally scribbles something on one of them with his red pen. A handful of students occupy the room. Ayla and Katsu sit side by side in front of an open laptop. When I clear my throat, they look up.

"Guys . . ." Ayla stands up and pauses dramatically, waiting for the other students in the room to look at her. "This is my friend, Emilie. Some of you have met her."

When she stops, everyone in the room speaks in unison. "Hi, Emilie," they say, like they're reading from some kind of support-group script or something.

I chuckle as Ayla pulls me toward Katsu and their laptop.

"You came," she says.

"I told you I would."

She nods, seeming pleased. "Yes, you did."

Katsu offers me a blue plastic chair, which I accept.

"We just need to finish this blurb on the theater department's next musical," Ayla says. "Then I can introduce you to Mr. Johnson."

"Sure," I agree, even though I have no desire to meet Mr. Johnson, who I assume is the teacher.

Katsu runs his hand through his spiky black hair. "This would be much easier if the drama director had actually chosen a show someone had heard of."

I lean forward for a better view of the image on the screen and smile. "You haven't heard of *Hello, Dolly!*?"

"No," Katsu says.

Ayla shakes her head.

"Yes, you have." I hum a couple of lines of the *Hello, Dolly!* chorus.

They smile patiently but obviously don't recognize the song.

"It's one of the longest-running Broadway shows ever. It won ten Tony Awards," I explain.

Katsu shrugs.

"It played two thousand eight hundred and forty-four times." I can understand that they've never seen it—it's not like a lot of shows come through our town. But to not even know it exists? My dad hated musicals, but even he would sometimes be caught whistling the famous tune.

"Um, yeah. Never heard of it." Ayla smiles at me, then turns back to the laptop to type a few lines.

"Why do you know so much about this show?" Katsu asks as he leans forward to read what Ayla typed.

"I just like musicals and movies and books. I'm kind of an arts-and-entertainment geek." I shrug.

"So you can write. You're an arts-and-entertainment geek. Any other hidden talents or stores of knowledge?" Katsu laces his hands behind his head and leans back in his chair.

"I kind of like history and politics," I say, like it's no big deal. And with them, it's not. It feels perfectly natural to open up to them.

He sits up, leans forward, and looks down his nose at me—all fatherly all of a sudden. "You, my friend, should join the quiz bowl team. I think arts and entertainment is one of their main categories. Or maybe the debate team if you know as much about history and politics as you do obscure Broadway shows."

I open my mouth to argue. If I'm not careful, these two will have my face plastered all over the yearbook in extracurricular photos.

Before I can respond, I hear Maddie's voice interrupting us. "Did I hear someone say 'debate team'?"

I cross my arms and let my eyelids droop, hoping my cool posture is more noticeable than the fire burning the tips of my ears. I never even heard her enter the room.

"What do you need, Maddie?" Katsu asks.

"Mr. Simpson asked me to give you the dates for the next round of debates." She pushes a sticky note with some dates written on it in Ayla's direction.

"Emilie here is a history and politics whiz if you need an alternate or something," Katsu says, tapping the back of my chair.

Maddie's eyes widen as though he said I'd won a Nobel Peace Prize for Literature or the Miss Universe Pageant and she'd only gotten second place. "That's cool, but it requires a lot of time and studying." She backpedals a step toward the door.

"That's the point. I don't think Emilie would have to study that much—especially not for the historical and political topics."

Maddie's face puckers like someone poured pickle juice in her Cap'n Crunch. "The team's full," she says, and heads to the door without a backward glance.

Ayla presses her teeth into her bottom lip, holding back a smile until Maddie's footsteps recede down the hall. "If I didn't know better, I'd think she felt threatened, Emilie."

"I don't think so." I shake my head. Ayla's observation couldn't be farther from the truth. Beautiful Maddie, with her stellar grades and cute spirit wear, is about as likely to be scared of me as she is to run screaming from a marshmallow. But I don't argue. Instead, I kick back and people watch while Ayla and Katsu finish their write-up about the play. The room and the kids in it are comfortable with themselves and with each other.

I could almost see myself comfortable here too.

Almost.

CHAPTER EIGHT

Our journey had advanced—

EMILY DICKINSON

It's been seventy-eight days since my last seizure. Chatham and Ayla and the lapse in seizures are weakening my defenses. I could be lured into believing I have a shot at normal. But the last time I traveled that road, it didn't end well.

Last time I went two and a half months without a seizure, Mom and I got a little confident. We drove Dad's truck up to the four-wheel-drive area of the beach on a fall afternoon. We pretty much had the place to ourselves. It was gorgeous. The wild ponies grazed the dunes. The weather was perfect.

We sat on the tailgate, ate extra-crunchy PB&J sandwiches and salt-and-vinegar potato chips, and drank root beer. And held hands as the tide came in. Then without any warning, any aura, any anything—*bam*. I seized. Mom's phone didn't have a signal. The beach was deserted. She says she screamed for help. Nobody came. The seconds ticked toward the five-minute red zone as the seizure continued, then moved into the 911, life-or-death zone. If a park ranger hadn't been patrolling the beach, if he hadn't had a radio, if an EMT hadn't been close by, I don't know what would have happened.

After that, Mom and I agreed to be more careful. And until recently we have been, despite Dr. Wellesley's encouragement to "participate more actively in life." But with each passing day, the temptation grows.

Chatham called tonight. He just had a grammar question about a paper he's writing for US History. But still, North Ridge's most valuable player and Mr. Most Likely to Succeed called *me*.

While I was sitting in the counseling office the other morning, I flipped through last year's yearbook. Chatham's picture decorated every other page. There were pictures of him on the basketball court, in a classroom dressed as a Greek god, and on the dance floor dipping an ancient but smiling assistant principal.

He has that effect on people, which is why I'm sitting here on the couch still grinning like crazy after hanging up the phone. Hitch nestles his head in my lap as I contemplate my good fortune. It's the first day since I started at the Ridge that I've come home with enough energy to make it through the afternoon and evening without a nap.

My phone rings for the second time tonight, and Hitch's brow furrows. It's sad that my dog looks confused when my phone rings, like he's baffled by my blossoming social life.

When I answer, Ayla launches into a breathless summary of the discussion she just finished with Katsu about a new opinion column in the magazine. "He wants a new perspective from someone who hasn't lived in Crystal Cove their entire life." She pauses significantly.

"I *have* lived in the Cove my entire life." I sigh. Ayla and I have been through this before.

"But you're an out—" She trails off.

"Outsider." I don't try to conceal the edge in my voice.

"You know what I mean. You're new to the Ridge." She shuffles papers while we talk. "Just think about it."

"Ayla, I'm honored. Really, I am. But I'm not sure about this."

I don't want more connections to North Ridge. I'm already obligated to Chatham for this Dickinson project and for tutoring. And Ayla is definitely creeping into friend territory. The more I let myself get sucked into their sphere, the harder it's going to be to break free.

At some point, the fake life I'm leading is going to come crashing down. I've been tricked before into thinking my seizures were gone, but they always return at the worst possible times—like at a public swimming lesson or the time I slept over at a friend's house in sixth grade, seized, and wet the bed.

"Just think about it."

I don't respond. Ayla's dad says something in the background. I slump into the couch and try to ignore the hole in my heart. Tonight is Mom's night to close up at the library, so Hitch and I are home alone—again. If I happen to need help with homework, I'm on my own. I picture Ayla and her dad seated at the kitchen table, puzzling through an equation, laughing at some inside joke, her mom standing at the stove transferring cookies from the pan to a cooling rack.

I stare at the ceiling as Ayla rattles off a list of things she needs to do for school tomorrow, including finding a childhood picture for the genetics project I almost forgot. When she hangs up, I drag myself off the couch and flip on the overhead light. Dad's beach glass glimmers in the windowsill above the sink. I blow him a kiss and head down the short hall to Mom's room and the boxes full of photographs stored in the back of her closet. I might as well find a picture for my own project while I'm thinking about it.

Hitch pads along beside me and I squeeze his ear, telling him what a good man he is.

Mom's bedroom door is cracked. I push it open, heading across the darkened room to the master bath without turning on any lights. It's still hard to look at Dad's empty side of the bed. I spent every Saturday morning of my childhood wedged between my parents, watching *Scooby-Doo* reruns on that bed. When I was sick or scared, they always made room for me. The first time I walked into this room after the funeral, Dad's keys were still on the nightstand beside a row of pill bottles. For one second, I forgot he was dead. Then a wall of grief hit me so hard I ran to their bathroom and puked my guts out.

The memory causes my stomach to twist in on itself. I swallow the saliva pooling in my mouth. I need to find a picture and get out of here.

Hitch's nails click on the cold tile floor as we shuffle through the bathroom to the walk-in closet on the far side. I loved this closet when I was a kid. It was the best hiding place in the house. I spent more winter afternoons than I can count curled up with a flashlight and a book behind Dad's shirts.

Without any windows, it's pitch dark in the closet. It doesn't matter. I could find the light switch blindfolded with my hands tied behind my back. But when I flick the switch, I pause, blinking. Something's wrong. Dad's side of the closet is empty, except for the "World's Greatest Dad" T-shirt I gave him the summer before he died and a couple of boxes labeled *Jim's clothes*. I hold the doorframe for a second before sliding to the floor. Hitch whines.

I sit, leaning against the wall, my knees squeezed to my chest. Mom asked me a couple weeks ago if I wanted any more of Dad's shirts, but I didn't think anything about it at the time. When the initial shock passes, I crawl toward the first box, untucking one of the flaps and pulling it open. I gasp. For one second, Dad's in the room with me—at least the faint smell of him is.

I pull out an L.L. Bean hoodie, burying my face in the soft cotton. A hint of the Calvin Klein cologne my mother bought him every year for Christmas mixes with the memory of wood shavings from his shop in the storage room, and the apple-scented shampoo he used for as long as I can remember. I clutch the sweatshirt to my chest, hot tears forming in my eyes, too upset to respond when Hitch nudges my cheek.

Images of my mother from the last few weeks flash in my head—the unrecognized number on her phone, her polished nails, my dad's clothes boxes. Then it hits me: What if she's moving on? What if she's *dating*?

It all starts to make sense. She keeps saying we need to work on *my* emotional and social well-being, but that's not it at all. She's starting a new life for herself, packing up Dad's things and sending me off to school.

Every time I think I have my life figured out, something rocks my world. One minute I'm a happy-go-lucky second grader, the next I'm epileptic. One day I have a pretty normal family, the next I've lost my father. I thought Mom and I had settled into our sad little existence without Dad, and now she's going to have some kind of midlife crisis or something. I can't deal. And this time, instead of avoiding an argument, I'm going to tell her what I think.

I'm halfway through a *Full House* rerun I've seen twenty times when the Honda putters into the carport under the house. One good thing about living in a house designed to withstand hurricanes and floods is the elevation. By the time Mom climbs the stairs to the front deck, I've turned off the TV and organized my interrogation about the mystery caller, the manicure, and the midlife crisis.

As the front door swings open, I suck down a steadying breath. A warped spring in the sofa creaks as Hitch jumps down to greet Mom. She enters in a swoosh. Rustling plastic grocery bags hang from one arm. A stack of DVDs nestles in the crook of the other.

"It's not Monday, but who cares?" She glances across the room at me as she jiggles her key from the lock.

"Mom, we need to—"

Before I can finish my sentence, she presses her lips into a thin smile, the way she did when she held Dad's hand during his chemo treatments. Her whole body tightens like she's bracing for a disappointment. *The Wizard of Oz* slides from the top of the stack and slaps the wood floor. "Oh, okay. I understand. I should've given you a heads up. I just thought . . ." The crow's-feet at the corner of her eyes deepen.

Hitch whimpers, looking from the movie on the floor to my face. Well . . . great. Just great. With a sigh, I throw the blanket off my lap and cross the room to help her. A colorful Dorothy, skipping along the yellow-brick road with her new friends, smiles up at me. I hand the DVD back to her, grab the grocery bags, and head to the kitchen.

"Gummy bears, Twizzlers, *and* Skittles?" I ask as I unload the first bag.

She smiles, revealing a hint of teeth this time. "And I thought we'd go to Fat Boyz for ice cream before the movie."

That's two smiles in as many days. I almost hate to burst her bubble. Almost. "Mom . . . we need to talk."

"About chocolate chip cookie dough?" She lifts her eyebrows teasingly as she straightens the pile of Disney movies she rented.

I stack the bags of candy on the bar, then cross my arms. Her smile falters, and Hitch glances between us, whining. The bag of Skittles slips off the counter. When it hits the floor, we both flinch.

"What's going on, really?" I ask.

She shakes her head like I've sprouted a third eye. "Emilie, we've been through this. I love you. I just want us both to be well—physically . . . and emotionally."

I want to believe her. I want to believe in fresh starts and bright futures. But experience has taught me that stuff only happens in fairy tales, and I'm no Cinderella.

She reaches across the bar to rest her hand on top of mine.

"So what's the special occasion?" I ask, concentrating on not pulling my hand away.

"I just want to spend time with you."

I want to spend time with you too. The words form in my brain but stick in my throat. Hitch's heavy breathing is the only sound in the quiet room.

Twenty minutes later, we're turning into Fat Boyz and I haven't said a word about the potential mystery boyfriend. So much for the great inquisition. I'm a wuss.

The parking lot's empty except for a rusty Jeep and a gold BMW. We park and walk up the steps to the take-out window beneath the rounded pink overhang.

"A double scoop of chocolate chip cookie dough in a waffle cone, rocky road in a cup with two spoons, and French vanilla in a doggie bowl," Mom orders, and drops a dollar in the tip cup in front of the window.

"Thanks, Mom." I force myself to meet her eyes as I grab an extra handful of napkins. It's the least I can do. She's spent a lot of this week's gas budget on our little outing tonight.

"You want to sit on the deck or walk on the beach?" she asks.

The hulking man behind the counter bends down to pass our order out the window. I immediately grab mine. "How 'bout the pier?" I ask around a mouthful of deliciousness.

"Great idea. We haven't walked the pier since . . ." Her voice trails off.

Without speaking, we sit on the bottom step and wait for Hitch to finish his French vanilla. Mom hands me one of her spoons to taste test her rocky road.

I lick and nod. "It's good."

Our eyes meet. The sugary goodness dissolves the edges of our awkwardness. When a twenty-something couple comes tumbling around the corner from the side deck arm in arm, we smile at them. The guy brushes Hitch's ear as he passes. The girl grins. They half walk, half run to a Jeep and rumble out of the parking lot.

They look like the kind of couple who would ride bikes in the rain and write each other letters on vintage stationary.

My teeth sink into a chewy gob of cookie, and I try not to compare my life to theirs. Sometimes I just wish I could drive

myself somewhere or swim in the ocean at night. Or even—
gasp—drink a beer beside a bonfire way out in the middle of
the woods. But I have to be six to twelve months seizure-free
and have a certificate from my doctor before I can think about
a driver's license. Plus, I know I should be grateful. There are
people less fortunate than me—girls whose medicines don't
control their seizures.

"That's it, big guy." Mom reaches down for Hitch's empty
bowl as I lick the ice cream dripping down the side of my cone.
A few minutes later, we cross the beach road to the pier. Mom
pays the attendant the walk-on fee, and we find a bench halfway down where we can watch for dolphins and finish our ice
cream.

"We should do this more often," Mom says as a man a
couple of yards down instructs his curly-headed son on how to
cast his line.

I nod and lick a drip of ice cream from my thumb. Mom
savors tiny bits of rocky road, rolling it around on her tongue
before swallowing, as I study people on the beach beneath us.
There's something familiar about the broad shoulders and
messy light brown hair of a boy on the packed sand near the
water's edge. Trailing a few feet behind him is a little girl with
pigtails in a pink sundress. She takes extra-long strides, trying
to follow exactly in his wet footprints.

As I watch, a wave rolls in farther than the others, taking
her by surprise, and she drops her red Popsicle. Before it hits
the sand, she's crying. I hear her even over the surf and wind.
The boy turns.

Chatham.

He jogs back to her, scoops her up, and swings her over

his head. She laughs, the Popsicle already forgotten. A man I hadn't noticed ahead of them turns back, frowning. He has the same light brown hair and strong features. But his jaw has a sharper edge, and his eyes are a little closer together, giving them a kind of pit-bullish look.

Another rogue wave rushes in, catching Chatham off guard. He leaps toward dry sand, trying to keep the little girl aloft, but stumbles and falls to his knees. When he stands, his jeans are soaked and caked in sand.

The man, who must be their father, throws his hands up in the air, mumbles something under his breath, and storms away from the water toward the parking lot beside the pier. The little girl's cheeks puff like she's about to lose it again. But Chatham drops back to his knees in the wet sand in front of her, gently tilts her face up to his, and plants a kiss on the tip of her nose.

"What movie do you want to watch?" Mom asks, interrupting my little stalker fest.

"Whatever you want," I say with a small smile.

She's trying really hard. I decide to play along.

At least for tonight.

CHAPTER NINE

Finite—to fail, but infinite
to Venture—

EMILY DICKINSON

n the morning I trudge down the hall to second period, missing being at home in my pj's with Hitch. Morning person I am not.

"What's up?" Chatham asks, ignoring my crossed arms and clenched jaw as he slides into the seat next to me in English class.

I can't deal with Chatham's enthusiasm today. The bags under my eyes prove it. I spent most of the night tossing and turning and second-guessing myself about when and how to confront Mom. "Why are you so happy?" I shoot back.

"Well, let's see. The sun's shining." He looks around the room. "And you should be happy too. You get to sit beside the hottest guy in class."

"Oh, where is he?" I glance around the room, fighting back the smile already pulling at my lips. Chatham's currently the *only* boy in the room. Most of Ms. Ringgold's students will come sliding in seconds before her and the tardy bell. Since

I don't have any distractions, aka friends, in the hallway, I'm usually the first person here.

When I peek out from behind my hair, Chatham's beaming.

"Okay. Maybe not the hottest but . . . the funniest?"

I raise a skeptical brow without meeting his eyes. Seated, I'm eye level with his chest and snug T-shirt. I try not to stare.

"You like it?" He pulls the prewashed cotton away from his chest.

My cheeks burn. "Yeah, ha-ha." I smile, pointing at the water glass on the front of his shirt and the handwritten notes out to the side labeling the water at the halfway mark and the air at the full mark. The inscription under the glass reads *Technically, the glass is always full.*

From what I've seen of Chatham, that could be his motto. Some people see the liquid and think half full. Others see only the air and think half empty. Sometimes I get the sense Chatham sees it all, which is kind of terrifying. I don't know if I want him to see me—the real me.

"I've been studying the notes you gave me on those American authors." He wags his pencil at me. "I'm going to blow your mind this afternoon."

My stomach drops like a deep-sea anchor. I forgot I told him I'd tutor him again today. I open my mouth, but before I can formulate an excuse, Ms. Ringgold breezes into the room carrying a lopsided pot overflowing with purple violets. She adds the flowers to the row of healthy plants already crammed on the windowsill as the rest of the class scurries in behind her. The cheery plants match the spring in her step.

Maddie and a friend sashay past my desk, whispering

behind cupped hands. I fiddle with my ring binder, turning pages, pretending I've misplaced my notes.

Ms. Ringgold walks to the back of the room to shut the door as Ayla darts in. Even with blue paint splattered on her white eyelet tank and a smudge on her forehead, Ayla looks confident. She's comfortable under the spotlight or blending in with the scenery. In fact, I can't imagine her being awkward anywhere. And I'm starting to think she's super talented too. I saw a self-portrait of her displayed beside the counseling office. From a distance, it looks like a charcoal sketch. When you get closer, you realize it's a collage. The whole thing is made out of symbolic words clipped from newspapers and magazines. I can't even imagine how she thought of something so original. It belongs in the North Carolina Museum of Art, not North Ridge High School.

Ms. Ringgold clears her throat. "Since I've been out, we have lots of catching up to do for the test on Monday."

The guys sitting in the back row grumble.

"We missed you, Ms. Ringgold." Maddie flashes her syrupy smile.

"I missed you guys too." Ms. Ringgold walks toward the group of boys in the back, patting Chatham on the shoulder as she passes.

"Even me?" Derek, the football player I was supposed to be partners with, asks. Several people laugh.

He is obnoxious in the history class we have together. He questions the teacher on everything. I'm pretty sure the boy could argue with a stop sign. With Ms. Ringgold, it's different. He jokes around with her but never messes with her in a disrespectful way.

"But you know my motto: family first." She flashes Derek a smile but ignores his question. Instead, she closes the *Sports Illustrated* on his desk without giving him a hard time or threatening to assign detention and heads back toward the front of the room. "Sean needed me yesterday." She points to a picture on her desk of a smiling boy with almond-shaped eyes and a round, flattish face. "He was running a fever and wanted his mommy."

I swallow hard, looking down at my hands. Ms. Ringgold's son obviously has Down syndrome. That has to be tough—way tougher than epilepsy. At least no one can look at me and see my disability. But she tells us how much fun they had watching old cartoons like it's no big deal and paraphrases Katharine Hepburn—something about "if you obey all the rules, you miss all the fun."

"Let's forget about the test and focus on the fun," Derek jokes, tossing her words back at her.

"No can do." She smiles, passing study guides to the kids seated at the front of each row.

The next forty-five minutes fly faster than the pages on Ms. Ringgold's slideshow. The only sound in the room when she stops talking is the psychotic scribbling of thirty-something pens as we finish filling in a graphic organizer with the characteristics of every American period of literature from colonialism to modernism.

When the bell rings, Chatham reminds me to meet him in the media center after school for tutoring. I should object, but I don't. How much harm could one more study session cause? Plus, if I kill some time with him after school, that's less awkwardness at home with Mom. I still need to talk to her at some point, but last night was kind of . . . fun. Kind of like the old days.

And I dread squashing our tender shoot of new growth.

Weaving my way toward the door, I squeeze by Ms. Ringgold's desk. She and Maddie are deep in conversation. I try to ignore them, but Maddie talks so loudly that I'm pretty sure she wants me to hear her announcement. She even pauses to make eye contact with me before continuing what she was saying to Ms. Ringgold. "I knew you'd want to know I was selected for the Yale Law School Camp."

"Oh, Maddie. That's great. You'll be perfect for that." Ms. Ringgold pulls her in for a hug.

I don't know Maddie that well, but it's pretty obvious Ms. Ringgold is right. The girl has strong opinions, she's not afraid to share them, and she seems pretty determined to get her way. I can totally see her swaying juries, maybe even judges.

When I finally make it to the noisy hall, Ayla and Jules stand outside the door talking. They pause when I join them.

"Hey, Emilie. I hear you're thinking of joining lit mag." Under the double rows of fluorescent lights, smiling at me, Jules practically glows with her purple hair and pale skin.

"Yeah. I've been thinking about it." Which is not a lie. I have been thinking about it. I'm just not ready to make any more commitments or connections right now.

Ayla glances at the time on her phone. The bell will ring in a minute or two. "Jules, don't forget to find out how many cans we've collected for the canned-food drive."

"On it." Jules squints like she's making a mental note, taps her temple with a shiny black fingernail, and scurries off toward the main rotunda.

Ayla tugs me in the opposite direction. Our next classes are beside each other at the far end of the hall. "And don't you forget, Miss Renaissance Girl—who is a wealth of knowledge in all things literary, arts and entertainment, and history and politics—that you promised to help me with my writing this weekend."

"On it." I squint and tap my temple, copying Jules and wondering what's happening to me. In some ways it feels like the most natural thing in the world to hang out with Ayla and Jules and Chatham. In other ways I feel like the biggest imposter on the face of the planet. Take the whole Miss Renaissance Girl thing, for example. Ayla, Katsu, and Chatham think I'm some kind of genius, as if I've made a life of some scholarly pursuits. The truth of the matter is I know all this stuff because I've spent so many hours holed up with the TV and hiding with my nose in a book.

Ayla and I part ways at my next class. I take a deep breath. As I enter the room, questions swirl in my head. I slide into my seat wondering—am I Renaissance Girl? Or Imposter Girl? Or someone else completely? Do I want to fit in or fade out?

Who am I?

CHAPTER TEN

The Soul selects her own Society . . .

EMILY DICKINSON

I don't like this." Mom wrings her hands as we wait for the light to turn green. The beach road is deserted at nine o'clock Saturday morning. By ten, it will be jammed.

"You'll leave me home alone, but you don't want me to go to a friend's house?" The rhetorical devices we're studying in Ms. Ringgold's class are improving the quality of my counter arguments.

"You have Hitch at home." She waits for a heavyset woman in a floral maxi dress to cross before entering the intersection. "Have you even told this girl about your epilepsy?"

"Her name's Ayla, and no, I haven't." Ayla's the closest thing I've had to a friend in years. There are several reasons why I *should* tell her—not just because Mom expects me to, but also because it's the safest thing to do if we're going to be friends and hang out regularly. But I can't. How do you just drop that into a conversation about homework or lit mag? *Oh, by the way, I have epilepsy. If I start thrashing around, just roll me on my side and call my mom.*

"You need to tell her, Emilie."

"I know." I glance out the window. She may be right. But I've made up my mind. I'm not telling Ayla anything.

"I still think I should come in and talk to her mother." She tightens her grip on the steering wheel.

"Please, Mom. You're only going to be at the library for a few hours. Dr. Wellesley said you have to let me have some control. I'll text you every thirty minutes." I rip the hangnail on my thumb with my teeth. "This is part of my social development. Right?" Oh, good one. I mentally pat myself on the back when my mom is forced to nod her agreement.

We turn down a narrow side street between the beach road and the bypass. Bungalows on pilings, barely larger than our house, huddle together without an ocean view in sight. We find Ayla's and pull in. Her weathered gray home is not what I expected. I know it's stupid, now that I'm spending more time out in the real world, but I pictured everyone at the Ridge living in houses nicer than my own. Clearly, I've spent too much time living in my head with unrealistic images reinforced by my TV and movie obsession.

Vowing to be more open-minded, I step out of the Honda. As I climb the steep stairs to the front deck, I gesture for Mom to leave. She doesn't budge until Ayla comes out and acknowledges her with a wave.

Mom rolls down her window. "The library closes at one."

"Okay." I grit my teeth. The library has closed at one since before Dad died, when the economy first took a downturn.

"I'll be back right after that. Text me in a little bit." She waves, but the Honda's still in park.

I will her to leave. "See you later."

Ayla opens one of the sliding-glass doors leading directly

into the main living area of her house. I follow her into a high-ceilinged room that includes what appears to be their living, dining, and kitchen areas all in one.

"Your mom seems nice." She smiles over her shoulder as she opens a squat refrigerator that looks like something out of a *Leave It to Beaver* rerun and grabs two Cokes.

I lean on the bar, taking in her house. With the exception of a few functional chairs, two wrought iron barstools, and a table in the kitchen, the house is bare. But what Ayla's home lacks in furniture it makes up for in color. Murals cover every square inch of wall space. The ceiling is fuchsia. "Your house is awesome."

"Thanks. I painted it myself."

I gape at an ocean scene painted on the back wall of the living room. It's done entirely in shades of orange and red. The sun's maroon, the water salmon, the sand apricot. "Amazing. My mom won't even let me hang posters on the walls."

"It's one of the few perks of having a single dad." She shrugs.

So much for the picture-perfect family with the stay-at-home mom I envisioned.

She leads me down a sky blue hallway to her room. "Thanks for agreeing to help me with my writing. Chatham says you're an amazing tutor."

"He said that?" I perch on the edge of her white bedspread. Her bedroom is the complete opposite of the living room. With the exception of the weathered pine boards on the floor and pops of red pillows and a massive red throw at the foot of her bed, everything in the room is either bright white or black.

"Yeah, he sits beside me in science. He said it's the first time he's ever understood anything he's read for English." She pulls back filmy white curtains to open the window.

I smile at the memory of Chatham's creased brow as he puzzled through one of the Dickinson poems we chose to annotate.

"So I can't wait for you to give me some feedback on my poem before I enter this contest. I feel better about the visual part than the written part." She grabs a composition book off a white wicker desk in the corner, clutching it to her chest. "Do you want to see the painting first?"

"Sure." I've never given someone feedback on creative writing before. What if her writing is horrible? I shake my head. It won't be. Even if it's only half as good as her artwork, it will be amazing.

She opens the closet, dragging out a large canvas draped with a sheet. Two dirty feet, painted in oil, peek out from under the white material. "Ta-da." She whips the cloth off the painting.

Wow. I lean forward to study it more carefully. A little girl seated on weather-beaten steps, leading down to the beach, watches what appears to be a mother and daughter playing in the surf. The sun shines on the pair frolicking in the water in their bright bathing suits. The little girl on the steps sits in the shadows of the handrail. Her frayed denim shorts and dingy T-shirt blend in with the shadows and the worn wood of the boardwalk.

My heart aches, but I'm not sure why. "She's sad."

Ayla nods. "It's called *Forsaken*." She hands me the composition book, opening it to the first page. The title "Forsaken" is centered at the top in Ayla's calligraphy-like script. "Read it."

My eyes float across the page. The free verse poem tells the story of a little girl whose mother drowned. She's grief stricken and wants to walk out into the choppy waves until the water covers her head and she joins her mommy. My chest tightens. I swallow, looking up into Ayla's eyes, wondering if I can finish without crying. She nods encouragingly.

After I read the last line, I look up at her, speechless. One side of her mouth turns up in an uncertain smile.

"Ayla, this is amazing." My voice cracks. "How did you write this?"

"It's kind of personal." She studies her hands, avoiding my eyes. "My mom didn't die. She left us when I was little."

I don't know what to say. For the second time in less than half an hour, I'm reminded not to assume things about people.

"We were at the beach. Dad and I were digging a moat around this elaborate sand castle. The sun was shining. Kids played in the surf near us. Mom said she was headed to the corner market for chips and drinks." She pauses to meet my eyes.

I hold my breath.

"She never came back."

I sink to the edge of her bed. "What happened?"

She shrugs, but pain tugs at the corners of her mouth. "She just left. We called the cops. It was terrifying. We thought she'd been abducted. But when we got home, she'd left a note saying she needed to follow a dream—a dream that didn't involve us. It involved New York and performing—like on a stage, not like the acting she'd done pretending to be a dutiful wife and mom."

My arms ache to hug her, but my heart wimps out. I've forgotten how to reach out to others.

"Sometimes people with these really raw emotions pop

into my head," she continues, saving me from my indecision. "I have to paint or write them in order to get rid of them, or they'll take over my life." She straightens a charcoal sketch on the wall beside her bed of an old man walking in the rain.

The way she explains her feelings reminds me of how I start worrying about seizing in public or how Dad would feel about Mom moving on with her life. Of how my thoughts snowball into obsessions and how the next thing I know, I'm clenching my teeth or gnawing at my fingernails—my two worst habits.

"It's kind of therapeutic." She pulls the sheet back over the painting. "So, any suggestions?"

"Nothing major." I skim the words on the page in front of me for a second time. "I love that it's written in first person. You could add more description to the first stanza to set the tone. I think you'll win anyway."

She shrugs. "If I don't win, it's not meant to be."

Ayla's amazing, and I'm a jerk for stereotyping the entire North Ridge student body as a bunch of spoiled rich kids born with silver spoons wedged in their whitened teeth. My chest tightens. I need to tell Ayla about my epilepsy—not because of Mom or because of safety concerns but because Ayla trusts me. She shared this really personal poem with me and the thing about her mom. I should open up to her. That's what friends do.

My lips part. *Do it.*

I can't. I'm trapped inside my shell like the hermit crabs Dad and I used to collect on the beach behind our house. We'd put them in a sand-filled aquarium on the counter, feeding them fruit and leftover fish. I always wanted to keep them as pets, but Dad would make me take them back down to the beach after a few days. They need lots of humidity—more than an air-conditioned house—or they'll suffocate, and Dad couldn't stand the idea of keeping anything caged. But hermit crabs are never free, and neither am I. We're both timid little creatures happier in tight, dark little spaces than out in the big world where we're likely to be stepped on and crushed.

I shut my mouth, squeezing back into the safety of my shell before Ayla or anyone else can crush me.

CHAPTER ELEVEN

Adrift! A little boat adrift!

EMILY DICKINSON

I hate Mondays. I skipped breakfast because I stayed in bed with Hitch for too long. Our school lunch is unreasonably early, so I barely nibbled on the imitation cafeteria food. By the time school ends, I'm starving and my stomach's growling. I glance around the media center to make sure the handful of kids studying or using the computers don't hear it and remind myself to eat something—anything—for dinner. I tell myself to load up on veggies and hummus like Ayla. No matter how hectic my new schedule, I can't afford to skip meals. Bad eating habits can interfere with the effectiveness of my meds. Dr. Wellesley and my neurologist would flip if they knew I wasn't making nutrition a priority.

For the twentieth time I peek at the clock above the checkout desk, wondering if Chatham's going to stand me up. He's seven minutes late.

Maybe he won't show. We took our literary time periods test this morning, and he was grinning from ear to ear when he walked out of Ms. Ringgold's room. Maybe he realized he doesn't need my help after all.

I check my phone again to see if he texted me. Nothing. If he's not here in three minutes, I'm leaving.

I shuffle my notes on postmodern literature, trying to look busy, which is pointless, as I'm pretty invisible to most everyone at this school. I should be happy. A couple of weeks ago, I would rather have died than be here. Now, I'm not so sure. I still think it's better to keep my connections to a minimum. If Chatham fades out of the picture, that only leaves Ayla to explain my departure to, and I'm pretty sure I still want a departure.

When I glance at my phone again, I see a missed-call notification from Mom. My hands tighten like fists. Last night, an unfamiliar number popped up on her phone again.

"Who is it?" I asked, sounding way less concerned than my insides felt.

"Wrong number," she answered without much thought.

"You've been getting a lot of those," I said without trying to hide the edge to my voice.

Her head snapped toward me. Our eyes locked. My stomach tightened, warning me to proceed with caution, but I barreled right ahead.

"You seem to have a lot of new stuff going on in your life lately," I hedged.

"What does that mean, Emilie?" She enunciated each word carefully.

"It's just an observation, Mom."

Tense silence draped every molecule of oxygen in the room. She blew on her chai tea and started to take a sip.

"And then, you know, there're also the manicure and sundress . . ."

She paused mid-sip, peering at me through the steam rising from her cup.

"... and Dad's clothes all boxed up in the closet." The words came out all jumbled together in one incomprehensible mess.

She struggled to swallow, then carefully placed her cup on the table. "First of all, Emilie, I am an adult and your mother. I do not have to explain myself. But I will, because I love you. Some things are changing around here—your school for one. Change is not always fun, but it is a part of life."

When she started quoting Dr. Wellesley, I gritted my teeth and tuned her out.

I'm not buying it. Something's up. The thought that she might be interested in someone—a man other than my father—makes me squirm in my seat. The only good thing that came out of my little confrontation was she was eager for the change of subject when I also brought up applying to North Ridge's online-learning program. She said we'd discuss it at the end of the three-month trial period, which was an improvement from the last time I brought up taking virtual classes.

Two minutes since the last time I looked at the clock, the media specialist announces that students should begin making their final checkouts. I take that as my cue to tuck my papers into my backpack and head for the door. I'm texting Mom to tell her I finished early when a familiar gray T-shirt that reads *Dare to Soar* in front of a picture of the Wright Brothers on Jockey's Ridge stops me in my tracks. The air whooshes from my lungs.

"I'm sorry I'm late." Chatham smiles down at me. "Don't leave."

"Oh ... I ... uh." I bite my lip. I sound like Dad's bad Elmer Fudd imitation.

Chatham guides me back to one of the empty tables in the center of the library. "Coach Carnes stopped me in the hall," he explains as he unzips the messenger bag slung across his chest. "He wanted to know about my English grade. I told him 'No worries—I have a tutor now. I'll definitely be eligible.'" The table squeaks when he drops his heavy bag onto it.

The media specialist scowls down her nose at us.

Chatham pulls out a rectangular package wrapped in papers from the funnies section of the Sunday paper. The gift is sealed with enough tape to secure two or three Christmas presents. He places it on the table in front of me.

"What is it?" I ask, sitting with my hands folded in my lap under the table, uncertain. What do I say? I haven't exactly been showered with gifts from hot guys in the past.

He laughs. "Open it. I found it at The Potter's House." He pushes the package toward me. "My mom and I volunteer there twice a month."

I don't know what surprises me more: the fact that Chatham York bought me a present or the fact that he volunteers with his mom at a thrift store for battered women and children.

I slip a finger under a loose piece of tape, tearing back a corner of paper, expecting a toy snake or something to pop out and scare me. But it's not a joke. It's an old book. I peel back the rest of the paper to reveal the title: *Collected Poems of American Authors*.

I'm speechless.

He leans across the table to inspect the book with me.

Careful not to crack the brittle spine, I open the front cover. Inscribed in Chatham's blocky handwriting on the first page is a Walt Whitman quote: *Keep your face always toward the sunshine—and shadows will fall behind you.*

"I thought you'd like it," he says. A flash of doubt flickers in his eyes before being replaced by the confident spark I've come to recognize.

"I love it." I concentrate on enunciating each syllable to cover the shakiness in my voice. "But you didn't have to buy me anything." I thumb through the old book in an effort to avoid his eyes.

"I know I didn't have to." He pauses, resting his elbows on the table. "I wanted to."

Suddenly I'm on high alert. Chatham's normally in constant motion. I don't think I've ever seen him sit so still. When he moves his hand across the table toward mine, I freeze. There isn't much physical contact in my life. Dad was the touchy-feely one in the family—always hugging me and Mom and rubbing my back after a seizure.

I want to meet Chatham halfway, but I promised myself I'd be careful—keep my distance. I feel like reaching out would be compromising my principles, crossing some invisible line in the sand. Plus, I can't stand the thought of Mom or Dr. Wellesley smiling at me with their smug I-told-you-so-Emilie smiles.

Instinct tells me to run while I can—that I'm about to be in over my head, about to be sucked out to sea in an undertow, about to drown. If I stick around too long, I'll make a fool of myself. It's inevitable. I need to escape with my dignity while I have a chance. So I just sit there like a lump of petrified driftwood on the beach. I want to run, but my feet feel like lead bricks.

I want to touch his hand, but I don't know how to reach out.

"Thanks," I whisper.

He pushes his chair back, coming around to my side of the table and pulling me to my feet. His hands rest on my hips.

When I look up at him, the left side of his mouth creeps up in a mischievous smile.

I slip one tentative arm around his waist, inhaling the smell of him—soap, oranges, and boy. I'm in heaven with my head against his chest. If people are watching, I don't know, because the entire library has blurred and faded into the background, like some special effect in a movie. I pray for time to stop right now while I'm wrapped safely in Chatham's arms. Despite all my promises to myself to keep my distance, I'm tired of bobbing around alone in the ocean, about to capsize. I want to grab on to Chatham like a life preserver.

He leans down, his mouth so close his breath tickles the sensitive skin in front of my ear. "Let's do something this weekend." His lips brush my earlobe.

I pull back, confused. "Like . . . like a date?" I ask, untangling myself from his arms.

The librarian steps out from behind the counter. She's wearing a disgusted "I'm about to write you up for PDA" face. Chatham smiles at her sheepishly. "Sorry, ma'am," he apologizes, and the woman retreats.

How does he do that?

He studies my face and nods, like he's just made an important decision. "Yeah. Like a date."

"Um . . ." This stuttering thing is getting out of hand. *Please say yes, please say yes, please say yes,* my heart begs. But as usual, my brain steps in to protect me from myself. "I, uh . . . I . . . My mom said something about family day this weekend." *Lame,* my heart screams. *That's the best you can do?*

"I'm flexible." He grabs my finger, wiggling my arm. "Let's climb Bodie Island Lighthouse."

I squirm free, my chest tightening at the thought of climbing anything higher than the steps to our front deck. It's too risky. What if I seize? "I don't think I can. I actually have to get going."

"But we didn't even have time to study."

"Sorry." I grab the poetry book and scraps of paper off the table. "It's too late to get started now. The media center's closing in a few minutes."

His face falls. "What about another day this week?"

"I'll let you know tomorrow." I press my lips into what's supposed to be a smile. "Okay?"

I don't wait for an answer, turning to go, hurrying past the onlookers who've been gawking at us. When the media center door closes behind me, I groan. It's been eighty-something days since I've seized. Maybe I should just take a leap of faith and say yes.

CHAPTER TWELVE

The Brain— is wider than the Sky—

EMILY DICKINSON

On Tuesday, Ms. Ringgold returns our literary time periods tests. I earn a ninety-eight and a note in purple glitter pen saying how much she enjoys having me in class. Chatham receives a ninety and a pat on the back.

"I got an A—a ninety. A big, fat nine zero." He waves his paper in the air, and the entire class cracks up.

"Seriously, dude? You're making me look bad," Derek complains, but he's smiling as he flips his messy brown curls off his forehead.

Chatham winks at me, and the trembly feeling I've come to associate with being in the same room with him flickers in my belly. He hasn't confronted me about another tutoring session this week or about a date this weekend. If he does, I don't know what I'll do. One minute, I think I should just do it. The next, I know the risk is too great.

"Your grades were good." Ms. Ringgold pauses. "So good, in fact, I'm going to let y'all have the rest of the period to review for another class or work on your annotations and analysis essays." She beams as she rotates a pot of violets in the windowsill. The woman must have two green thumbs, because the flowers are plump and cascading over the sides of their mismatched pots.

A few people get up to go work with their partners. Chatham slides his desk up to mine, his knee grazing my leg. We're both wearing shorts, hanging on to the last days of warm weather before the wind off the Atlantic rushes in with her biting teeth.

"So, partner, thanks for tutoring me." He drapes an arm across the back of my chair while I try not to stare at the ropey muscles in his forearm.

"There's no need to thank me." I open my notebook, flipping pages, looking for my Dickinson quotes.

His hand brushes the back of my neck as he removes his arm, placing a palm on my papers, stopping me mid-page turn. "Sure, there is. Making an A is huge."

"Why? You seem really smart." I glance around the room to see if anyone's watching us.

"I am pretty smart when it comes to playing basketball, or even with math and science," he says, picking up my pen and doodling a picture of a lighthouse in the margin of my paper. "Not so much with reading."

With his head bowed, I can't see his eyes.

"When I was in first grade, I had a hard time learning to read. My mom took me to all these doctors. We found out I had tunnel vision." He stops drawing for a second to study my face. "It sucked being the only kid reading those little phonics books when everybody else had moved on to Magic Tree House."

I can't help smiling. Jack and Annie were my best friends in first grade, the year before I was diagnosed with epilepsy, back when I still believed magical tree houses packed with books could transport me to faraway lands.

He goes back to his sketch, filling in the horizontal black bands around the lighthouse.

"But you didn't give up on reading." I've only known Chatham for a few weeks, but a few weeks is long enough to know he's not a quitter.

"Nope, and look at me now—making As, hanging with the smartest girl in class." He's writing something under the lighthouse sketch.

I tilt my head to read his words. *Bodie Island Lighthouse? Please?*

"Oh. Uh . . . I have that family-day thing with my mom." I shove my hands under my thighs.

The thing is, I really, really want to say yes. On one hand, all I ever do is wish for normal. Cute high school boy, plus crush, plus fun outing, sounds pretty normal. On the other hand, saying yes is opening myself to serious physical and emotional peril. I've weighed the consequences, and no amount of normal is worth the risk of humiliating myself in front of Chatham. It would be bad if we were at school and I seized. It would be worse than horrible if we were alone somewhere without any adults trained to handle a seizure, and he had to care for me while I puked or worse.

"Which day?" He watches my face as he leans over to pull an orange out of his backpack.

"Saturday." I pause. "My mom's super strict about stuff like that." A burst of citrus invades my nose when his thumb punches through the thick skin and into the heart of the fruit.

"What about Sunday?"

"I have plans on Sunday too." I draw a dark cloud above his lighthouse without explaining that my unofficial plans involve an eight-year-old and a game of Monopoly.

He crosses his arms, his brow creased.

Somehow, I doubt Chatham has much experience with rejection. I open my mouth to apologize, but before I can, Derek lumbers over.

"What's your secret, dude?" He props himself on the corner of my desk, smiling. "I thought we had this unspoken agreement to maintain the status quo, the mediocrity, to not stand out academically."

"You're looking at it." Chatham gestures toward me with both hands, like one of those TV hand models on the Home Shopping Network Mom loves to watch even though she never has the money to buy anything.

Derek sits up, his eyes wide. "Really?"

I flip a page, trying to look focused, and wish his voice weren't quite so booming. When I look across the room, I notice Jules and the girl sitting beside her watching us, like they're studying us for a piece of creative writing or maybe a nonfiction piece on dating rituals.

"How about you share the love, man?" Derek slides off the desk, squatting so he's eye level with us. "My GPA could use a boost."

"No can do. She's all mine." Chatham grins, but his jaw is set, his eyes firm.

Derek throws up a hand in quick surrender—like he doesn't want to mess with bowed-up, ready-to-spring Chatham.

Chatham's last three words thaw the frost around my heart a little. *She's all mine. She's all mine. She's all mine.* I feel like that bacon-craving dog on the Beggin' Strips commercial—panting, *Bacon, bacon, bacon.*

When I look up, Ayla's watching too, smiling from ear to ear. She wiggles her eyebrows like she can read my mind, and I laugh.

Chatham and Derek turn in unison to face me.

"What's funny?" Chatham asks, squinting, obviously trying to read my thoughts.

"Nothing." I uncurl my spine. My shoulders rise higher than usual. Chatham and Derek couldn't appreciate the irony of the situation. Maybe Ms. Ringgold could, if this were a scene in a book. She'd probably say it was a cliché, though—the two cutest guys in the class vying for the awkward, bookish girl's attention. Or, in this case, her tutoring abilities. It's like my own strange little version of a fairy tale, and I want to freeze it in time to smile over once I've left this place.

When the bell rings, the fairy tale continues. "I'll walk you to class," Chatham says, grabbing my hand.

I breathe slowly, picturing a brown bag expanding and deflating in front of my mouth, so I won't hyperventilate. "Cool."

The one-word response doesn't sound cool at all. I make a mental note to work on my vocabulary. Thankfully, the hall is too loud and too crowded to carry on a conversation.

As we approach the door to my next class, Chatham squeezes my hand, stopping me in my tracks. We're pressed together against the lockers by a river of bodies.

Chatham studies my hand. "You don't seem like the kind of girl to play hard to get." The corners of his mouth turn up in a half smile.

If the situation weren't so unbelievably insane, I'd laugh out loud. Me play hard to get? "No, it's not like that at all." I glance toward my class. "You wouldn't understand."

"How do you know?"

The scene unfolds like a movie in my head. I'm having this whole out-of-body experience, watching myself from above as I interact with the cutest boy in eastern North Carolina. Except I don't know what my next line is. Though I can tell you it's definitely not "I can't go on a date with you because I have epilepsy."

The bell interrupts us. "You're going to be late. I've got to go." I pull away, telling my feet to move, but they ignore me. It's like the few times I've braved standing at the water's edge. A wave washes over my feet, warm and frothy. I freeze, standing perfectly still. Even though I know I'm not moving, it feels like I'm slipping forward toward the sea when the wave recedes, sucking at the sand around my feet. Chatham's like that: an invisible current, a swell of floodwater threatening to wash out my foundation. If I don't reinforce the levees around my heart, I'm going to float away. Or drown.

"It's just my mom's crazy protective." I tell myself it's not a total lie and avoid his skeptical gaze. When my science teacher pokes his head out in the hallway, shooting us the evil eye, my feet decide to cooperate, dragging me into the lab and away from Chatham. I mouth the word "Sorry" as I slip inside the classroom.

CHAPTER THIRTEEN

An awful Tempest mashed the air—

EMILY DICKINSON

A t home, after the world's longest day at the Ridge, Hitch and I cuddle on the couch. Our sofa wasn't meant to support me and eighty-something pounds of squirming golden retriever, but I don't have the heart to tell him to get down. He's the one thing in this crazy world I can always count on—my rock, my best friend. When we were first introduced at Canine Companions four years ago, it was love at first sight. Dad used to tell anyone we met this story about how Hitch and I were like an old, married couple. From the moment we laid eyes on each other, we were *hitched*. People would shake their heads in confusion. Then Dad would explain the bad pun on Hitch's name.

I used to cringe when Dad told personal stories to the mailman or to strangers in line at the hardware store or when he sang along to his favorite eighties songs on the radio. Now I'd give anything to hear him. A dull ache pulls in my chest when I try to recall his voice. My shoulders slump as I hug myself, trying to block out the emptiness.

It's weird. I can remember every detail of his tan face, the indentation in his cleft chin, even the way the sun glinted off his five o'clock shadow when he didn't shave, but I can't recall his voice. I mean, I'd know it in an instant if I heard it, but I can't quite re-create it in my head. When I try, it's hollow, distant, like the summer I was seven and we made a homemade telephone out of tin cans and a piece of string. For an entire summer, I carried around my contraption. Dad was the only person who didn't get tired of talking to me with a can to my ear. He'd whisper entire bedtime stories to me that way, long after Mom refused to communicate via the rickety apparatus.

The only way to smother the pain rising from my chest to my throat is to think about something else. I stare at the Whitman poem Ms. Ringgold assigned, but my mind keeps wandering. Every once in a while Hitch sighs or nudges my hand, reminding me to keep petting him.

I'm highlighting an implied metaphor in a line of poetry when the phone rings. The fluorescent pink marker jags across the page. I hurry over to the bar, grabbing the cordless phone. The number on the caller ID looks vaguely familiar, so I answer. There's a long pause before a male voice asks to speak to Mom.

"She can't come to the phone right now," I lie. If I made the effort to stick my head out the front door and call for her, she could come to the phone. She's only walked downstairs to check the mail.

"You must be Emilie." The voice tries to strike up a conversation.

I picture a flat-faced, smiling pug of a man hitting on my mother and almost throw up a little in my mouth. "Do I know you?"

Hitch jumps off the couch, coming to stand at my side, alert to the ice in my voice.

"I'm Roger." He breathes into the phone as he speaks. "Your mother's friend Roger."

He emphasizes the word *friend* as I concentrate on not puking.

"I've heard a lot about you." He hesitates, like he's choosing each word carefully. "All good, of course."

I roll my eyes, digging the fingernails of my free hand into my palm, willing myself to at least be polite if not sociable. "Really? I haven't heard anything about you." Ouch—I don't mean to be rude. It's just . . . this is too weird.

Mom dating.

Me not.

Roger gives up on the friendly chitchat. I glance at Hitch, who does this thing where he raises one eyebrow, then the other, and lets his lower eyelids sag. He's obviously disappointed by my lack of social graces. If Hitch were a person, he'd be Mother Teresa or Gandhi or someone who treated all living creatures with the respect they deserve. It's depressing how my dog is a better human being than I am.

Before Roger can sputter out another cheery response, I mumble a quick good-bye and something about giving Mom the message he called, then shove the phone down on the charger. Bracing myself against the counter, I close my eyes and exhale through my nose. Specks of light flash on the back of my closed eyelids.

Hitch whines as I wipe my palm on my ratty sweatpants, but he doesn't tug on my clothing in an effort to pull me to a safe place, which means I must just be overstressed and freaking out and not about to have an actual seizure. I open my eyes and study the sea oats outside the kitchen window, swaying on the dunes out back. My breathing begins to slow until the back door opens and Mom comes breezing in with a handful of envelopes and sale flyers.

Then all my pent-up emotions erupt. "Your *friend* Roger called," I hiss, fists balled at my side.

A furniture advertisement slips from her hand, swishing to the floor. "Okay. Thanks." She bends to pick it up, avoiding my eyes. "I'll call him later."

"I can't believe you're doing this." I stomp my foot like a spoiled five-year-old who didn't get the toy she wanted in her Happy Meal.

"Doing what, Emilie?" When she looks up at me, the ceiling light casts shadows on her face, accentuating the dark circles under her eyes.

Swallowing the lump in my throat, I spit out the *d*-word we've both been avoiding: "Dating." We lock eyes. "Mom, you're dating."

"Is that really such a horrible thing?" There's heat in her voice, and I withdraw a step, afraid I might have awakened a sleeping dragon. The color drains from the hand she uses to grip the mail. Her nostrils flare. "Your father loved me. He would want me to be happy."

"No." I choke on the argument. "He told me you were like geese, that you mated for life."

Her free hand clutches her stomach like I punched her. She steps toward the breakfast table, grabbing one of the ladder-back chairs for support. "We *were* geese, Emilie. We did mate for life." Her voice is barely more than a whisper. "But your father . . . died." She turns the chair around, sinking into the sagging, woven seat, her eyes fat with tears. "He left *me*, Emilie. He left *me*."

When her shoulders sag, Hitch pads across the room to lay his big head in her lap.

"It wasn't his fault!" I scream, swiping my palm along the windowsill above the sink. Dad's collection of beach glass slaps the counter, clatters in the stainless steel sink, and crashes to the hardwood floor. "And—you're a liar. All this crap about emotional development has nothing to do with me. It's all about you and your . . . your *friend* Roger."

Mom flinches but stays in her seat. Hitch's eyes ricochet nervously back and forth between our faces. I run to my room, slamming and locking the door behind me before throwing myself face-first on the bed.

I hate her. I hate my life. Most of all, I hate myself. I'm being immature. What kind of teenager is jealous of her own mom? But Mom had the love of her life once already. Now, she's going to start dating again. My forty-two-year-old mother is going to find another goose and soar off into the sunset. I'll be an armadillo or something equally hideous for the rest of my life, burrowing around in my shell, too afraid to take a risk on a relationship. I'm a coward.

And I'm always going to be miserable if I don't do something about it. Soon.

CHAPTER FOURTEEN

Much Madness is divinest Sense—

EMILY DICKINSON

Hitch scratches at my bedroom door around eight that night. I open it to let him in, relocking the door behind him. He jumps on the bed, and I lie down beside him, draping an arm across his chest. We lay like that for a long time. When Mom jiggles the doorknob and whispers my name around ten o'clock, I pretend to be asleep. Hitch whines but doesn't get up.

By eleven, Mom's room is quiet, and it's pretty obvious I won't be falling asleep any time soon. I flip on the bedside lamp, glancing around the room for a distraction, and on the nightstand, there's the little book of poetry Chatham gave me, staring me in the face. Anything is better than thinking about the scene I caused in the kitchen tonight. So I open the cover, careful not to damage the fragile spine.

Chatham's bold handwriting grabs my attention. *Keep your face always toward the sunshine—and shadows will fall behind you.* A smile pulls at the corners of my lips. The first time I read the inscription in the media center, I was too overwhelmed by Chatham's physical closeness to really comprehend the message. But now, in the quiet of my room, the irony hits me. The first time I met him, he reminded me of the sun. How I would love to keep my face toward that flaming ball of light and let the shadows created by epilepsy, Mom, and all my insecurities fall behind me.

If I were a glass-is-full kind of girl like Ayla, I would take Chatham up on his invite to Bodie Island Lighthouse. If I were a glass-is-full kind of girl, I would believe Mom and Dr. Wellesley when they said my seizure meds were working. I'd be optimistic about not having an episode in almost three months—at least one that I'm aware of. There's always a chance I could've seized in my sleep. But Hitch is super reliable about waking Mom, and that hasn't happened.

I kick my legs over the side of the bed, pulling open the drawer of my bedside table and fumbling around until my hand grazes the spiral notebook I'm supposed to use to journal about my seizures.

My neurologist seems to think I might be able to ward off some of my seizures by controlling my sleep, diet, and stress levels. Personally, I think he's crazy. I've never been able to determine any rhyme or reason to what triggers a seizure. They just happen. They're like storms during hurricane season—inevitable. I can try to lessen the damage by boarding up the windows and barricading myself in the house, but all the plywood in the world won't push back the gale-force winds or the rising tides of a grand mal seizure.

I flip toward the back of the notebook in search of my last entry—July 15. Glancing at the golden retriever calendar hanging on the back of my closet door, I realize it's the fifteenth of October. It's been exactly three months since my last seizure. I can't believe Mom and I both forgot my three-month anniversary.

Ugh. I want to run into her room, jump on her bed, and do a little victory dance. But I can't since we're not speaking— well, since I'm not speaking to her. The last time I went three months without a seizure was before I was diagnosed with epilepsy when I was seven years old.

When I bounce on the bed, Hitch lifts his head. "I haven't had a seizure in three months," I whisper, squeezing his jowls and laughing at his scrunchy fish face. "Hitch, what if my meds *are* working?"

He raises his left brow, placing a paw on my thigh.

I bend down to kiss the top of his blond head, then float across the room to grab my phone off the dresser, my heart racing. This is huge. I need to celebrate, to face the sun, to let the shadows trail behind me.

Before I can second-guess myself, I open the contacts in my phone and scroll to the Cs. My finger develops a mind of its own and presses the message button. Are you awake? I hit Send, instantly doubting myself. What have I done?

Yes

Crap. Crap. Crap. I rack my brain for a clever response. I'm an idiot. I should turn off my phone and pretend I never texted Chatham. But I'll see him in class tomorrow. My pulse throbs in my neck. What do I say? He has to know something's up. I've never called or texted him first.

Hello?

I have to say something. I stare across the room. When I blink, my vision clears. The dog on the calendar smiles encouragingly. It's been three months, I remind myself. Channeling my favorite butt-kicking Disney princess, Mulan, I start typing. Hey, do you still want to go to Bodie?

My phone's dead weight in my damp palm. I've lost my freaking mind. It's taking too long for him to respond. My free hand hovers at my neck as I inhale through my nose. If I don't relax, my heart's going to thump out of my chest.

Hitch whimpers.

When I squeeze my eyes shut, an image of a sleepy Chatham, lying on his bed, his sandy-brown hair mussed, flashes in my head, and a little groan escapes my lips. He's changed his mind, invited someone else, decided I'm not into him. He's laughing at me, toying with me.

The phone vibrates. I jerk, bumping Hitch with my elbow. He narrows his eyes.

"Sorry, Hitch. I'm an idiot."

He rests his head on his front legs with a sigh.

I've been reprimanded by my dog. Squinting with one eye, I dare to peek at the phone.

What about family day?

Crap. What about family day? What about family day?

My mom had a change of plans.

And now I'm lying to the nicest boy on the face of the planet.

Great! Saturday at four?

Stop! Abort! the voice in my head commands, like Captain Kirk from the helm of the *Enterprise*. But do I listen? Of course not. I lack even one tidbit of Spock's logic.

Yes. Saturday at four. :)

My plan is riddled with more holes than a duck brought down with one of Granddaddy Day's shotguns. I don't know whether to be more worried the buckshot will maim my relationship with Mom, who has no idea I'm putting myself out there on the dating front, or that I'll mortally wound myself.

One thing's for sure: I'm taking risks, and Dr. Wellesley seems to think that's what's going to lead to me breaking out of my shell. But taking risks also leads to skydiving accidents, motorcycle crashes, and brain injuries. I guess one way or another other, I'll develop or die.

When Hitch stands, scratches the quilt where he's been lying, circles a few times, and collapses in a lump back in his original spot, I know it's my signal to go to sleep. And I try. I really, really do. But I end up tossing and turning until the alarm clock buzzes at six thirty, forcing me to face the day, my mother, and eventually Chatham.

CHAPTER FIFTEEN

The Heart asks Pleasure—first—
And then—Excuse from Pain—

EMILY DICKINSON

On Wednesday, Chatham suggests we move our study session to the picnic tables behind the cafeteria. I'm feeling braver, and I'm a sucker for the mid-October temperature. If I'm going to follow through on this Bodie thing—I guess it's a date—I'd better get used to spending time alone with Chatham.

We have the place to ourselves except for three kids from the middle school next door involved in a vicious game of keep-away on the soccer field. The sand dunes, extending from Jockey's Ridge along the spine of the island, rise up behind them to the west, where the grass ends. In a couple of hours, the sun will turn orange, then red, then maroon, like the mural in Ayla's living room, before dipping behind the creamy ridge of sand in the distance.

"Have you started your essay?" Chatham asks. "Mine's done, and you're going to be impressed." He smiles, leaning over to dig it out of his backpack.

This is not the language arts student I met my first day at the Ridge—the one who fidgeted nervously while Ms. Ringgold returned papers. This boy is the bold MVP who sees a challenge and meets it head on.

The afternoon sun highlights the streaks of blond in his light brown hair. Another reason to love October, when all but the last tourists have left for the season. Something about the slant of light just makes everything look better, softer somehow.

"Yes." I lie. I have no idea what I'm going to write about, but I'm not telling him that.

Ms. Ringgold assigned this five-hundred-word essay, due tomorrow. Her lecture today included a twenty-five-slide PowerPoint detailing Jack London's life. According to Ms. Ringgold, London was everything from an oyster pirate—whatever that is—to a gold prospector before settling down to a life of professional writing. She gave us the spiel about the importance of pursuing our dreams with a "single-minded focus"—her words, not mine—and expects us to write an expository essay by tomorrow explaining what we want to be or do when we graduate.

Apparently, the assignment was much easier for Chatham than for me. He lays his crumpled two pages on the table in front of me, smoothing the wrinkled corners with both hands. "I've known what I wanted to do since seventh grade."

I imagine the typical teenage-boy scenarios—soldier, professional athlete, astronaut. As usual, Chatham surprises me.

"I want to go to Chapel Hill and get a degree in counseling." His chest inflates. His shoulders rise, like he's just announced he's going to discover a cure for cancer or something. "I want to be an elementary school counselor when I graduate."

"That's pretty specific." I remember him saying something about volunteering at The Potter's House when he gave me the poetry book in the media center, and realize yet again what a genuinely nice guy Chatham is and what a jerk I've been for withholding the truth.

"Yep." He pushes the paper toward me. "My little sister was diagnosed with Asperger's when she was three."

My mind flashes to the serious little girl on the beach as I try to remember where I've heard of Asperger's. I come up blank.

"It's a high-functioning kind of autism. It makes her a little clumsy and affects her social skills." He shrugs. "Mom and I love her. We don't care, but kids can be cruel."

"What about your dad?" I ask. The man on the beach didn't seem like he'd have much patience for imperfection.

"My dad's not around much unless sports are involved." He pauses to watch the kids horsing around near the goals. His normally bright eyes darken, his face hardens.

I try not to stare.

"My parents kind of do their own thing. Since Mary Catherine was diagnosed, that means Mom does everything for my sister and Dad spends all his time at his office working. My dad says he hates quitters, but he totally quit on Mary Catherine when times got hard." His hands ball into fists—tight white against the weathered gray boards. "I do *not* quit. Plus, I'm pretty good at the whole man-of-the-house thing."

He twists his lips into a smile as he shrugs, obviously uncomfortable with his show of emotion and ready for me to read his work.

I'm starting to believe that everybody's life might be a little messed up—maybe even as screwed up as mine. Ayla's mom walked out on her and her dad. Chatham's parents "do their own thing." His sister has Asperger's. Ms. Ringgold's son has Down syndrome. I mean, what the heck? Where are the Cleavers of the world?

I blink, focusing on his writing. He starts with an anecdote about Mary Catherine repeatedly falling and bumping her head when she was two, long after most kids have mastered walking. I feel his warm eyes on my face as I read, and I swallow. He proceeds to share another situation with an insensitive woman in a restaurant who insulted his mother's ability to discipline her own child. He goes on to explain how he wants to educate patients, families, and the public to help make the world more tolerant of people with special abilities and needs. I insert a missing comma in a compound sentence, break one really long paragraph into two, and make a few other minor revisions. All in all, the essay is well done and touching. I'm speechless.

When I look up, he's smiling.

"Do you like it?" he asks.

I nod, blown away by Chatham's big heart. Which is weird, because the first time I saw him, I assumed it was his Abercrombie good looks, not his heart or his mind, that made him so appealing to students and teachers. "Yeah. I corrected a few grammatical things, and that's it. You want to look at my comments and see if you have any questions?" I hand over the paper, focusing all my energy on my left hand so he won't see how unsteady I am in his presence.

He glances at my notes. "I got it." He shoves an open palm in my direction. "So? Let me read yours."

I shake my head, sliding my hands back toward my

stomach. One of them scrapes the weathered boards, and I wince. Yanking my palm toward my mouth, I blow on the jagged line of splinters piercing my skin. But before I can do more, Chatham grasps my hand and runs a finger along the slivers of gray wood. I flinch.

"Watch the kids." He waves in the general direction of the soccer field.

When I turn, he gently pinches the first splinter from my palm.

"Then at least tell me what you want to do when you graduate," he continues as he presses the inside of my hand with his thumb, plucking the remaining gray flecks from my skin. When he massages my palm with his warm index finger, the hyperactive hummingbird in my stomach takes flight.

There's no way I'm telling him I just want to be normal, to be safe. That I don't want to have epilepsy. Short of that, who knows? I used to think I wanted to be a recluse and stay holed up at home with a dog and my books. But then I'd miss days like this. "I really don't know," I finally say.

His shoulders sag a bit. I should've said I wanted to join the Peace Corps or become a pediatrician or something half as noble as his life plan.

"What are you interested in?" he asks, his eyes searching my face.

I want to turn away, to stop my front teeth from pulling at my bottom lip. "Books," I blurt before I can help myself. Chatham has that effect on me—this need to bare my soul. Books? That's all I can come up with?

He perks up. "Reading them or writing them?"

I don't know. I chew on the inside of my cheek instead of

my lip, trading a visible bad habit for one I hope Chatham can't see. Taking a deep breath, I mentally scramble for the right answer. "Um, reading them, I guess." I'd love to be a writer, but I'm no Jack London. What kind of life experiences would I write about—homeschooling with Mom, vegging on the couch with Hitch? Hiding in plain sight?

"Maybe you could be a librarian." He lifts a brow, resting his chin on his hand as he studies my face.

I shrink away. "Uh, no."

"If you love books . . ." He shrugs, then pauses. I know he's waiting for me to explain.

"It's just my mom's a librarian."

Don't get me wrong, I'd love to be surrounded by books all day, every day. I'd be good at it too. It's just . . . I need to be different from Mom. I need to be brave and stop living in everyone else's shadows, following *their* footsteps. I need to venture out on my own. I'm tired of being a caterpillar—I want to be a butterfly.

My phone vibrates on the table and I jump. It's Mom. I glance at her text, breathing a sigh of relief. How ironic that I'm actually happy to be saved from this way-too-personal conversation by my mother. "Oh, uh, that's my mom." I stand, pushing back from the table and slipping my phone into the back pocket of my shorts. "She's out front. I've got to go."

As I sling my leg over the picnic table bench, he stands, bending down to lift my backpack from the sandy ground. When he leans forward to slip it onto my right shoulder, his face lands inches from mine. In the late afternoon sun, his blue eyes turn violet. I think I might swoon like one of the heroines in the racy novels Granny Day keeps tucked under her bed. If he kisses me, I'll die—whether from shock or ecstasy, I'm not sure.

He smiles, seeming to sense my rising panic. "I can't wait till Saturday," he whispers, his voice hoarse as he pulls me in for a hug.

A cloud of heat blossoms in my lower belly, like the atomic mushroom clouds we studied in physical science when we learned the difference between fission and fusion. I melt into Chatham's chest as Ms. Ringgold's SAT Word of the Day flashes in my head: *nirvana*. "Me either," I murmur, and I really, truly mean it. I can't wait. Epilepsy, fear of heights, overbearing mothers—nothing will stop me.

When my phone buzzes a second time, he releases me, and I scurry toward the pickup line at the front entrance on a puff of optimism. Mom's face snuffs the hope flickering in my chest faster than a fire extinguisher on a candle. Before my butt hits the seat, we're involved in a game of twenty questions—all directed at me.

"What took you so long?" She swivels to study my face.

"I was helping a friend with an English paper." Not a lie; I mentally pat myself on the back.

"Oh?" She pauses, her eyes all squinty as she taps her pink fingernails on the steering wheel. I know she's trying to decide whether to be happy I've made another friend or worried that I might be slipping farther out from underneath her thumb.

"How was *your* day?" I turn the conversation back on her. "Did you see your *friend* Roger?"

She mumbles something about him stopping by the library to pick up research materials. Whatever. We head up the beach road toward home in the quiet abyss that's come to represent our relationship.

CHAPTER SIXTEEN

I breathed enough to take the Trick—

EMILY DICKINSON

Miracle of miracles, the bell rings a minute early Friday afternoon, releasing me from a torturous hour of Music Appreciation. I had no idea music could be so boring until I met Mr. Bottoms. The man stands in front of the room and *talks* about music fifty minutes a day, five days a week. You'd think he might do something crazy like *play* a piece of music every once in a while. But no, he's still talking when kids storm out the door and into the hall.

Grabbing my binders and backpack, I rush to follow them. "Excuse me," I mumble, squeezing alongside a group of surfers planning some bonfire shindig. I've got my own plans with Ayla tonight, which I'm actually looking forward to. I asked her to help me pick out something to wear to Bodie tomorrow and to coach me on the whole hair and makeup thing.

Look at me being social.

Ayla's waiting for me outside Music Appreciation. "Is he over there?" She cocks her head toward the double doors leading to the pool.

"Maybe." I shrug, falling in with the rush of students

flowing in the direction of the nearest escape, praying she'll follow. But she grabs the sleeve of Dad's hoodie, which I've been wearing a lot lately, halting me in my tracks.

"Let's watch." She tugs me toward the pool. "I told Katsu I'd check out their swim practice some time."

Ayla swears she and Katsu are just friends because of lit mag, but I've noticed how she gets all animated and starts talking with her hands when he's around and how he's always watching her out of the corner of his eye at lunch. There's definitely chemistry there.

"I'm allergic to chlorine," I blurt, unsure there's even such a thing as a chlorine allergy, but desperate times call for desperate measures.

Her brow furrows skeptically. "You might see Chatham in his swim team suit."

As tempting as that sounds, I can't do it. Ayla and Chatham would freak if they knew I've lived in Crystal Cove— on an *island*—my entire life, facing the Atlantic Ocean every day with my back to the Albemarle Sound, and can't swim. So if anyone saw how nervous I was near water and asked, I'd have to lie and act like I *can* swim. And I'm a terrible actress. Maybe a little better than when I started at the Ridge, but the drama kids aren't exactly begging me to join the thespian society.

"Come on, Ayla," I beg, inching toward the exit, crossing my fingers she'll follow. "Another time, I promise." I bite my lower lip, my eyes darting from her face to the door leading outside to the breezeway.

"Oh, okay." She falls in beside me. "But you're the one missing out. Chatham York looks good in that little wetsuit thingy."

I squeeze my binder against my chest. I have no doubt Chatham looks amazing.

The swarms of students thin when we reach the back parking lot. A vintage Volkswagen Bug—not one of the revamped, shiny Beetles that most teenage girls cruise the beach road in—sits in the last spot. Without asking, I know it's Ayla's. It's a true Carolina blue that any Tar Heel fan would be proud of, and it's sporting whitewall tires like the ones Granddaddy Day always kept on his pickup truck.

"I call her Gussy or Gus." She pats the roof of the car before opening the creaky driver's side door and tossing her Wonder Woman lunchbox into the back.

I sink carefully into the passenger seat, and Ayla laughs.

"Don't worry." She jams a key into the ignition. After a couple of wet coughs, the engine sputters to life. "Gus is tough as nails."

Gus may be tough, but she's slower than the sea turtles Dad and I used to watch at the Roanoke Island Aquarium. We never actually hit the speed limit as we cruise up the beach road with the windows rolled down—literally rolled down, like with a handle you turn. The radio crackles and Ayla spins the dial until she picks up a scratchy version of Jimmy Buffet singing about cheeseburgers in paradise.

When we reach the house, Mom's car is gone. I told her last night Ayla was coming over for a few hours, and she said she'd stay at the library a little later to catch up on work. I didn't ask for details, and she didn't offer any. But I seriously doubt there are piles of work to catch up on at the public library in the fall when the year-round population consists of maybe a few thousand residents.

Ayla pulls under the house, and we climb the steps to the front deck.

"You're so lucky to live on the beach." She peeks around the corner of the house to the ocean beyond.

"It's pretty cool." I shrug. I've never thought of myself as lucky—until recently.

When we step into the tiny living room, Hitch greets us with a smile and his favorite stuffed duck clamped in his mouth. Ayla reaches down to pet him, and he adheres himself to her leg, thrilled with the attention. He glances over his shoulder, brows raised, anxious for me to recognize how wonderful he is at making new friends.

Ayla breaks away, twirling around the room, arms outstretched like she's landed in a castle. Hitch and I watch, amazed by her enthusiasm. "This room makes me want to dance," she explains, gliding to the kitchen window. "Look at how the light touches everything."

She's right. She sees room to dance and opportunities to paint. And I've spent so much time focusing on a faded floral slipcover and a once-white kitchen table that's now more cracked and peeling than painted.

She caresses a piece of Dad's beach glass resting in the windowsill above the sink. Mom placed Dad's treasures back in their original arrangement—except for the largest pink piece. When I slung the collection across the kitchen the other night, it shattered. My chest tightens at the sight of the jagged shards sitting in a fruit dish beside the sink—broken, the way I pictured myself that night.

"Who found all the sea glass?" she asks, running a finger

along the flat green piece near the ledge and peering out at the dunes.

"My dad. He was the lucky one." It's true. He was the only one of the three of us to ever find a four-leaf clover, the only one to win thirty straight family-game-night Monopoly matches, and the only one in the family to ever score a piece of beach glass.

Ayla turns to face me. "'Was'?"

"Yeah." I paste on a smile, rubbing the tender hangnail on my index finger with my thumb. "He died three years ago."

She steps around the bar, heading toward me, but stops when she sees me flinch.

"I'm sorry." She offers a simple apology, and I love her for it. Most people would ask a million questions or give some lame bit of advice like "He's in a better place" or the one that really makes my blood boil: "It gets better with time." Those people don't understand how full of life my dad was, how he was the energy that kept our family on track and in motion, how empty and alone I felt after he died. They talk to comfort themselves because they don't know what else to do. I wish they'd just be quiet.

"He had lung cancer." I bite the inside of my cheek, willing myself not to cry. I can't believe I'm talking to Ayla about Dad. "He never even smoked." The words shoot out of my mouth like darts.

She opens her mouth to say something but stops. After a second's hesitation, she continues. "That sucks."

Only Ayla could sum it up like that. I laugh, and when I do, my shoulders relax and my hands unclench. For the first time since Dad died, I'm opening up to someone, a friend, and I'm laughing, not crying. Dr. Wellesley would be thrilled.

Ayla steps toward me, arms open, her flip-flops slapping the weathered boards beneath her feet.

I let her hug me. "You're right. It does suck."

I don't know whether it's the hug or the confession, but my chest expands. For the first time in three years, there's a fullness in my abdomen, like someone just released a vise on my lungs. And I'm sucking in deep lungsful of air and wondering why Dr. Wellesley or Mom or some other adult didn't think to remind me to breathe years ago.

CHAPTER SEVENTEEN

Are Friends Delight or Pain?

EMILY DICKINSON

By the time we take Hitch for a walk on the beach, organize the tray of snacks we raided from the pantry, and head to my room, the sun is dipping on the horizon.

Ayla turns on the overhead light and the lamp on the nightstand, then opens the blinds. "The *Mona Lisa's* the *Mona Lisa* wherever you hang her, but even the *Mona Lisa* looks better under the right light, in a room that accentuates the dimensions of her frame. So let's get cracking on highlighting your best features."

She gestures toward the chair with the painted butterfly seat at the little desk in the corner. Compared to Ayla's sleek white bedroom with its splashy red accents, my room is a throwback to a decades-old *American Girl* magazine. It's too late to worry about that, though, so I follow orders, sliding my butt onto the butterfly's smiling face. In addition to hiding, I realize I'm also good at following directions.

My earlier confidence falters under the glaring lights and Ayla's squinty inspection like a storm-swept piece of seaweed. To her, I am just a blank canvas.

"Ayla, I've changed my mind," I start to protest.

"Shh." She grips my jaw between her thumb and fingers, tilting my head from one side to the other, her brow furrowing. "Good bones," she murmurs, more to herself than to me.

"Great. Maybe Chatham's more into skeletons than facial features," I mumble, unable to enunciate clearly with her fingers pinching my chin.

"Bone structure's everything." She ignores my humor, obviously serious about emphasizing my best features. "We just need to pluck a few brow hairs to frame your eyes and highlight your high cheekbones with a little bronzer."

I kind of doubt it will be that simple. But I hate to deflate her enthusiasm, seeing as how she's my friend, so I keep my mouth shut.

"This will be a piece of cake." She steps across the room and opens the sliding door on my tiny closet. Her face falls when she spots the collection of graphic tees, khaki shorts, and jeans, but she doesn't miss a beat. "Let me run downstairs. I have a couple of emergency wardrobe items in my car."

Hitch raises a skeptical brow in my direction when she leaves. I shrug and reach for Ayla's makeup mirror, studying my reflection. Maybe it's not so bad after all. "You don't have to say anything. I know it's crazy."

It's hard to believe a few short months ago my mom was so worried about me becoming a pajama-wearing recluse, she upped my counseling sessions. It's like the chicken-or-the-egg paradox. Did I start feeling better because I got out of the house and out of my pj's, or did I start taking better care of myself because I was forced out of the house?

Hitch sighs, stretching out on his side, laying his big head on my pillow, content with the fact that he's right and he tried to warn me.

Ayla returns with a gold-sequined tank top, a strapless red sundress, and a couple of colorful tops with a pair of jeans.

"Sequins? To a lighthouse?" My nose curls. There are enough sparkles on that shirt to bring on a seizure.

My colon ties itself in a knot at the word *seizure*. I still haven't told Ayla about my epilepsy. She deserves better, and I really, really think I can trust her.

"Yeah, it would've been a stretch." She tosses it on the bed. "How 'bout the dress?"

"It's . . . tiny."

"Exactly." Grinning, she shoves the soft cotton at me. Hitch eyes the dress distastefully as she holds it up to my chest.

"Umm . . . not exactly lighthouse appropriate either. Plus, strapless isn't really my style."

"Oh, okay. You're right. You should be comfortable." She selects a shirt with rolled-up sleeves that ties at the waist and the very skinny jeans. "Royal blue's better for winter anyway."

I glance out the window. The wind's a little cooler, and it's getting dark a little earlier, but it's barely fall. "It's not winter."

"No. *You're* a winter." She brushes a strand of platinum hair off her forehead, smiling and shaking her head. "Your dark hair and fair complexion give your skin a cool tone."

How appropriate—my chilly temperament matches my skin tone. I tug on a wisp of hair near my cheek, wishing I could be warm and sunny like Ayla and Maddie and all the other beauties prancing around Crystal Cove. Or bold and confident like Jules with her purple hair. "Is the cool tone the reason I don't tan?"

"Pretty much." She twists the side bangs away from my face and secures them in back with two crisscrossed bobby pins. "But who cares about a tan when you have this flawless skin?" She skims my cheek with her fingers.

Whoa, flawless? The ocean breeze through the window must be going to her head.

"Seriously. It's porcelain-doll smooth." She pulls a little pouch of makeup out of her bag and unzips it, retrieving a pair of tweezers and going to work on my eyebrows. Pressing my lips together, I concentrate on not whining as she plucks stray hairs. She pauses every few minutes to study her work. I sit up a little straighter.

"That's it. Look at you. I've barely done a thing. It's more about how you carry yourself than it is about the makeup or clothes." She smooths my brows with her thumbs. "Quit hiding behind your hair, throw your shoulders back, and ditch the lifeless beiges and blacks. They're washing you out." She grabs the shirt from the foot of the bed, dangling it in front of my face. "Put this on."

"It's so . . ." I pause, searching for the right adjective. "Bright."

"You have to choose something." She glances from the royal blue shirt to the little red dress.

I accept it before she tries to choose for me.

"The color's perfect. The jewel tones will make you glow." She tosses me the jeans.

I scrunch my nose but drag myself out of the chair.

"Trust me," she says, digging through the lip glosses in her little bag. "I'm really good at this." She squints to read the color on a tube of lipstick. "Wait till you see yourself with lip gloss and earrings."

I shut myself in the bathroom. I want to believe her, but I have a hard time seeing myself the way she does. Ayla's awesome but also way overly optimistic.

I slip out of my tan fitted tee and denim shorts, then pull the top over my head and yank on the jeans, ignoring the reflection of graying bra and white granny panties. If Ayla dislikes my nondescript wardrobe, she'd be traumatized by the state of my underwear. I've just never seen any use for frilly bras and panties. What's the point when no one's ever going to see them?

A knock on the front door interrupts my thoughts. "Who's that?" I wiggle, trying to make sure no skin shows between the shirt and jeans.

Ayla's soft footsteps pad to the front of the house, followed by Hitch's clacking nails. "A little girl."

I frown. It must be Cindy, though I'm not sure why she'd be here tonight.

Mentally shrugging, I glance at myself in the mirror . . . and my jaw drops. Ayla's right. The blue of the shirt lights up my skin, turning it from *pale* to *alabaster*. The V-neck draws attention to my collarbone, lengthening my neck. With my hair off my face, my jaw and cheekbones look sharper, more defined. Ayla's an artist in more ways than one.

I can't imagine what Cindy will think when she sees me like this, but she must need me if she walked over here this late on a Friday evening. By the time I venture out of the bathroom to join them, she and Ayla are in the kitchen. Cindy kneels with her back to me, talking to Ayla, her arms wrapped around Hitch's neck.

When I enter, Ayla's face brightens. "You look gorgeous, darling." Her French accent is atrocious, but she's beaming like a proud grandmamma when she steps toward me.

I can't help giggling . . . until Cindy turns to face me. When I spot the angry bruise on her right temple, the laughter dies in my throat. "Sweetie, what happened?" I reach toward the fist-sized black-and-yellow oval marring her face, and she shrinks from my touch.

"Nothing." She pulls her mouth into something resembling a smile, but the pained look in her eyes doesn't fade. "I was playing hide-and-seek and ran into a door." Her hand shakes a little when she tucks a tuft of curly blonde hair behind her ear.

I glance at Ayla. Her facial expression perfectly sums up my feelings. Something's up. I've never seen Cindy this nervous before, and Hitch won't take his eyes off her face either.

"Mom wants me to borrow some packing tape if you have any." Standing with her hand on Hitch's broad head, she looks like a delicate sandpiper ready to scuttle away from the threat of an incoming wave or a predatory bird.

"Sure." I rummage around in the junk drawer in the kitchen, trying to buy time. "What're y'all working on?"

"Mom's just packing some boxes." Cindy runs her fingers through Hitch's thick mane without meeting my eyes. "She said it's okay if you don't have any." She steps toward the door.

"Wait." I hold up a yellowing roll of tape. "I found some." If I didn't think she'd run, I'd pull her in for a hug. But if anyone knows how it feels to want some space, it's me, so I give her what her stiff posture says she needs: room to breathe.

"Thanks." She accepts the tape, tilting her head back to examine my hair and outfit. "You look really pretty, Emilie." The angelic smile I'm familiar with lights up her face.

"Smart girl." Ayla nods approvingly, putting Cindy at ease with the same calm energy that washes away my self-doubt.

Two words from Ayla, and Cindy's posture improves too. Now she looks less like a shorebird and more like a little girl.

"Why don't you stay?" Ayla asks, moving toward the hallway. "You can help with Emilie's makeup and jewelry."

"Uh . . ." Cindy sighs, shuffling her feet, glancing from Ayla to the front door. "I better not. Mom's waiting."

I follow her as she inches toward the door, still eyeing her bruise. "Come see me tomorrow. Okay?"

"Okay." She slips out the front door and down the front steps. As her little blonde head fades into the evening light, my stomach tightens. Watching her go, I wonder what's causing the uneasy feeling in my gut. Kids run into stuff all the time, right? Still, I hope she does come over tomorrow. Maybe then I can figure out what's wrong.

Hitch whines, and I blink.

"Earth to Emilie." Ayla waves a hand in front of my face as she reaches to close the door.

Crap. I lost a minute there. Somehow, Ayla and Hitch crossed the room without me knowing. Did I just zone out for a second, or was that an absence seizure?

"Are you all right?" she asks as the door clicks shut.

"Um . . ." I have to tell her *something*. This episode could be nothing. I've been under a lot of stress with school and Chatham and this whole coming-out-of-my-shell thing. I could just be overly tired. Or it could be the precursor to something else—something big, like a grand mal seizure. My shoulders droop. It's now or never, and never's not really an option any longer. I owe Ayla the truth.

"Ayla, we need to talk."

CHAPTER EIGHTEEN

My friends are my "estate."

EMILY DICKINSON

I sit in the corner of the couch with a throw pillow clutched to my chest and Hitch curled at my feet. Ayla perches on the edge of Mom's old recliner opposite me, obviously anxious to hear whatever it is I have to say.

"I have epilepsy." I spit the sentence out in one big word: *Ihaveepilepsy.*

She exhales softly. As her face relaxes, she settles back into the worn upholstery. "Thank God."

"Thank God?" I knew Ayla was laid-back, but now I think she's lost her freaking mind. Digging my fingers into the pillow, I resist the urge to gnaw on my nails.

"Yeah, I thought you were going to say you were moving— or dying or something." She swings the lever on the side of the chair, extending the footrest. "You should've seen the look on your face."

My heart races and I try swallowing around the lump in my throat. "I don't think you understand what I'm saying. I have a seizure disorder—convulsions." If this were a cartoon, my high-pitched voice would shatter the glass in the windows.

"That's awful." She kicks the footrest down, gets up, and steps around the coffee table, joining me on the couch, resting a hand on my knee. "I'm so sorry you have epilepsy. But I can't help it—I'm relieved you're not going to die on me." Clasping my chin between her thumb and pointer finger, she angles my head so I'm facing her. "You're not going to die on me. Are you?"

I can't help it. I smile. If Dr. Wellesley or Mom tried this positive, reverse-psychology crap on me, I'd be furious. But coming from Ayla, it's funny in a kind of morbid way. Maybe she's right. I could have one of those brain-eating amoebas I saw on the Discovery Channel or cancer like Dad.

Secretly, though, I believe death is harder on the living than the dying. I think survivors experience the pain in its sharpest, rawest form. Dad looked pretty peaceful the night he closed his eyes in his hospice bed, with the soft cotton blankets pulled to his chin, and drifted away from us for the last time.

I shake off the memory before it progresses to the part where the funeral home came to pick up his body and the reality of our loss set in. "No, I'm not going to die on you."

"Then let's go teach you how to do your makeup while you tell me what I need to know."

And that's what we do. In my room, I tell Ayla what it's like to live with epilepsy. As she brushes my cheeks and nose with bronzer, I explain what kind of first aid she needs to be aware of if I seize: to make sure my airway is clear, roll me on my side, and basically ride it out—unless it lasts longer than five minutes. Then she needs to call 911.

As I stare at the ceiling, she glides her mascara wand along my upper lashes, and I describe the worst-case scenario: a grand mal seizure, when a person can puke or lose control of her bladder or bowels.

She nods and murmurs the occasional sympathetic sound, encouraging me to keep talking. "Who else knows?" she asks when I finish and she caps the tube of black noir mascara.

Every muscle in my body tenses. I try to speak, but my jaw's locked like the deadbolt on our front door. I know where this is headed, and I don't want to think about it.

A heavy stillness hangs over my room. The rustle of wind through the sea oats outside my window and Hitch's steady breathing are the only sounds in my universe—well, those and the voice screaming excuses in my head for why I haven't told anyone else yet.

Ayla finally breaks the quiet. "Emilie, does Chatham know?"

I lick my lips. The taste of the thick gloss caking my tongue makes me want to gag. I'm naked with my side bangs pulled back from my face. I shake my head.

She sinks to the bed beside my chair. "You've got to tell him." Her words dangle in the quiet room.

"I can't," I mumble, studying my hands.

"Why?" She scoots forward to the edge of the bed, angling her body so I have to face her.

"Because . . ." I lift a hand to my mouth to chew on my nails, think better of it, and fold my fingers in my lap.

"Because why?" She jiggles my knee, her eyes searching my face.

If she leans any closer, we'll be breathing the same air. "Because . . . I like him. I really like him." There. I said it.

There was this boy I really liked in elementary school—Nicholas Wilkins. I thought he liked me too. But a few days after my first seizure, I heard him making fun of me in the media center. Boys circled around him laughing while he rolled his eyes back in his head and flung his arms around with his tongue sticking out. They never even saw me behind the magazine rack.

Not long after that, I started homeschool.

It's stupid to compare Chatham to Nicholas Wilkins. But Chatham's not a girl—he's not Ayla. Friends can accept stuff like this better than potential boyfriends. I just need more time to figure out how to tell him.

Hitch jumps down from the bed, coming to sit with us, his ears raised.

"Emilie, Chatham York is one of the nicest guys I know." Ayla rubs the soft fur between Hitch's eyes. His ears relax. She even quiets my dog with her composure. "You're not giving him enough credit."

I'd give anything to experience her tranquil calmness for one day. How can she be so confident, so serene?

"I just can't. Not yet." I've deflated. My shoulders sag. The heat's gone from my voice.

"If he cares about you, the epilepsy won't be an issue." Her soft words loosen the knots in my head.

I wring my hands. "I know, but that's a big *if*."

"You have to have faith in him." She squeezes my hand. "Promise me you'll tell him tomorrow."

I've never been too great with the whole trust thing. Before Dad got sick, we used to go to this little Episcopal church on the beach road. In fifth grade, when I didn't want to go to children's church because I was worried about seizing, my parents talked to one of the Sunday school teachers about putting me at ease. She gave me a really great piece of advice. At snack time, while the other kids were wolfing down Goldfish crackers and Kool-Aid, she pulled me to her rocking chair in the corner and asked me if I prayed. When I nodded, she smiled like I'd given the correct response and then spewed this little nugget of wisdom: "If you pray, don't worry; if you worry, don't pray." She said worrying was like praying for what you *don't* want. Even in my ten-year-old mind, her advice seemed really astute.

I've always wanted to do that—pray, not worry. But it seems like the harder I try not to worry, the more I do. My chewed lips and ragged cuticles are the visible signs of the stress that's eating me from the inside out.

So Ayla's advice about having faith in Chatham is going to pose more than a bit of a problem. The probability of me all of a sudden learning to trust is about as likely as me finding a big lump of orange sea glass—the coveted color that eluded even my charmed dad.

But Ayla looks so hopeful that I can't disappoint her. "I promise. I'll tell him."

And just like that, my mouth makes an oath I'm not sure the rest of me can honor.

CHAPTER NINETEEN

My River runs to thee—

EMILY DICKINSON

Chatham will be here in less than an hour and Mom is irritated. I don't know whether she's more upset with me or the situation, and I'm not sure I care. She created her own catch-22. She wants me to branch out, to pursue this great social and emotional journey of self-discovery, but she's not willing to give me the freedom I need to grow.

If she's surprised by my social life, I'm not sure what she'll think about the royal blue shirt and the earrings.

Not long after Mom came in last night, Ayla bolted, so we never had time to accessorize. But she told me to wear something silver or platinum. No gold. I inventory the sparse accessories in my jewelry box for the third time as if the perfect necklace or earrings will magically appear if I just keep looking long enough. In the top tray, there's some costume jewelry from elementary school and a pair of pearl earrings Granny Day gave me for my thirteenth birthday. I grab the studs, sliding the first silver post through my earlobe and looking away from the little black pouch resting in the lower tray of the box.

Inside that bag is a charm bracelet. Other than the pearl

earrings, it's the only really expensive thing I've ever owned, and it's silver. Ayla would love it, but I can't wear it. My vision blurs just thinking about opening the drawstring on the velvet bag. I haven't looked at it in ages—not since Dad died.

I've had it for as long as I can remember. Dad swore it came from Santa Claus when I was a baby—that it just appeared in my stocking on my first Christmas. All my life charms have materialized on special occasions. Some kids got money from the tooth fairy or candy from the Easter bunny. I got those things too. But I also frequently found sterling-silver charms tucked under my pillow when I lost a tooth and hidden in the tippy toe of my stocking every Christmas morning.

The baubles always held some significance. When I started kindergarten, I found a little silver school bus in my Crayola pencil pouch. The year Hitch and I were matched, there was a golden retriever charm in my stocking. The last charm came on my birthday in eighth grade, a few weeks before Dad died. It was a white-enamel dove. I hung the symbol of peace on my bracelet, but after Dad died, I tied the whole bracelet up in the little bag, where it's stayed buried ever since. I'd give anything—anything—to have received just one more charm from Dad and have the opportunity to tell him how much I loved him.

My heart jumps into my esophagus when Chatham knocks on the front door. I consider faking a violent illness. But I can't do that to him. I have to save him from Mom's unavoidable interrogation and buy myself some time to tell him about the epilepsy on my own terms before Mom scares him to death.

Without a backward glance at my pulled-back hair or the little blue shirt, I march out to the living room to run the gauntlet past Mom. Chatham's shaking her hand when I reach the living room, and she hasn't eaten him. So, all in all, we're off to a decent start. More than anything in the world, I wish Dad were here to send me off on my first date. He'd crack a corny joke to put everyone at ease, and I wouldn't be standing here worrying about cardiac arrest.

Shaking off the wistfulness, I lift my shoulders and clear my throat. They both turn to face me. Mom's eyes bulge at my appearance, but they don't actually fall out of their sockets. Chatham's lips part, then squeeze shut, like when you recognize someone at the grocery store but the person's name stays lodged on your tongue until you're pulling out of the parking lot.

I swallow, careful not to let my jaw drop at the sight of him standing in my living room petting Hitch, who's plastered himself to Chatham's calf. Ralph Lauren and Calvin Klein would both be impressed by the way Chatham's broad shoulders fill out the simple white button-down and the way the khaki shorts hang from his narrow hips.

After his Adam's apple travels the length of his neck, he murmurs, "Hello."

The two-dimple smile sends my insides into a tailspin. "Hi," I whisper, reminding myself to maintain eye contact. "Well, I guess y'all have met." My hand flicks back and forth between the two of them.

"We have." A muscle twitches in Mom's jaw. "So . . . uh . . . ," she mumbles, twisting her hands. "You know the rules, Emilie."

At least I'm not the only one who's nervous. If I didn't know better, I'd think she had steel rebar for a spine—her posture's that stiff.

"Yes, Mom." Now my jaw's the one flinching. If she

embarrasses me, I'll never forgive her. When she stuck her head in my room last night to say good night, she snuck in about fifteen questions about this outing. I promised I'd already discussed the epilepsy with Chatham. I'm dead in the water if she asks him straight out.

"I want you to text me when you get to the lighthouse and when you're headed home." She speaks to me, but her eyes drill Chatham's face.

To his credit, his smile barely falters, like he's used to dealing with girls' parents. "Mrs. Day, I promise to take good care of her." He grabs my hand, lacing his fingers through mine. "You ready, Emilie?"

This is my shot at brave. This is my three-months-seizure-free celebration. My time to live a little. And Chatham York is holding my hand.

Breathe. Breathe. Breathe.

"Yes." I force a smile, concentrating on the one-word response. I'm not sure I'll ever be ready. But here goes. I set this whole mammoth wave in motion when I texted him the other night. And it's not stopping until it breaks gently on the shore—or crashes into something.

Mom follows us out onto the front deck, arms crossed, lips pressed together, a haunted expression on her face—the way she looked for the first twelve months after Dad died. A microscopic sliver of guilt stabs my heart. Dad's gone, and I'm leaving her.

No, I'm not leaving her. I'm going out with Chatham for a few hours. She's the one who wanted me to branch out and make friends, to put away the pajamas, to live. So she should be happy. This is exactly what she wished for. No turning back.

And besides, if she would've remembered my three-months-seizure-free anniversary, I never would've planned my own celebration.

Now that I'm really heading out of the house, I'm feeling a little better. I'd be safer in my room with Hitch and a good book, but what are the chances that something will actually go wrong the few hours Chatham and I will be gone tonight?

Chatham follows me down the front steps to the black SUV waiting in the driveway. His car is as masculine as he is, with a rack on top for surfboards, a rack on the back for bicycles, and some winch-looking thing on the front big enough to pull wildebeests out of the Nile.

He opens the passenger door for me, gesturing toward the leather seat. "Your chariot awaits."

"Thanks." I try to look graceful hoisting myself into the vehicle. "I've never ridden in a chariot."

"Today's special, and special days call for special transportation." His eyes twinkle as he waits for me to buckle up. The car's so high, he's practically eye level with my thighs. My cheeks warm when he looks up from my legs to my face. "You look beautiful, by the way." He smiles sheepishly, shutting the door and walking to the driver's side.

I tug on my shirt, making sure it's covering my waist, cursing Ayla for talking me into trying something new. I should've stuck with my uniform: shorts and a tee.

He slides behind the wheel, and I try to repay the compliment. "Thanks. You . . . uh, look nice too." Nice? That's the understatement of the millennium. I abhor the way I revert to the monosyllabic vocabulary of kindergarten when I'm around him. If it gets much worse, I'll be *goo-goo*-ing and *ga-ga*-ing like an infant.

He slides the gearshift into Reverse. Swiveling to check traffic before backing out of the driveway, he places a hand on the rest behind my head. Twisted in the seat like he is, with his face inches from mine, I forget to breathe. But I notice every detail of the damp hair curling at the nape of his neck and the way the pink sunburn on his nose highlights the blueness of his eyes. When I remember to breathe, my head fills with the orangey citrus of his shampoo.

"You can change the music if you want." He points to his phone, resting in the console between the seats, as he pulls onto the beach road.

I rest my hands in my lap, trying to look casual. "This is good."

Thankfully, Chatham's great at making conversation. We talk about Hitch and Ms. Ringgold's assignment. I even ask a few intelligent questions about basketball.

"Not many kites today." He points at Jockey's Ridge as we head south into Nags Head. "I guess it's too windy."

I've been so distracted by his closeness, I missed the breeze picking up and the dark clouds moving in from the sound behind us. Normally the massive dunes, the highest in the eastern United States, are covered with people flying colorful kites and even speckled with the occasional hang glider. But today, with the exception of a few touristy-looking types on foot, the ridge is deserted.

"Maybe we should try Bodie another day," I suggest. I haven't been thrilled by the idea of climbing a one-hundred-and-sixty-five-foot lighthouse, but I kept telling myself retirees and kids do it all the time. Plus, this is my big day—my day to have fun, to take chances, to live a little.

But I probably should've stuck with baby steps—something along the lines of a walk on the beach or strolling up to the Wright Brothers Memorial. Climbing Bodie on a windy day with the possibility of a storm on the horizon doesn't seem like such a good idea.

"No way." The car slows as he takes his foot off the accelerator to glance at me. "I checked the weather. There's only a small chance of isolated showers."

Yeah, but I've been the girl with the black cloud hanging over her head for so long that I can't help being a little skeptical. Me and Murphy's Law have been best buds for a while. I've even been his poster child. He loves me because if anything can go wrong with anyone, it generally will with me.

"But those clouds look like they're moving kind of fast," I say.

"I guess we could go to Fat Boyz for ice cream or something instead." His tone is upbeat, but his smile wavers. He wants me to climb Bodie to have this great experience so he can feel like he's repaid me for the tutoring, which is entirely unnecessary.

Chatham glances at me, eyebrows raised. "So what's it going to be?"

"Let's do the Bodie thing." I lift the corners of my mouth into something that I hope resembles a smile. When I grip the door handle, it squeaks beneath my wet palm.

The fifteen-or-so-minute drive south on Highway 12 feels more like three. Chatham entertains me with action-packed stories about surfing in pre-hurricane tides, and before I know it, he's flipping his right turn signal at the Bodie entrance. The bold black-and-white stripes of the tower rise up behind the white keeper's house. Bright October sunbeams shimmer on the road leading up to the lighthouse, and slate gray clouds tumble around on the eastern horizon. It's like two worlds are about to collide, and the universe wants to draw attention to its stark contrasts—the differences between light and dark, fair and foul, Chatham York and Emilie Day.

But I've made a decision, and I'm going to follow through, barring any unforeseen disasters.

CHAPTER TWENTY

*We never know how high we are
Till we are called to rise.*

EMILY DICKINSON

W ell, if it isn't one of my favorite volunteers," a park ranger says to Chatham as we approach the front desk.

"I'm one of your *only* volunteers, George." Chatham offers his hand to the man behind the counter.

"We haven't seen you enough lately."

"I've been volunteering at Potter's House since you guys finished the renovations here."

"Of course you have. Well, with all the hours you put in here last year, you've more than earned a free ticket for you and your lady friend." George hands over two complimentary tickets, winking in my direction. "And I think you know enough of the history and safety regulations to guide your own tour."

My ears perk up at the words *safety regulations*.

"I've always wanted to be a tour guide." Chatham grabs my hand. "You're going to love this, Emilie." His smile lights up the visitor's center.

George's face turns serious as he levels his gaze on Chatham. "Your dad made another generous donation. Please tell him again how much we appreciate his support."

Chatham tugs on my hand, stepping toward the door. "Yeah, I will," he mutters without enthusiasm.

George says we're lucky to have the place practically to ourselves, but I don't feel as lucky as I did last night with Ayla. In fact, the deserted atmosphere seems like another bad omen, if you ask me. The Outer Banks lighthouses generally draw substantial crowds even in the fall. It's odd there are no tourists around. Do they know something about the weather that Chatham and I missed?

"This is awesome," Chatham whispers, placing a warm hand on my back as we cross the threshold into the tiny lighthouse foyer. He's back to his cheerful self. "It's like we've stepped back to nineteen hundred and we're the keepers."

"Except I'm pretty sure keepers weren't teenage girls who were terrified of heights," I mumble, turning to face him at the base of the two hundred and fourteen rickety steps leading up to the light. I've researched every detail about the lighthouse, down to the three hundred and forty prisms of the Fresnel lens lamp. It probably wasn't one of my wiser decisions, considering I now know all the tower's features, from the swaying spiral stairs to the dim interior lighting. The paragraph about the multimillion-dollar renovation to firm up the unstable structure and replace the rusted-out stairs didn't do much to calm my fears.

He places a gentle finger underneath my chin, tilting my face toward his. "Are you okay?"

I nod. "I'm a little afraid of heights." I almost laugh at the understatement. It's like saying a great white shark is just a little fish or a Komodo dragon is only a little lizard.

He loops an arm around my waist, pulling me in for a side hug. "Me too."

"You don't look scared." Somehow, I forget the suffocating fear when I look into the placid waters of his eyes.

"That's because I know what's at the top is worth the climb. And because my dad has zero patience for fear or hesitation." He tweaks my nose, nudging me toward the first step.

When Dad used to pinch my nose, I hated the way it made me feel like a child. When Chatham does it, my heart softens. "Okay, but if I die, you have to live with the guilt."

He chuckles as I mount the spiral staircase. I'm half listening to his history lesson as I climb. One detail I overlooked in my research is the fact that the metalwork on the steps is comprised of an intricate woven pattern, which is really pretty but also really transparent—as in you can see through the swaying stairs to the black-and-white-checkered floor below.

While Chatham talks about the granite-block foundation, I focus on counting steps. We're somewhere around sixty-seven when my legs start shaking. At seventy-three, I stop, interrupting him mid-sentence. "I . . . I can't do this." I turn to face him.

His hand falls from the rail to his side as he studies my face.

My legs quake like Granny Day's Orange Delight Jell-O Salad. "I think I need to sit down."

"Okay." He reaches for my hand. "You'll feel better after you rest for a minute."

I kind of doubt that.

I carefully lower myself to the iron step. Chatham follows

my lead, stretching his long legs out in front of him. The spiral staircase stops swaying.

Now that we're seated, I'm frozen in place. The thought of descending is almost as horrifying as the remainder of the climb. I'm sitting eye level with an ancient-looking screw bolted to the wall. The thing looks original. I can't stand the thought of what might happen if one of those screws comes loose. "I don't think I can do it."

"No big deal." He jiggles my knee. "We'll just—" He's interrupted by the ringing of footsteps on metal and muffled voices.

The stairs swing a fraction of an inch. I swallow the fear rising in my throat.

When a little girl with chocolate-brown ringlets rounds the bend in the staircase and spies me seated on the steps, her brow creases. She turns back to her dad and the ranger guiding their tiny tour. "What's wrong with that girl, Daddy?"

The ranger's eyes widen when he spots us seated on the black iron steps. "What's going on here?" he asks, ignoring the little girl's question and examining my face.

"Just taking a little rest." Chatham smiles, and the lines around the guide's tight mouth relax a little. Recognition lights in the ranger's eyes.

"Hey, Big C, do y'all need help?"

Everybody here knows Chatham—just like school, where teachers, student athletes, and band kids all call him by name.

"How's your dad?" The guy seems to have forgotten me.

"Great." The short tone's returned to Chatham's voice. It seems to go hand in hand with any mention of his father. "We've got this under control." He looks away from the ranger, nodding at me as if his enthusiasm will somehow fix *my* problems.

The guy can't seem to take a hint. "I can call someone for you."

"No, really, we're fine." Chatham's jaw twitches, like the day Ms. Ringgold returned his failing quiz. Except for that day in English class, I've never seen this curt side of Chatham.

Now the girl moves in, descending the few steps separating us and plopping down beside me. "Don't be scared."

Is my fear that obvious? I tighten my death grip on the step under my sweating butt cheeks, praying that the little cherub will quit wiggling and that these well-meaning people will just leave us alone.

"You have to go up." She glances back over her shoulder to her father. "Right, Daddy?"

"It is beautiful, but . . ." His voice trails off.

The girl laughs. She can't be a day over seven, and she's laughing at me. "There's nothing to be scared of. That's what Daddy said."

When Chatham chuckles, I shoot him the best evil glare I can muster, careful not to move my head too fast and risk sliding off my seat.

"I'm not—" My voice cracks. I swallow again. But my mouth's bone dry, and my tongue's swollen like a waterlogged sponge. "—scared."

The little girl's eyes narrow, like she's totally on to me.

"I'm fine—really. See?" When I release my hold on the metal step, my upper body lists to the side.

"Uh, yeah." She looks toward her father for guidance. He offers his hand, and she stands to take it. They move to squeeze by us, followed by Mr. Overly Eager Ranger Dude. I hold my breath when they pass, as if their movement may send me plummeting to the checkered tiles below.

"Well, enjoy the view, then." The ranger grins at Chatham. The three of them leave without a backward glance.

When I peek at Chatham, a mischievous smile breaks on his face.

"What?" I cross my arms.

"Nothing." He presses his lips together in a straight line, but the indentation popping in his left cheek is a dead giveaway that he's trying not to grin. "I'm just glad to hear you're not scared, that's all."

"I'm not scared." Huffing, I force myself to my feet. The step under my foot sways, and I grab the handrail to steady myself. Curse Chatham for being so cute. Curse Mom for forgetting my anniversary. Curse my pride.

I'm climbing this lighthouse if it's the last thing I do. And it might very well *be* the last thing I do. But at least if I'm pushing up daisies at the Motel Deep Six, I won't have to worry about seizing anymore.

I heave one leg up to what I'm calling the seventy-fourth step and occupy my brain with simple mathematics. Seventy-one steps is about one-third of the way. If I can get to one hundred and eight, I'll be past the halfway mark, and then it will all be downhill.

Actually, it'll be all straight up. My math is better than my analogies.

I focus on placing one foot in front of the other, avoiding the views out the occasional peep windows. The last thing I need is a visual reminder of the heights we're reaching. Dragging my white-knuckled hand along the rail, I pray I'm not leaving behind a trail of moisture and that Chatham can't see my legs shaking beneath my jeans.

"Almost there," he chirps, obviously unfazed by the height. There's definitely a disconnect between my definition of "afraid of heights" and his definition of "afraid of heights." In any case, I ignore his optimistic outlook. A little over halfway is not almost there.

Don't look down. Don't look down, I remind myself. *Left foot, right foot, left foot, right,* I chant to myself, so focused on not looking down I forget to not look up either. When my chin tilts up and back past the ninety-degree mark to survey the remaining distance, the close walls swim before my eyes.

I pause. Not good. Black spots whirl across my vision, and Chatham bumps me from behind. My heart skips a beat as my chest constricts. "Oh, my gosh! You scared me."

"Sorry." He looks away, his smile wavering.

I really, really want to sit down, but I can't even do that because my knees are locked like steel traps. To top it off, I've lost track of the number of steps again. I suck down a lungful of marshy air, willing my knees to unlock. Miracle of miracles, they do, and I hoist a leg up to the next woven tread.

"Hey," Chatham whispers, careful not to scare me a second time. "I can see the top."

I resume counting but have to start over because of all the interruptions. *One. Two. Three. Four.* I drag myself upward with the clumsy gait of a zombie. I will not be fooled into looking up again. If that dizzy vertigo feeling hits a second time, they'll have to call in emergency personnel to get me out of here.

At twenty-seven, I estimate that with all my stops and starts and miscalculations, we must be at least three-quarters of the way to the top. I'm rechecking my addition when all of a sudden the dim interior brightens. I lift my eyes a fraction of an inch. We're nine steps from the top landing.

A sudden rush of air escapes my lungs. My spine straightens. If someone didn't know me, they'd never guess how terrified I was. They'd see this normal-looking girl in trendy clothes with a cute boy at her side, climbing a lighthouse.

I pause on the landing opening up to the lantern. Outside the watch room is a narrow balcony with these wimpy iron spindles that look like something off one of the colonial homes we toured on vacation in Williamsburg, Virginia. I'd expect a lighthouse built to withstand hurricanes to have something a little more substantial separating me from the one-hundred-and-sixty-five-foot plummet of death.

"You did it," Chatham whispers, wrapping his arms around my waist from behind and resting his chin on my shoulder.

It's really hard to breathe with nothing but Ayla's shirt and his white button-down separating us. "I told you I wasn't scared." My voice shakes a little too much to convince even myself. How can I possibly be expected to think with him pressed against my back?

"Right." He laughs, his soft breath tickling my ear. "I forgot."

I don't dare move.

"And since you're not afraid, we're going to check out the balcony." He nudges me gently across the threshold.

Hormones must have hijacked my better judgment, because I step out onto the gallery. If this was an essay, Ms. Ringgold would ding me for the cliché, but I can't help it: the view literally takes my breath away.

Looking out over the pine trees and the marshland to the

Atlantic Ocean beyond, I feel like Leonardo DiCaprio on the prow of the *Titanic* shouting, "I'm the king of the world!"

"It never gets old," Chatham whispers, sensing my awe at the raw beauty of the land and water surrounding us and my need to devour the scenery with all of my five senses.

"How could it?" I murmur, drinking in the scene. This place is a maritime garden of Eden. It's a place for new beginnings where anything is possible, a place to take a leap of faith—the place where I should tell Chatham about my epilepsy. I can almost feel a miniature cartoonish Ayla perched on my left shoulder chanting, *Tell him, tell him, tell him.* But I don't. There's still plenty of time on the way down or on the ride home. Right now, I just want to enjoy the moment.

When Chatham laces his fingers through mine, I don't freak out. For once in my life, I don't worry about sweaty palms or chewed fingernails. I just relax and enjoy being on top of the world with the most wonderful boy in the history of the universe.

"And look what you've accomplished." He gestures with his free hand to the horizon. "You conquered your fears."

"Yes." I meet his direct gaze. "Yes, I did, didn't I?"

"Emily Dickinson would be proud of you." He squeezes my hand.

"How's that?" I follow his gaze out to sea.

"Remember that quote we annotated? The one about fortune befriending the bold?"

I smile, nodding. "Yeah."

"She was right. You know? If you hadn't been brave enough to climb this lighthouse, we wouldn't have been fortunate enough to be up here together."

He slips his free hand behind my neck, pulling me toward him. Before I have time to worry about being awkward or not knowing what to do, he's leaning in for a kiss.

On the lips.

My lips.

Instead of being clumsy like I imagined it might be, I realize it's a lot like breathing or blinking or any other involuntary process. Or maybe it's just that Chatham's mouth is warm and he tastes like oranges and the beach. Whatever it is, my lips part instinctively as I melt into his chest. My heart bangs against my ribs, and it has nothing to do with my fear of heights and everything to do with the boy in front of me.

I remember something else Emily Dickinson said, about how she knew it was poetry when she felt physically as if the top of her head were taken off. And I totally get it, but it's not poetry that's blowing the top of my head off.

It's Chatham York. It's like I'm a balloon, and Chatham's the oxygen. The more I hang around him, the more I stretch and grow.

Please, God, please, I pray for the first time in a really long time. *Let this balloon last.*

CHAPTER TWENTY-ONE

*That it will never come again
Is what makes life sweet.*

EMILY DICKINSON

The first plump raindrops of the approaching shower force us back inside the watch room and down the winding stairs. When my legs shake, I focus on Chatham's back and the way his shoulder blades move beneath the white button-down. Compared to the climb, we descend in record time. On the way, I even pause to check out the view from one of the peep windows. The forests are just as green and the water just as blue, but somehow it's not the same as it was from the lookout up top. It's like the difference between a Hershey's Kiss and a Godiva chocolate.

By the time we reach the ground, angry black clouds chase the gray skies I noticed back at Jockey's Ridge toward the ocean. The few raindrops have turned into many.

"Should we go home?" I ask, shivering. The temperature must've dropped fifteen degrees in ten minutes.

"Not yet." He grabs my hand, pulling me out into the deluge. Ice-cold water splashes our legs as we run for the keeper's quarters where we got our tickets. Laughing like preschoolers, we tumble onto the front porch of the visitor center, where we spend several minutes trying to shake rain from our clothes and hair.

I clench my jaw in an effort to disguise my chattering teeth. But Chatham's not fooled so easily.

"You're freezing." He reaches for the door, ushering me inside. Little brass bells hanging on the back of the door tinkle as his eyes travel the length of my body.

"I'm okay," I lie, glancing down at myself and realizing with horror that my wet shirt is clinging to my skin like Saran Wrap. So much for leaving anything to the imagination.

I wrap my arms around myself, wishing I could fold inward and disappear behind one of the racks of postcards. Ranger George talks on the phone behind a glass display case of seashells and souvenirs. He nods at us, chuckling, as if he can read my mind.

Chatham holds up a finger. "Wait. I've got this."

I don't move.

He hurries over to a stack of hunter green sweatshirts, grabbing one without looking at the price and heading over to the register.

George hangs up. "Y'all got wet, huh?"

You think? I rub my upper arms, trying to warm myself and biting back the snide comment on the tip of my tongue.

"Yeah." Chatham slaps several bills on the counter, turns his back on George, and trots back to me. "Ta-da." He unfurls a Cape Hatteras National Seashore hoodie and hands it over.

"Thanks." I slip it over my head, camouflaging my wardrobe malfunction, thankful for the warmth. "You're a lifesaver."

"I try." He pulls me into his arms and against his chest, rubbing his warm hands up and down my back. The muscles in my lower back unclench, setting off a chain reaction of warm tingling that radiates up my spine to my tight shoulders. The tension in my body melts away.

I try to remember the last time anything felt so delicious. Maybe the Saturday morning a few months ago when I woke from a pleasant dream to a sunny bedroom with Hitch at my side. I lay there, drifting in and out of sleep, relishing the lazy morning—until I thought of Dad and a wall of grief came crashing down on my chest, suffocating me.

That's happened several times since he died. I'll forget for a minute he's gone. Then the realization hits like a landslide, uprooting everything in its path, and I have to relive the pain that threatens to drag me along the ocean floor and dump me out in an expanse of water where I can't touch and I can't swim.

What's wrong with me? Am I seriously comparing Chatham's embrace to cuddling with Hitch? No. Today's the first day of the new me. Today's the day I put grief and fear behind me. Everyone I know has lost someone or is dealing with some challenge. They're all moving forward, and so am I. Right now.

I inhale the smell of Chatham's laundry detergent and the rain on his wet shirt, living in the moment. But it's not meant to be. A loud clap of thunder breaks the stillness of the visitor center, and I jump out of his arms. Every muscle in my body contracts.

George clears his throat. "Guess y'all won't be leaving for a bit."

Thank you, Captain Obvious.

A corrugated jag of lightning cracks open the sky.

"Y'all should check out the new Graveyard exhibit." He waves to a room in the back corner of the refitted keeper's house. "Your dad's donation paid for most of it." He straightens the stacks of brochures on the counter without taking his eyes off Chatham, who's leading me toward the rear of the house.

"Your dad must be really generous," I say as we step into a room filled with artifacts from the sunken ships of the Graveyard of the Atlantic.

"My dad does things for one reason." He shakes his head. "No, make that two reasons: profit and prestige. Donating to the lighthouse does both. It helps the county, which makes him look good, but more important, it brings in tourists. Tourists bring money, which creates jobs and loans for the bankers and the mortgage brokers, who then refer lots and lots of business to my father's real estate company." The tendon in the side of his taut neck twitches.

I press my hands into the front pocket of the hoodie, turning to examine the plaque beside a picture of some old ship, not quite sure how to handle what Chatham just said. "The exhibit's cool even if his intentions weren't."

"I guess." He shrugs. "Did you know more than two thousand ships have sunk here in the last five hundred years?" he asks, pointing to the photograph in the glass case in front of me.

Pine trees outside the window bend to the howling wind as I scan the placard above the picture of the USS *Monitor*. The first ironclad warship commissioned by the US Navy during the Civil War sank on the reefs just outside the house where we stand. I wish I could make some intelligent contribution to the conversation about the place I've called home my entire life. "That's depressing."

Not exactly sparklingly witty. I'm not doing much to show-case my talent in the stimulating-conversation department.

"That's why they call it the Graveyard of the Atlantic." He points to a diagram of the coast of North Carolina.

Neither the conversation nor the weather are doing any-thing to thaw my freezing hands. "I do remember studying some of this in North Carolina History in eighth grade." I point to the sketch of the ocean currents just off the coast.

His eyes follow my finger. "Isn't it crazy that the collision of those two bodies of water is what makes this place both loved and feared?"

"I never really thought of it that way," I say, trying not to stare as I turn to study his profile. I never really thought of a lot of things until I started hanging out with Chatham and Ayla.

He traces the wavy line moving south from Canada. "If you think about it, the arctic water from this Labrador Current colliding with the warmer water of the Gulf Current is what creates the great fishing and surfing that make the Outer Banks so popular. But it's also what causes the severe weather and fog that has sunk so many ships and killed who knows how many people."

A cold draft brushes my cheek, and I shiver. He's right, of course. And what's really scary is how those colliding currents are a perfect metaphor for our relationship. My frigid current smashing into his warm world could make for rough waters and eventual breakup, like the two thousand splintered ships and countless drowned sailors who've lost their lives in these waters.

No. I won't let that happen. I haven't had a seizure in ninety-plus days. I just conquered my fear of heights. Like the

Shakespeare quote on Ms. Ringgold's wall says, the world is my oyster.

It's time to look for pearls and ignore the tumultuous seas.

At the thought of turbulent waters, an image of my anxious mother flares in my head. "Oh, crap," I groan, biting my lip.

Chatham's eyes widen. He must recognize the look of horror on my face. "What is it?" His eyes search my face.

"I forgot to text my mom." My pulse accelerates. I'm dead thanks to Ayla's cute shirt that wouldn't cover my phone in my pocket. I had to leave it in the car. I should've asked Chatham to carry it for me.

He glances out the window at the pine trees doubled over under what must be gale-force winds. "My phone's in the car too. You can text her when the storm lets up." He squeezes my upper arm.

I know I'm supposed to appreciate the comforting gesture, but nothing—I repeat, *nothing*—can lessen the dread roiling in my belly.

I'm a dead girl.

CHAPTER TWENTY-TWO

Will there really be a "Morning"?

EMILY DICKINSON

Your mom wouldn't want you to head out into that." Chatham points through the foggy window to the monsoon outside.

"A Category Five hurricane won't stand between me and my phone." I inch backward toward the front door as I speak. "If there's any chance of me stepping foot outside the house again before my fortieth birthday, I need to call home *now*."

"Okay, then." He waves a quick good-bye to George and shepherds me through the rain to his car. "I want to see you again before you get wrinkles."

I try to ignore the guilt chewing at my insides as he stands in the rain holding the door open for me, but I don't pause to apologize. Instead, I snatch my phone from the cup holder and hit Escape, ignoring the text box announcing the seventeen missed messages. My fingers fly in a flurry of activity.

Mom, I'm fine. I'm so sorry I forgot
to text. Headed home now.

My stomach sinks at her short response.

Good. We need to talk.

Chatham inches along at a reduced speed because of the weather, heading north on the bypass at a nice, safe thirty-five miles an hour. I try really hard not to lean forward in an effort to will the vehicle to higher speeds.

Chatham can't possibly understand the severity of my panic, which is probably why he's so focused on the road and we're draped in silence. The only sound penetrating our private little world is the scrape of the windshield wipers in their losing battle against the sheets of rain pummeling the glass. When we finally turn right off the highway onto my road, I'm wound so tight tension coils in my shoulders.

I have to do something. I've got less than two minutes to tell him about the epilepsy. "Chatham, I, uh . . ." I pause, realizing in the middle of the awkward silence I should've thought through this confession ahead of time.

"Look at that." He whistles, taking a hand off the wheel to point at a swarm of blue lights up ahead. Several dark-colored sedans and SUVs block the road.

For a second, I think the cops have descended on my house. "What the . . ."

Chatham rolls to a stop, and I see they're swarming Cindy's house. I open the passenger-side door, jumping down to the sand at the edge of the road. But before I make it two steps from the car, a granite block of a buzz-cut officer cups my elbow in his meaty paw, pushing me back into the car.

"The suspect's in custody," a gruff voice barks from his walkie-talkie.

The suspect? It sounds like a reality cop show. Suspects aren't taken into custody in Crystal Cove, North Carolina— not unless they're teenagers driving under the influence.

"Ten-four," Concrete Cop snaps, then turns on me. "Do you live here?"

"I, uh . . ." I shake my head. "I live next door."

"Then you need to get on inside." He presses me into my seat, ducking his colossal head inside the car to speak to Chatham, who's leaning over the console, eyes wide, mouth half open. "Son, get her home." He gestures toward my house with his thumb.

Chatham nods, his face washed out by the flashing blue lights.

"But, wait." I grab the sleeve of the man's navy blue uniform. "I'm friends with Cindy, the little girl who lives in that house. You have to tell me if she's okay."

"Miss, I don't *have to* do anything." He gently pries his arm free and steps back toward Cindy's house. "But I'll tell you she and her mom are safe."

Thank God.

"You need to get home." His radio crackles as he fiddles with one of the dials. "I'm sure Ms. Blackstone will check in with you when the situation is resolved."

I shut the door, praying that Mom has some information about what's going on. Images and snippets of conversations pop in and out of my head, waving red flags I should've listened to over the past several months—the angry bruise on Cindy's face, the frightened look when her mom called down to her on the beach, the heated argument between her parents in the sterile kitchen. I promised Mom when they'd moved in that I'd mind my own business. But now I'm second-guessing myself.

"You know that family?" Chatham asks, squeezing around a police car, creeping toward my driveway. Every light in my house is on. He parks, turning off the engine and reaching for his door handle.

"Mostly, I know the daughter. The parents, not so much." I place a hand on his upper arm, stopping him before he steps out of the car. "I think it'd be best if I go in by myself."

"Okay." He places a warm hand on top of mine. "I hope your mom isn't too mad."

"She'll be beyond mad. I hope I survive this." Before opening the door, I take a minute to memorize his face, the straight line of his jaw, the wave in his still-damp hair, even the faint smell of his citrus shampoo. I don't want this day to end. Standing out on that balcony with Chatham was the high point of my post-dead-dad life—a living, breathing fairy tale. The bad weather, the irate mom, the blue lights—these things don't belong in that story.

"Thanks for today. It was . . . special." I lean across the console to brush his cheek with my lips, and my head spins at the bold gesture. It's like I developed a backbone all of a sudden and morphed into Molly Ringwald in the closing scene of *Pretty in Pink*. Okay, that might be a bit of an exaggeration. But still.

I pull back a fraction of an inch, prepared to step out of the car and face my impending doom. Before I can escape, Chatham cups my face in his hands, pulling my mouth to his. His hands wrap around my neck, tangling in my rain-matted hair, and I forget about the crowd of police officers, my angry mom, and the promise I made Ayla. A pinwheel of flickering lights sparks on the backs of my eyelids and bursts into fireworks inside my head. His kiss is like the Fourth of July finale at the Nags Head Pier Spectacular. When he pulls away, it's as if someone's thrown cold water on me to douse the flames.

It takes me a second to realize the flaring lights weren't in my head. Mom's backlit in the glass of the front door flipping the porch light on and off like the captain of a foundering ship signaling the coast guard. I push open the door, motioning for her to stop the psychotic flashing. If I could, I'd disappear inside the oversized Cape Hatteras National Seashore sweatshirt, but it doesn't belong to me. I start to pull it over my head.

Chatham stops me. "No. Keep it." He turns the key in the ignition, and the engine roars to life. "It looks good on you." His smile brightens the dim interior of his car. "Go—before your mom comes out here to get you."

Good advice. I head up the stairs to the front deck, looking over my shoulder, watching as he backs out of the driveway. When he taps the brakes, the red lights on the receding black SUV flicker through the fog like a scene in a cheap horror movie.

Before my feet hit the bottom step, Mom opens the door. Hitch charges down to meet me, then escorts me up to the house, attached to my thigh like a suckerfish on the underbelly of a shark. I brace myself for the oncoming assault. But instead of the irate tirade I'm expecting, I'm greeted with a bearlike embrace. Mom and I haven't had this much physical contact since her genius idea to "immerse me in life and in an authentic high school experience." I mean, we've exchanged some awkward hugs, maybe even pecks on the cheek, but nothing this heartfelt, this genuine.

After my initial shock, I settle into her arms, catapulted back in time to a real family with real emotions who comforted each other in their times of need—unlike the robotic, disjointed interactions she and I have suffered through more and more frequently since Dad died.

"Oh, Emilie, sweetie." She caresses the back of my damp head, hanging on to me for dear life. "Thank God, you're okay. I was so worried."

The skin at the base of my neck tingles, coming back to life. Muscles in my shoulders relax, the way they're supposed to under a mother's soothing touch. My heart unknots.

"You are okay, right?" She pushes me away to examine my face.

"Yes, I'm fine." And I kind of am. Despite my concern about what's going on next door, I feel like I've made some kind of breakthrough today—first with Chatham, now with Mom.

"Then why didn't you call?" Her voice catches on the last word.

"I should have. I'm sorry. Chatham and I both forgot our phones in the car. Then it rained . . ."

"I was so worried—between the weather and you not calling. And now this thing next door." She gestures toward the blue lights.

"What *is* going on next door, Mom?" I ask, steering the conversation away from my mess-up, and needing proof that Cindy's okay.

"I don't know exactly." She tucks a wild sprig of hair behind her ear. "About an hour ago, the first two cops showed up."

I step toward the glass door for a view of Cindy's driveway while Mom closes the blinds on the front windows.

"Cindy and Debbie left with a female officer before I could get down to them." She shakes her head as if she can't wrap her mind around the night's events.

The stocky officer glances up at me from where he stands in the driveway. When we lock eyes, I step back as if I'm the one caught in a crime instead of the suspect at the Blackstone's house.

"The next thing I know, policemen are breaking in the front door with one of those battering-ram things." Her shoulders shrink inside Dad's faded OBX T-shirt.

Hitch abandons me to nuzzle his head under her hand. When she runs her fingers through the blond fur on his head, I notice her nails are bare. All traces of the pink nail polish have vanished. Dark circles bruise the puffy skin beneath her eyes, aging her face.

A stitch of guilt pricks the edge of my heart as I scoot around the couch for a better-camouflaged view through the blinds. Mom squeezes in behind me. We peer down at Cindy's house without talking. A minute later, Mr. Blackstone staggers out the front door, his hands cuffed behind his back, followed by two stern-faced officers.

Mom gasps. "What in the world?" She pulls me back against her chest, wrapping me in her arms, the way she did before our constant bickering.

When Mr. Blackstone looks up at our house, I let the blinds close all but a fraction of an inch. He'd have to have X-ray vision or super powers to see our eyes through the tiny slit in the blinds, but I still shiver. How could I be so blind to have never noticed the nasty glint in his eye? And to think I was jealous of Cindy's life next door. How could I have thought having a Y chromosome in the house would magically make life better?

My views of people and the world are changing so fast, my head spins in an effort to keep up. The family I thought I envied is crumbling before my eyes. I climbed a one-hundred-and-sixty-five-foot lighthouse today and kissed a boy I wouldn't have had the confidence to make eye contact with a month ago. Even Mom and I are reaching out to each other.

I strain at my too-tight shell, my hermit crab body preparing to molt, ready to shed this skin in favor of a larger shell that will accommodate my new growth. It's time to head out into the aquarium unprotected in search of a better fit, time to quit burrowing down into the same old sand and hiding from the world.

CHAPTER TWENTY-THREE

Each Life Converges to some Centre—

EMILY DICKINSON

M om calls the Crystal Cove Police Department while I change into sweats and wash my face. But they won't tell her what's going on with the Blackstones. As she refills Hitch's water bowl, I boot up her old laptop and search for information online. Our Wi-Fi creeps like some sort of pre-historic slug. After several minutes, aggravation gets the best of me, and I give up. Mom and I agree the media isn't likely to report on Crystal Cove anyway.

"We can go to the police station in person tomorrow," she says as she heads down the hall to the linen closet.

I prop myself in the corner of the couch, motioning for Hitch to join me. "I just hope Cindy's okay."

Mom walks toward me with our favorite blankets. "They weren't physically harmed, from what I could see. But the police were there a long time, like they were looking for something."

She pops *Freaky Friday* in the DVD player, then piles onto the couch with me and Hitch. We nibble Twizzlers. Neither of us laughs at our favorite scenes. Even the "fun-sucker" exchange between the mom and daughter fails to earn a chuckle. We take that as a sign to admit defeat and head to bed.

⁂

In the morning, I brush my teeth and throw my hair into a messy ponytail. Twenty minutes later, we swing by the police department on our way to the library. The lady at the front desk refuses to give us any information other than to say, "Mrs. Blackstone and her daughter are safe."

Mom and I ride to the library in silence.

"The whole thing is just weird," I say as we let ourselves in through the employee entrance. The hush of the library and the familiar smell of books does little to calm my nerves.

"It is, but we're just going to have to accept that it's none of our business." Mom heads toward the back room and the book drop. She's assumed her no-nonsense librarian persona, and I've been dismissed.

I open my mouth to argue, but my vibrating phone distracts me. Pulling it from my pocket, I head across the lobby to log in to a computer. My cheeks warm when I read Chatham's text.

> **Busy with fam last night. Hope you survived the Wrath of Mom.**

> I did.

> **Good. Want to see you again this decade.**

I smile. Heat prickles my neck and cheeks when I think of his hands on my waist . . . and my lips on his. Me too.

I close my eyes, trying to forget my promise to Ayla about being honest with Chatham.

Another reply comes in. Today or tomorrow?

> Tuesday, actually. Out of
> school for appointment
> tomorrow. With Mom today.

Okay. Can't wait. Peace out.

My chuckle sounds out of place in the empty library, but I can't stop myself. I picture Chatham tapping his chest with his fist and flashing the peace sign like Kip in *Napoleon Dynamite*. Chatham knows his movies, that's for sure. And I know what our next date should be: a classic-movie marathon.

Typing my library code into the computer with one hand, I press my phone against my chest with the other and consider the seriousness of this observation. I'm kind of amazed at myself for contemplating a next date with Chatham—that sounds more like a glass-half-full girl than the Emilie Day I know.

It sounds like a girl with plans. It sounds like a girl with a future.

I'm not sure how long I've been daydreaming—long enough to need a second to compose myself when my phone vibrates against my chest. Somehow, I manage to avoid falling out of the library rolly chair when I nearly jump out of my skin.

It's Ayla, which makes me both immensely happy and immensely sick to my stomach. I don't know how to explain it exactly. I can't wait to tell her all about last night, but I dread telling her I wimped out on telling Chatham about my seizures.

I swipe my phone to accept her call.

"What're you doing?" she asks when I say hello.

"I'm at the library with Mom." I lean back in the chair, studying my smooth cuticles.

"That's crazy about your neighbors. Are you sure everyone's okay?" she says. She texted me last night when I was looking for information about the Blackstones on the Internet. I told her I'd have to talk to her today.

"I think so, but just the thought of that creep and I feel sick," I say.

"Me too. Hey, I don't have long to talk. Dad and I are headed to Virginia Beach to meet a woman about displaying some of my stuff in her gallery."

"Oh, Ayla! That's awesome."

"Yeah, but I want to hear about the date. How was it?"

"Amazing." I tilt my head back and spin in the rolly chair.

"Did he kiss you?"

"Um, yeah." I spend the next several minutes describing how perfect it was. When I share the poetry analogy—the Emily Dickinson thing about the top of my head lifting off—Ayla laughs.

Her dad says something in the background, and she pauses. "What did he say about the epilepsy?"

I take a deep breath before responding.

"Emilie?"

I don't know what to say.

"You didn't tell him. Did you?"

"No."

"It's going to get harder the longer you wait."

"I know."

She's right, of course. But she doesn't know how hard it is. She could have pretty much any guy she wants if she ever decided she wanted a relationship. I haven't had that luxury. And Chatham is so nice. I don't want to scare him away. I want to enjoy what we have. Is that so awful?

"He deserves better." Her voice drops, like Mom's when I've disappointed her.

"I know." My voice cracks. I do know. I feel terrible and deceitful, and now she's adding guilt on top of that.

Her dad says something else.

"I have to go. Can we talk tomorrow at school?" she asks.

"I'll see you Tuesday. I have appointments with Mom tomorrow."

I know her dad's waiting for her, and she has to leave. But it still feels like I'm being brushed off. A few minutes ago, I felt so normal texting Chatham and answering Ayla's call. Now I feel fake, like I'm pretending, like I'm watching an alternate version of my life play out on screen. But this isn't a fantasy like *The Lord of the Rings* or *The Princess Bride*.

This is real life.

My life.

And Ayla's right. If I'm going to have a relationship with Chatham, I'm going to have to quit pretending to be someone else.

CHAPTER TWENTY-FOUR

For each ecstatic instant

We must an anguish pay . . .

EMILY DICKINSON

Monday morning I wake confused by the light streaming through the window. Rubbing sleep from my eyes, I reach for my phone on the nightstand. It's nine o'clock. I'm beyond late. Hitch lies on the floor, head raised on high alert, sphinxlike, waiting for me to drag myself out of bed.

When I swing my legs to the floor, the fog in my head clears. Ugh. Mom let me sleep in because I have an appointment with Dr. Wellesley.

I fall back on the pillows, not sure if I have the strength to prove my emotional growth this morning. Hitch jumps up on the bed, licking my fingers and face, wiggling his nose under my hand, unable to stand my laziness any longer.

"What a good man," I coo, patting the bed beside me.

He plops down on top of the quilt, curling into the angle of my hip, and I pull all eighty-five pounds of him into my chest. My heart tangles when I think about how much I love him. If anything ever happened to him, I'd die.

"I love you, Hitch," I whisper, tugging at a tuft of velvety hair in front of his ear.

He exhales—the contented sigh of a dog happy with life and satisfied with the quality of his work. I concentrate on his breathing, trying to block out the anxiety snowballing in my chest. My sleep's all messed up. I have no answers for the questions about Cindy and her family that have kept me up the last two nights.

Hitch and I are inhaling our fourth synchronized breath when Mom pushes open the bedroom door. "Let's hit it," she says. "We need to leave in thirty-two minutes."

I can almost bear the hour-long counseling sessions. It's easy enough to tell Dr. Wellesley what he wants to hear to inflate his ego. He so needs to believe he's guiding me through my grieving and out of my depression. What gets me every time, though, is when Mom comes in for the last fifteen minutes. It's way harder to convince him of my emotional and social improvements when Mom's in the room ready to call me out on every mood swing and snide comment.

I take my time getting ready. The sound of her rattling keys sends me into one final flurry of activity—rubber-banding my ponytail, throwing on the Cape Hatteras National Seashore hoodie, and sliding into the first pair of matching flip-flops I manage to dig out of the closet. Hitch follows me from the bathroom to my room to the front door in hopes we'll take him with us. Without asking Mom, I grab his service collar and leash and slide into the backseat with him. She starts the car, and we head north wrapped in silence.

We're crossing the northbound bridge headed for Elizabeth City when she smiles at me in the rearview mirror.

"What?" I meet her reflected gaze, wondering what happened to the closeness we shared Saturday night. Part of the problem is my lack of sleep and resulting crankiness; I know that. The other part is we've been distant for so long that one or two nights of connecting again can't erase it all.

The woman driving this green Honda is not the same woman who demanded we sit down together for family-style meals my entire childhood—the woman who moved a card table into the master bedroom so she and I could eat every meal with Dad when he was too exhausted from the chemo to make it to the kitchen.

"I was just going to tell you the school board made a decision." She pauses to glance at me through the mirror, eyebrows raised expectantly.

"And?" I know what she's going to say, but I can't stand the suspense. I have to hear it.

"And . . ." She pauses, turning to look over her shoulder. "And . . . Hitch can go to school with you." She bounces on the driver's seat.

When I don't respond, she repeats the "good" news. "Hitch can go to school with you."

I pull Hitch to my side, burying my face in his neck without answering.

"Aren't you excited?" she asks, settling back into the faded upholstery.

"I am. I just . . ." I speak into Hitch's fur, unable to put my conflicting emotions into words. She wouldn't understand anyway.

"Just what?" she asks, her voice rising. "I thought you'd be thrilled. He's your best friend."

Ouch. "He is. I just . . ."

"What's wrong, Emilie?" Her knuckles whiten on the steering wheel.

I have to do something to release the tension building in the car. "It's just I don't know what everyone will think."

"Why would you care what anyone else thinks?" She changes lanes to let someone pass. "Plus, you've already told your friends."

When I don't respond, she takes her foot off the gas, craning her head around to look directly at my face.

Uh-oh.

"You said you told your friends." There's ice in her voice. "You have, right?"

Crap. I resist the urge to cross my fingers behind my back the way I did in elementary school. "Yes, Mom." I have told Ayla. And Chatham's technically more of a crush, right? So it's not exactly a lie. "I've told a few people. But I don't know that many people very well. I'm not sure I want to answer all their questions."

"We can't pretend you don't have epilepsy." Her voice squeaks on the word *epilepsy*.

I sigh. "You're right, Mom. We can't. Can I just wait a few more weeks, please? I want people to judge me for me—not because of my seizures."

She meets my gaze again. "What if you seize at school?"

"Maybe I won't. Maybe my meds are working." I fiddle with the tag on Hitch's collar. "It's been three months since my last seizure."

A hand flies to her mouth. She stomps on the brake, veering toward the shoulder of the road. Hitch and I flop against the seat when she stops short. I peek out the back window to make sure we're not about to be rear-ended.

"Oh, Emilie." She turns in her seat to face me, reaching for my arm. "How did I miss that?"

I pull back a couple of inches and look her square in the face. "Maybe because you were so busy boxing up Dad's stuff and hanging out with your *friend* Roger."

Did I just say that? What's wrong with me? She was trying to be nice, trying to connect with me.

Her arm falls short of mine. Cold, hard silence pierces the Honda's interior. We sit frozen in time until an eighteen-wheeler whooshes past, shaking us out of our petrified stillness.

"Mom, I'm sorry." I reach for her shoulder this time.

She scoots away before my fingers make contact, turning back to the wheel and flicking her turn signal so hard I can't believe it doesn't snap off the steering column. The Honda lurches back onto the highway, and neither of us speaks until we're turning into the hospital parking lot.

"We'll just see what Dr. Wellesley thinks." The actual words sound harmless enough, but the tone feels like a noose tightening around my neck.

I keep my mouth shut, which is what I wish I'd done earlier. Sometimes I fear she and I will never be in sync again without Dad. He was the fulcrum that balanced our out-of-whack see-saw, the counterweight that balanced our scales. Without him, there's no middle ground. When she's up, I'm down. When she's reaching out to me, I'm pulling away. When she's thinking logically, I'm thinking emotionally.

I swallow my feelings and pray for a miracle at Dr. Wellesley's office.

CHAPTER TWENTY-FIVE

Afraid! Of whom am I afraid?

EMILY DICKINSON

itch and I hold the door beside the tiny pediatric psychiatry sign open for Mom at Dr. Wellesley's office. She doesn't thank us. Bad omen—very bad omen.

I head toward the front desk to check in. She and Hitch find a seat in the tiny waiting room. I don't know how Dr. Wellesley manages his schedule, but in almost three years I've only run into another patient twice while waiting for my appointment. Everything about the place is designed to protect the privacy of his at-risk teenage patients. At the end of each visit, clients are ushered out the back door that feeds directly into the parking lot to avoid the risk of running into a familiar face. We have the place to ourselves again today.

When I return to where Mom sits, she doesn't take her eyes off the outdated *Sports Illustrated* clutched in her fists. Bad sign number two. Mom knows about as much about football as she does theoretical physics. She's upset. I overstepped my bounds with the Roger comment. Now there will be consequences. And I kind of deserve it.

"Emilie, Dr. Wellesley's ready," the secretary calls from behind the desk.

I reach for Hitch's leash.

"He can stay with me," Mom says without looking at my face. She's pulling out the silent ammunition. Withholding Hitch is her deadliest weapon. There won't be any guilt tripping or crying today—no bombs or hand grenades. What there will be is cold, hard sniper fire—a single noiseless shot to the head when I least expect it.

"Fine." I make my way to Dr. Wellesley's open door.

He stands when I enter but doesn't cross the room. I slip into one of the two chairs angled in front of his desk. Concentrating on not crossing my arms or legs, I fold my hands in my lap to camouflage my nails. He's a master at deciphering body language, and I don't want to send up any red flags.

"Emilie." He nods, folds his long avian body in half, and perches on the edge of his chair. Like the great blue heron with the long neck that nested beside our house the year before Dad died, Dr. Wellesley's motions are slow and deliberate, but I know better than to be fooled by the leisurely movement. Just like the skinny-legged bird with the sharp beak, he can strike lightning fast, snatching me up like an unsuspecting fish or gopher. Most days, though, he opts to peck away at my defenses with one probing question after another.

"So, how are things?" he asks, foraging for information.

Here we go. "Okay, I guess." I study my hands.

He waits.

I wait longer.

He picks up his pen. "Tell me about school."

Bam. "It's okay, I guess."

He stares, unblinking.

I hate this. "I'd rather be homeschooled."

"Why do you think that is?" He rubs his pointy chin between his index finger and thumb.

Well, let's see. Maybe because I have epilepsy. Maybe because Dad died. Maybe because I live in fear of being exposed. It wasn't all that long ago that people with epilepsy were believed to be possessed by demons and banished from their communities or isolated in mental hospitals for fear they were contagious.

Okay, I know people don't think that anymore—not really—but it isn't like having epilepsy is suddenly cool.

"Um, because I don't like being around a lot of people. I'm more comfortable at home." I have to be alert to my tendency to babble when I get nervous. My main goal is to survive the sixty-minute session and say as little as possible. But I have to be careful not to be so close lipped I get labeled as *confrontational* or *passive aggressive*.

He tilts his head to the side when he nods. "Talk to me about that."

"We've been through this before. I don't feel comfortable around strangers." I glance at my hands. Normally I'd pick at my cuticles and avoid the collage of happy family photos on the bookshelf behind his desk. But I don't have any hangnails. In fact, my hands haven't looked this good since before Dad's diagnosis. I settle for rubbing the tip of my index finger around the bed of my thumbnail.

"Have you made any friends?" He rocks back in his chair, crossing a foot over the opposite knee.

I picture a young Dr. Wellesley role-playing this nonchalant body language in shrink school. "A couple."

"Tell me about them," he says, pausing to glance out the window.

I shrug, trying to peek at the clock while he's not looking. "Well, there's this girl named Ayla."

He zeroes in on my face. "Mm-hm."

"She's on the lit mag. She's cool—she invited me to sit with her at lunch and we've been to each other's houses." I refold my hands and place them in my lap.

"So you feel comfortable with her? She's not a stranger?" His chair creaks when he leans forward, propping his elbows on the desk.

"Well, no, I guess she's not a stranger anymore. I feel comfortable with her." It's true. I do feel I can be myself with Ayla. Granted, I felt better before she started laying on the whole guilt trip about not telling Chatham.

Dr. Wellesley jots a note on a legal pad on his desk. I hate it when he does that. I lose track of my thoughts and become hyper focused, trying to figure out what he's writing, whether I said something sane or insane.

"So you've told her about your epilepsy?" His eyes narrow on my face.

I look him dead in the eye. "Yes. Yes, I have." So there. I stop just shy of poking out my tongue.

He waits. I spend the next several minutes explaining how the conversation with Ayla unfolded. When I admit it felt kind of good to be honest with Ayla, he smiles. I'm not a shrink, but I'm pretty sure there was a tinge of told-you-so in his facial expression.

"So have you made any other friends?" he asks, eyes still

locked on my face without blinking. The man never blinks. Maybe that's another trick they teach in shrink school.

I glance at the clock. Twenty-nine minutes down, thirty-one to go. Actually, sixteen until Mom comes in. Then they'll kill a few minutes with idle chitchat till we get down to the real mother-daughter business.

I have to be truthful. This could be a trap. Mom may have already told Dr. Wellesley about Chatham. If she hasn't, she's bound to mention it when she comes in, so I may as well be honest. "Well, there's this guy, Chatham."

If Dr. Wellesley leans much farther forward, he'll be sitting in my lap. "Tell me about him."

I make a mental note to look into a psychology degree. Seriously. I may not be a real people person, but for one hundred and fifty dollars an hour, I think I can sit behind a desk and say, "Tell me about that. Tell me about how that makes you feel." "He's really nice—not what I expected from North Ridge guys."

He nods. Then out of the blue, he pierces my defenses with a sharp, pointed question. "So how did your *friend* Chatham take the news about your epilepsy?"

I grip the arms of my chair, trying to swallow around the cotton ball wedged in my throat. "Um . . ." My eyeballs bulge. "He, umm . . ."

I glance at the clock. The receptionist will send Mom back any second. She thinks I've told Chatham about the seizures. I hate liars, but I don't have a choice. I have to lie to Dr. Wellesley to cover the other lie to Mom. Plus, it's not exactly a lie, right? I just haven't told Chatham *yet*. But I am going to tell him—ASAP. I promised Ayla I would, and I will. Tomorrow. "He was . . . supportive."

The door creaks open at exactly a quarter till. I might have a lot of issues with Mom, but punctuality is not one of them. She's as reliable as the postman. I spend the next three and a half minutes petting Hitch while they talk about my social and emotional development like I'm not in the room. Roger, the boxes of Dad's clothes, and the pink manicure somehow never make their way into the discussion. With twelve minutes left until freedom, I settle back in my chair. This could've gone much, much worse.

I'm staring out the window at a heavy, lead-gray cloud, rehearsing my conversation with Chatham, when Mom pulls the trigger on her well-aimed sniper shot. "So, Doc, I have good news." She reaches over to ruffle the thick mane of yellow hair on Hitch's chest. "The school board has reviewed the Americans with Disabilities Act and has rewritten its policy on service dogs to include seizure alert dogs."

"Emilie, that's great." Dr. Wellesley unfolds his long body and walks around his desk toward me. "I know that was one of your main concerns about public school—not being able to take Hitch. Now you can. See, you stepped out of your comfort zone and took a risk, and now things are falling into place."

Oh, they're *falling*, all right.

He squeezes my shoulder with his bony hand. Mom and Dr. Wellesley decide—without my input—I should take Hitch to school next week. How thoughtful of them to give me a few days to publicize my epilepsy to my peers before I show up at the Ridge with Hitch in tow.

Things go from concerning to catastrophic when we step out the back door and into the parking lot. While my eyes are still adjusting to the now blinding sunlight, Maddie materializes from a candy-apple red Mini Cooper, eyes hidden behind a pair of oversized black sunglasses. I blink, hoping the yellow halo of light before my eyes is not her head but rather a figment of my imagination. Why isn't *she* in school? A look of shock crosses her face when she spots me, but she quickly smooths it away.

"Emilie, is that you?" She's all artificial sweetener when she holds a hand out to Mom. "You must be Mrs. Day."

Mom falls hook, line, and sinker for the sugar dripping from Maddie's tongue. She nods, beaming, clearly impressed at my newfound social abilities.

"We missed you at Daddy's shrimp boil." Maddie slides the sunglasses down her nose a fraction of an inch. The glint in her eye clashes with the cheery tone of her voice as she taps Hitch on the top of the head.

Any self-respecting dog person knows you offer your outstretched hand to the dog first or at the very least rub under the chin. But Hitch quietly accepts her dominant, need-to-be-in-charge gesture. I follow his lead, swallowing my disgust.

"How sweet that you bring your dog with you to the . . ." She peers over my shoulder to the door at our backs. ". . . doctor?"

"Yeah. He's awesome." I ignore the question implied by her tone, wondering what she's doing here but not wanting to prolong our conversation. I vaguely remember Ayla saying something about Maddie's dad owning a medical practice. "Does your dad work here?"

She pushes her sunglasses back up her nose. "He owns the building."

"Oh?" That means she's familiar enough with the place to

know I'm seeing a shrink. If she has more than two brain cells, she'll also make the connection that Hitch is a service dog.

She holds up a large manila folder. "And he's waiting on this. My mom let me take a half day to catch up on my beauty sleep, but I have to be at school by fourth period. I guess I'll see you at school, Emilie."

Mom beams, wiggling her fingers in a polite little wave.

Maddie may have my mom eating out of the palm of her hand, but she's not fooling me. I know she doesn't like me one bit. I also know if she felt so inclined, she could now destroy everything I've built at school with one well-placed rumor.

Just like that, the sand beneath my feet shifts again, and I'm being pulled out into choppy waters on a tide of white lies and half-truths. A tsunami-force wave barrels across the ocean toward my fake life at the Ridge with Chatham.

CHAPTER TWENTY-SIX

Silence is all we dread.

EMILY DICKINSON

After spending Sunday at home and most of the day Monday at the doctor and running errands with Mom, it takes a second to readjust to school Tuesday morning. I wave to Ayla in the hall when I see her.

She lifts her hand in a semi-wave. "I'll catch up with you later, okay?" she mumbles as she and her lit-mag buddy head up the hall. Feeling brushed off, I shuffle to my locker, head down, unaware of Chatham until I collide with his solid frame.

"I missed you yesterday." He grins, holding out a hand for me.

When our hands touch for a moment, I smile. Being this close to him sends my nervous system into overdrive. Sights and smells and sounds from Saturday bombard my senses— his warm lips on mine, the curl of damp hair on his neck, the touch of his firm hands on my wet skin.

"My appointment took longer than I thought, and then Mom wanted to hang out." I turn away, digging around in my locker, trying to come up with a plan. I have to be honest with him. I have to tell him about the epilepsy. Today. Before this relationship goes any further. No matter what, I'm not a liar. I need to be honest with him to make things right with Ayla, and to explain my situation before Hitch comes to school next week. Or before Maddie fills his head with rumors and speculation.

"Is everything okay?" he asks.

Am I okay? Well, let's see, that's way trickier than it sounds—yes and no. "Uh, yeah, it was just a . . . follow-up." A follow-up to almost a decade of neurological disorder.

"That's good," he says, catching a binder for me and slipping it back in place before it can hit the floor.

Squeezing my eyes shut, I try counting to ten. At three, I cave. "Listen. We need to—" I turn to face him and notice for the first time the black circles of exhaustion carved beneath his eyes. "Are *you* okay?" I ask, my disclosure conversation all but forgotten.

He shrugs. "Just tired. Mary Catherine's afraid of storms. I was up with her most of the weekend. Then we had late practice last night."

When he slings my backpack over his shoulder, I smile, remembering the first time I met him in the counseling office.

"Thanks to my awesome tutor, I'm back in the starting lineup." He hides a yawn behind his free hand.

"I'm sorry about your sister." I touch his arm—a pretty bold move on my part, I must say.

"No big deal." He loops the arm around my waist, pulling me toward him. "It comes with the territory."

No big deal? Walking around half dead, sporting industrial-sized black bags under your eyes, is just a part of loving someone with special needs. What would Chatham look like if I seized on him? If there's a nicer guy anywhere in the world who doesn't deserve to be weighed down by a disabled girlfriend, I can't imagine him.

I don't care what Mom or Ayla or Dr. Wellesley say. I'm not telling Chatham about my epilepsy today—not when he looks like one of the POWs we've been studying in US History.

"Since you're the one responsible for my improved grades and starting position, I thought you might want to come to our first game." His hand tightens on my waist. "I could save you a seat behind the bench."

I glance up at him to make sure I'm hearing this right. It's one thing to visit a lighthouse, just the two of us. It's something else to have him save me a seat behind the bench. It's so visible, so out in the open. It screams *relationship*. "Oh." My lips part. My brain forms a response, but the words lodge in my throat.

His hand falls from my side. "It's okay if you don't want to," he says, his voice barely audible over the noisy traffic in the hall. "Not everyone likes basketball."

I don't care much about basketball, but that has nothing to do with my hesitation. All I've ever wanted since I was diagnosed with epilepsy is to be normal, and this is my shot. It's just I don't know if I'm ready for it. I'm chest deep in rising water and don't know how to swim. The water's about to rush over my head, and I've got two seconds to make a decision: head back to safety or start pumping my arms and legs.

"No. It's not that." I'm on tiptoe, gripping the floor of the pool with my toenails. "I'd love to go." Just like that, the bottom recedes. My arms and legs are moving, but with more thrashing than pumping.

"Awesome. You can meet my parents."

I swallow a lungful of water. "Great," I gasp, forcing a smile.

He delivers me to math, where I spend the next fifty minutes trying to digest what just happened in the hall. Thankfully, I am so completely invisible to Mr. Gravitt that he fails to notice me. When he surveys the room for daydreamers, I shrink in my seat, scribble a random equation on my bare paper, and squint at it like Einstein puzzling through the theory of relativity.

The bell rings, and I scurry to the bathroom. I need a second to gather my thoughts before facing Chatham and Ayla in second period. And—my stomach tightens—Maddie. Who may or may not have figured out my secret. I bolt myself into the last stall, drop my bag on the floor, and collapse on the toilet. Digging my fingers into my thighs, I suck down a couple of steadying breaths.

When the bell rings a minute later, I jerk, and my butt lifts six inches off the toilet. Unfortunately, I snag my foot in the strap of my backpack, and before I can catch myself, my hand slips inside the rim of the toilet. I slide to the floor, disgusted with myself.

I drag my hand out of the toilet, push off the sticky floor with the other, and try not to gag. When I stand, I'm eye level with one of my favorite author's names written in silver paint pen. *Frances Hodgson Burnett*. In bubbly letters, some optimistic girl has scribed a quotation from *The Secret Garden*.

I remember how badly I wanted to be Mary Lennox when I was little and slip out of my life and into her magical garden of blossoming flowers with its friendly robin. Now I study the fat words meandering up the wall: *If you look the right way, you can see the whole world is a garden.* Oh, how I want to believe those fifteen words—or at least meet a teenage girl with that hopefulness.

Then I realize I *have* met a girl like that: Ayla. And she's sitting in second period disappointed with me. I can't blame her. After her mother deceived her the way she did, I'm willing to guess Ayla has zero tolerance for anything resembling dishonesty—even if it's not really a lie, even if it's just a lack of full disclosure.

I grab my backpack and head to the sink to wash my hands before moving out of the safety of the bathroom and into whole wide world, praying that Frances Hodgson Burnett knows what she's talking about.

CHAPTER TWENTY-SEVEN

Tell all the truth but tell it slant—

EMILY DICKINSON

Okay, so I'm a wuss. I don't head straight to Ms. Ringgold's class. I swing by the clinic with a lame excuse, knowing I'll be able to finagle a late pass out of Nurse Younghouse. "I'm feeling a little foggy," I tell her.

She presses the back of her hand to my forehead. "You don't feel warm." She flutters around my face in a cloud of lemons and Ivory soap. "Your color looks good."

I stare down at my clasped fingers in what I hope passes as pitiful or at least a little under the weather. If I'm feeling foggy, it's because I'm not sleeping enough and I'm stressing about how to handle things with Ayla and Chatham. My funk has nothing to do with illness or epilepsy.

"Your mom left Tylenol with your other meds. Do you need one?" She squeezes my hand. "You can call home if you need to."

I take a Tylenol and, more important, the pink slip she offers and head to Ms. Ringgold's room fifteen minutes late for class. When I slide into the room, Ms. Ringgold acknowledges me with a nod and a quick smile from her seat in the back of the room, then turns back to Derek up front. He and another guy stand on either side of a projected image of Ernest Hemingway.

I slip into my seat beside Chatham.

"You okay?" he whispers, raising an eyebrow.

I squeeze out a smile. "Yeah."

Ms. Ringgold shushes us and points to Derek. We refocus, which isn't difficult considering Derek's ability to captivate an audience.

"And that, my friends, is why he was called Papa—that and the fact that he was super smoo-ooth with the ladies." He slicks back his curly hair with two hands, swivels his hips, and gestures at the larger-than-life Hemingway photo.

The class erupts into laughter. Even Ms. Ringgold chuckles.

I can't help myself. I smile too. And it hits me—I like this class. I like Ms. Ringgold, and I like being a part of the group laughing with Derek. There are things I'd miss if I were at home alone. The number one reason is sitting beside me, of course. And I tip my head to the side to look at Ayla. I owe it to her to make things right.

When Derek and his partner head to their seats, Ms. Ringgold passes out half sheets of paper for peer evaluations of their work. She twists a pink pig kitchen timer on her desk and tells us we have six minutes to provide thoughtful feedback written in complete sentences.

I glance around the room, not sure where to begin after missing most of the presentation. Pens and pencils scratch out a feverish pace on the mini rubrics. As I contemplate what to write, I study Ms. Ringgold's violets in the windowsill. The pot on the end, the one that looked so cheery and plump last week, is now limp and withering. Shriveled blooms rest on drying brown leaves. Even Ms. Ringgold's optimism wasn't able to keep the thing alive once fall struck.

I lift my pen to write something constructive about Derek's use of humor. The pink pig dings a second later, and ink jags across my paper. I race to finish my sentence as Ms. Ringgold moves to the front of the room.

"Make sure your name and the names of the presenters are on the rubric and pass them forward face down." She turns her back to us and writes the names of students due to present tomorrow on the whiteboard, right beside an announcement for Thursday's opening basketball game against the rival War Eagles.

Luckily, Chatham and I are the next to last group and aren't scheduled to go until next week. The thought of standing in front of this group raises my heart rate and the moisture level of my palms. I pass my paper forward, pretending to reread Friday's notes and trying not to stare at Chatham. When someone crumples a piece of paper, I glance up. Maddie's walking my way, and she's smiling. Not good.

She pauses at my seat. Every eye in the back half of the room, including both of Chatham's, zeroes in on the two of us.

"I hope your appointment went well yesterday." She flashes me a blinding smile, then turns to Chatham. "You should see Emilie's dog."

Crap. She's pegged Hitch as an assistant dog. I should have known Miss Yale Law School Camp Girl would put two and two together.

"I have." The dimple in his left cheek pops. "When I went to her house."

A tiny crack fractures the foundation of Maddie's smile, but she barely misses a beat. "I met him leaving the *therapist's* office yesterday."

Chatham turns to me, confusion etched in his wrinkled brow, head tilted, studying my face.

"Yeah, everybody loves Hitch." I shrug, trying to look cool. "Spending time with him is really therapeutic for Dr. Wellesley's counseling patients." Hitch has passed the therapy dog test as part of his seizure-response training, so it's not a total lie. It's more of a half lie. Plus, I'm a counseling patient and his presence alleviates some of my anxiety, so maybe it's really only like a quarter lie.

"That's cool. I didn't know you and Hitch volunteered at a counseling office." Chatham looks impressed.

Maddie crosses her arms, squinting down at me. She knows I'm lying. I can tell by the frown on her face. She just hasn't figured out a way to disprove my story yet.

I look up front for Ms. Ringgold. What the heck's taking her so long? "It's no big deal. Hitch loves it."

"Maybe you could bring him to The Potter's House sometime to visit with the kids." He speaks to me as if Maddie's invisible.

"Yeah, maybe." I answer noncommittally, feeling like the biggest jerk known to mankind. Now, I'm lying about helping therapy patients to Mr. Volunteer of the Year himself, Chatham York.

When Ms. Ringgold addresses the class with instructions on how to annotate some obscure Hemingway short story, everyone in the room moans except for me. I exhale for the first time in several minutes, relieved to have something, anything, other than Maddie to occupy my attention.

"I'll walk you to third," Chatham offers when the bell finally rings.

"I have something I have to take care of." I smile, backing away. I need to catch Ayla before she dodges me again.

When Derek shoulder bumps Chatham from behind, I spy an opportunity for escape.

"Okay. Don't forget about the game Thursday," he says, untangling himself from Derek's playful headlock.

"Got it." I wave.

Derek drags Chatham into the hallway. I clutch my binder to my chest, waiting for Ayla to make her way toward where I'm standing near the door. She forces a little smile. Her tight lips clash with the pink flower clipped in her wispy blonde hair.

"Can we talk? Please." I touch her forearm, guiding her toward the computer table in the back of the room before she can slip away again. A smiling miniature of Dr. Wellesley, wearing a white robe, halo floating above his head, perches on my left shoulder. The real Dr. Wellesley would fall over if he saw me reaching out—physically touching people—twice in one day. First Chatham, now Ayla.

She places her free hand in her pocket. "Have you told Chatham?"

I blink under her stare. "No, but—"

She holds up a hand to stop me. "Emilie, I'm not trying to be mean." She hesitates. "I just know how much it hurts to be deceived by someone you trust. Chatham's a nice guy. Tell him. Everything will be all right." Her voice drops on the last sentence. "I promise." Now she's the one laying a comforting hand on my arm.

And I realize she's not mad at me so much as pushing me to do the right thing, like a mama bird nudging her baby from the nest so it will learn to fly. My shoulders slump as I shrink back into myself. I've been such an idiot. I came to the Ridge with these preconceived notions about the fake kids at this school who all look alike with their bleached teeth and their bleached hair, when I'm the biggest fraud of all, pretending to be something I'm not and condemning them.

I drag my eyes from the waxed tiles beneath my feet to her open face. "I was going to tell him. But then we had the thing with the neighbors Saturday and I had a doctor's appointment yesterday and he doesn't feel good today." The sentences tumble out of my mouth in one big glob without any punctuation.

She shakes her head. "Those are excuses."

I open my mouth to speak, then close my lips. Of course she's right. I'm lying to myself and to Chatham. I'm more worried about guarding this pseudo life I'm creating and protecting my own heart than I am about Chatham's feelings.

"I'll tell him Thursday after the game." My voice drops when Ms. Ringgold stands up behind her desk.

Ayla's hand falls away from my arm. "You need to tell him today. You're playing with fire the longer you wait."

"I can't tell him at school, Ayla," I whisper, avoiding Ms. Ringgold's questioning eyes. "I promise. I'll tell him Thursday."

She retreats toward the door, wiping at a smudge of paint on the back of her hand. "I hope that works out for you. I'll be at the game afterward if you need me."

"Why don't you go with me? He's saving seats behind the bench." I tag along behind her.

Ms. Ringgold steps around her desk. "Girls, is everything

okay?" I recognize the raised-brow, inquisitive-mother look on her face.

"Yes," Ayla and I answer in unison, our voices a little too high.

Ayla turns back to me. "I'll be there. Everybody will. We can talk afterward." She smiles at me, but her eyes are sad, like the little girl's in her *Forsaken* painting.

This is useless. I'm banging my head against a wall. She's not budging till I tell him—till I do the right thing.

She steps away from me, melting into the hall, and I have no choice but to head to third period.

"Emilie," Ms. Ringgold calls as I cross the threshold.

I pretend not to hear her as I walk away, kicking myself for being such an idiot. A few weeks ago, I didn't want to be here. I was positive I didn't want any of this—friends, crushes, teachers who care. Currently, I'm not so sure. I feel like I *should* be happy. But now I'm so desperate to hang on to these people, even if it means pretending to be something I'm not, that I can't enjoy their company. It's like a storm surge has ripped me off my foundation, and I'm spinning around in tumultuous flood-waters. I'm floating around aimlessly—adrift—when what I really need to be doing is seeking higher ground.

CHAPTER TWENTY-EIGHT

I should not dare to leave my friend ...

EMILY DICKINSON

Thursday afternoon, I'm filled with equal parts anticipation and dread. The butterflies in my belly wage war with the stomach acids threatening to make swiss cheese of my stomach lining. To make matters worse, Mom refuses to let me stay after school for the game. I could walk to the gym and watch the JV game and then Chatham's game, but she won't have any part of that. If I'm going to the varsity game, I'm going to come home first, suffer through some mother-daughter conversation, and choke down whatever healthy snack she's prepared.

"Why didn't you bring Hitch?" I ask as we turn left out of the parking lot.

"Well ..." She drums her nails on the steering wheel without answering my question.

My stomach drops at the sight of wine-colored nails.

"He's at home with Roger," she says without meeting my eyes.

My jaw drops. "Wh-at?" I choke on the last syllable. "You left Hitch at home with a stranger?" I turn in the seat to face her, my mouth hanging open.

She takes her eyes off the road for a millisecond to glance at my face before refocusing her attention on the after-school rush. "He's not a stranger. He's . . . my friend."

"Well, he's a stranger to me." I lean my forehead against the cool glass of the passenger-side window, pressing my fingernails into my palms. "And I don't want him messing with my dog."

"Emilie, Hitch likes him." Her quiet words are almost snuffed out by the hum of the tires.

I grit my teeth. Please, God, this can't be happening. I can't deal with this—not now, not today. I tap my head against the window.

"I really want you to meet him." Her jaw is so tight, the words grate against her teeth like sandpaper when she speaks. "We're going to Poor Richard's for crab legs after we drop you off at the game."

My jaw twitches. "I don't want to."

Mature. I know.

"Have you ever considered that maybe this is what *I* want?" There's no fight left in her voice—just defeat, followed by silence.

The quiet overwhelms me, and I feel kind of sick. Deep down, I know she's right. I'm being childish and selfish. I bite my tongue for the rest of the drive home and the long walk up the stairs to the front porch.

"Hi, Roger." Mom's voice and mouth smile when we walk in the house, but her eyes are still wary when she looks at me.

Hitch is curled up with Roger in my corner of the couch. His blocky head rests in Roger's lap, and it isn't moving. The traitor doesn't even rise to greet me. When I smile at him, he wags his tail and lifts his head an inch, but makes no effort to move until Roger stands to meet me with a smile and an out-stretched hand. "I've heard so much about you."

I force a smile, mumbling something unintelligible. He reaches for my hand, pumping it in the two-fisted handshake of politicians and pastors. His fingers and eyes are kind of warm, but it might all be a show for Mom—the way he's sucking up to Hitch and now me. He can't be that nice. Why would he want to get involved with a middle-aged widow and her depressed, epileptic teenager?

When Hitch finally pads over to me, I kneel down, nuz-zling his face with my cheek, trying to ignore Roger. But the man's too friendly to be ignored.

"I have a golden." Smile lines crinkle the corners of his eyes when he talks. "Her name's Bella. We should get them together sometime for a play date."

I smile and grunt noncommittally, wishing he was a jerk so I could hate him for something other than dating my mother.

"What can I get y'all to drink?" Mom asks, stepping around the counter and opening the refrigerator. She's only moved fif-teen feet, but I feel lost and alone, like that first day when she left me in the counselor's office at the Ridge.

"I'll have water." I pull out a stool at the bar to busy my hands and sit down.

Roger pulls out the seat beside me. Mom hands him a Diet Coke. I stare at Dad's beach-glass collection in the kitchen window, trying to ignore the weirdness of the situation. I don't know whether I'm more upset my mother knows what Roger wants to drink without him answering or more concerned she likes a guy who drinks Diet Coke.

Dad would've had real Coke, high-fructose corn syrup and

all. He'd never shy away from a few extra calories. His hair might have been thinning, but he loved to run barefoot in the sand until the chemo made him so weak he had to walk. Eventually he just had to watch runners on the beach from the bedroom window. But Roger looks a little soft, if you ask me. I guess his face is okay for an old guy, and he seems friendly enough.

But he's not Dad.

A lump forms in my throat, and I reach for an apple from the fruit tray Mom has arranged on the counter. But I can't eat it. An oncoming headache pinches my skull.

"So your mom says you like to read." Roger nibbles a handful of grapes.

I swallow a sip of water. "Um, yeah."

"Fiction or nonfiction?" he asks.

"Both."

We struggle through nineteen minutes of awkward conversation before I can't take it any longer. "This is the first game of the season. There will be a huge crowd. We'd better go," I say to Mom, moving toward the bathroom to brush my teeth before we head back out.

Hitch nudges the door open for me, and I hear Mom and Roger laughing nervously in the kitchen. I frown at Hitch, still shocked he hesitated when I came in. But when he wiggles his nose under my hand, I smile, hard feelings forgotten, and plop down on the closed toilet seat to hug him.

"You coming?" Mom calls a minute later.

I jump to my feet. When I do, the blood rushes to my head, and a wave of dizziness catches me off guard. "I'll, uh . . . be right there." I brace myself against the counter, taking a couple of steadying breaths. Hitch whines, but he doesn't pull on my sleeve or pant leg. So I square my shoulders, remind myself I haven't had a seizure in over three months, swish some Listerine in my mouth, spit, and head out to the living room followed by Hitch.

"It'll be okay, boy," I mumble as I head out the door, but my stomach tightens at the sight of his black nose pressed against the glass door. I blow him a kiss, telling myself he'll be fine on his own for one more night. Whether it's for the best or not, he'll be going to school with me next week.

The three of us pile into Roger's pine-scented station wagon and head back toward school. I turn away from Cindy's dark house when we pass and mentally rehearse walking into the gym by myself and taking my seat behind the bench. Going to this game would be much easier if I were with Ayla, or even better if I were any of the hundreds of ordinary North Ridge teenage girls.

But nothing about me is normal, so I do what my fifth-grade Sunday school teacher suggested: pray. I could really use a miracle with Chatham tonight and with the rest of the school on Monday when I show up with my furry, eighty-pound best friend in tow.

CHAPTER TWENTY-NINE

My Cocoon tightens—Colors teaze—
I'm feeling for the Air—

EMILY DICKINSON

The breeze off the ocean has turned chilly. I shiver as I wait my turn outside the crowded gym doors. Every person in line wears either North Ridge blue and white or War Eagle red. I, on the other hand, am dressed in my standard fitted black tee. At least I traded in the usual khaki shorts for cream-colored jeans and dusted off the black baby-doll flats Mom bought me to wear the one time we went to church last year. I even added a pair of dangly silver earrings I grabbed when Mom and I were in the drugstore Monday.

When I make it to the front of the line, I peek through the lobby to the packed gym beyond. A balding dad with a pot-belly takes my ticket and stamps my hand. The crowd pushes me forward. My pulse vibrates in rhythm with the pounding music of the pep band. Teenage boys circle both ends of the court tossing easy layups as they warm up. For a second, I panic—I don't know where to sit. I stand frozen and out of place, alone in the crowd.

After a minute, I thaw enough to survey the gym. When I do, I realize all eyes are glued to the guys on the court or on the cheerleaders' barely concealed behinds. The few people involved in conversation have to lean in to each other and strain to hear over the spirited chaos. No one's paying me any attention.

I exhale as a group of fans in front of me rushes toward the bleachers. When I spy two men in blue-and-white coaching shirts beside a row of folding chairs, I know where I'm supposed to sit. I just need to convince my feet to move in that direction when they really want to hide in the bathroom or duck outside and call Mom and Roger for a ride home. A vision of the two of them snuggled up against each other in a booth at Poor Richard's motivates me to inch forward. I mutter "Excuse me" a thousand times as I squeeze around the perimeter of the court.

Royal blue North Ridge towels mark either end of the first two rows of seats behind the bench. A couple of vaguely famil-iar ninth graders sit with racks of water bottles on the first row.

"Are these seats saved?" I bow down so they can hear me, ignoring the headache building behind my eyes and pointing to the wooden bench behind them.

"Officially, no," the taller of the two says, his close-set eyes trav-eling from my shoes to my chest. His gaze never actually reaches my face. "Unofficially, yes." He props himself on his elbows, block-ing the row where I'd hoped to sit, staring at my boobs.

Little creep. "Who are they *unofficially* saved for?" I ask through gritted teeth.

A warning buzzer sounds over the noise of the crowd. I jump, almost losing my balance. The only thing keeping me from falling into the players' folding seats below the bleachers is the creeper's bony little claw on my thigh.

Eww.

His hand slides a little too slowly down my leg, stopping on my knee. "Certain girls."

Pressing my lips together, I jerk my leg free. "Well, Chatham told me to sit here." I slide into the empty row behind him, ignoring his friend's bulging eyes and focusing on the guys on the court.

It takes me all of two seconds to spot Chatham shooting a three-pointer on the far side of the court. He moves like a dancer. When a teammate passes him the ball, his muscular calves contract. Ropey arms extend toward the ceiling. Large hands palm the ball until a perfectly timed release sends it sailing toward the basket, where it drops into the rim and swishes through the net. Transfixed by his beauty, I forget the pounding of the music and the noise of the crowd. I even forget the mounting pain in my head.

The referees take the court, and the head coaches call their players in. Chatham huddles with his teammates around the bench. He nods at something the coach says, then glances up at the stands. When he spots me, a smile cracks open his face, and the flock of birds in my belly takes flight when he winks.

Someone coughs beside me, and I look to my right. The birds in my belly drop like a Boeing 747 in a nosedive, crashing and burning on the runway. It's Maddie.

"Well, look who's here—it's Emilie." She elbows the friend standing beside her.

All of a sudden, I'm nauseous. Not like nervous-butterfly nauseous, but hang-your-head-over-the-toilet-and-puke nauseous. Nevertheless, I sit up relatively straight and meet her eyes. I nod but don't speak as they slide into the bleachers beside me. Creeper boy smiles at them without saying a word.

I'm seriously considering my escape options when the band stops. A voice booms over the loudspeaker, instructing fans to rise and introducing the senior who will sing the national anthem. When I stand, the gym spins. I place my right hand over my racing heart and breathe slowly through my nose in an effort to halt the swaying movement of the stands beneath my feet. My lips pucker at the sour taste on the back of my tongue. I'm fighting my own perilous fight when the singer hits her note on the line about the rocket's red glare and the bombs bursting in air.

All signs—the headache, the dizziness, the bad taste in my mouth—point to either an oncoming panic attack, which I haven't had since the year after Dad died, or an impending seizure. I scan the sidelines. I'm trapped by two rows of long-legged players, a handful of coaches, and three women sitting at the scorer's table.

The song ends, and Maddie leans toward me. My throat tightens in defense against her suffocating cloud of hairspray, shampoo, and perfume. "Chatham must really like you if he invited you to sit behind the bench," she says without taking her eyes off the court where the War Eagles' starting lineup is being introduced. I can't tell if it's curiosity or malice in her tone.

"I thought you'd be cheering," I say, trying to steer the conversation away from me and wracking my brain for an escape plan.

But Maddie just laughs, like I'm stupid or funny or both. "I'm not a basketball cheerleader," she says. "That's for girls who don't make the football competition squad." She shakes her head, flicking a strand of long blonde hair off her shoulder.

"Oh." I force a smile to cover my confusion. Who knew there were social classes within the cheerleading ranks? I thought once you hit cheering status, you were home free. Now I almost feel sorry for the beautiful girls with the big bows in their hair, bouncing on the balls of their feet at either end of the court. Do they understand their lowly status compared to Maddie and her crew?

The announcer calls the North Ridge starting five. The gym erupts, and I forget about the cheerleaders. Swarms of feet pound the bleachers. Whistles, cheers, and applause drown out any attempt at conversation. I clap for Chatham when they call his number and smile when he looks up in the stands. Maddie waves so hard, a puff of stuffy air brushes my cheek.

I'm thankful for a second to sit down and gather my thoughts when the referees and the tallest guys from each team take center court for the jump ball. I may not actually be able to play, but no one is born and raised in the Tar Heel state—the heart and soul of the ACC—without knowing a little about the game of hoops.

The tip goes to Chatham. He throws a beautiful bounce pass to one of his teammates. The guy lobs a quick three-pointer, and North Ridge is on the board. But the War Eagles are vicious. The Ridge never leads by more than three. The gym buzzes with electricity.

During the first full time-out, I survey the stands on the other side of the court in an effort to avoid Maddie's prying eyes. I spot Ayla sitting with Katsu, and my stomach tightens. I should be sitting with them. She glances my way and waves.

Once again, I wish she was on my side of the gym. I shouldn't be fighting off Maddie by myself, not when I could have a friend on my side if I'd just done the right thing.

"You want to hang with us after the game, since you're, um . . . alone?" Maddie asks me. For the second time, I'm unsure of her motives. Is she trying to use me to get to Chatham, or does she have a more sinister plan in mind? It's a little hard for me to believe that after weeks of the ice-queen routine she's actually being friendly.

"I'm leaving at halftime." I didn't even know I'd made the decision until the words plunge from my mouth. But now that I've said them, I know they're true. No matter how disappointed Chatham is or how concerned Ayla is, I can't risk seizing in this gym. As soon as the buzzer sounds for the second quarter, I'm texting Mom and telling her I'm ready to go. Then I'm texting Ayla and Chatham and to say I'm sick, which I'm pretty sure is about to be true.

By the time Mom and Roger get here, it'll be halftime. The sidelines should be clear enough with the players and coaches in the locker rooms that I can escape without falling over anyone.

Chatham passes the ball to our center—some guy named Eric—who scores an easy layup, bringing the lead back to two. My neck gets a workout, swiveling back and forth in an attempt to keep up with the lightning-quick game. The War Eagles force an aggressive press, racing the ball up court in an attempt to score before the halftime buzzer. Chatham steps in front of their point guard. The guy trips over Chatham's foot.

The ref calls a foul on Chatham, and the crowd boos.

"Get a pair of glasses, ref!" an angry voice shouts behind me. Chatham glances up into the stands, his jaw twitching.

I look over my shoulder, trying to identify the obnoxious fan, and spot the man I noticed that night Mom and I went for ice cream at the pier. Except for the bulging vein in the man's forehead, the stern cut of his jaw, and the pit-bull eyes, the guy's a forty-something-year-old photocopy of Chatham. I turn away, not wanting my mental vision of Chatham to be polluted by the image of his dad.

With four seconds left on the clock and the Ridge up by two, the War Eagles throw the ball from midcourt to one of their shooting guards. He snaps an overhead pass to one of their tallest players.

"Three, two . . ." The crowd counts down the clock.

My heart races.

My head pounds.

With one second to go, the guy launches a three-point shot. Time slows. The War Eagles cheer. North Ridge fans cringe. I cover my eyes with my hands, unable to watch. When I do, the world goes black.

CHAPTER THIRTY

Success is counted sweetest
By those who ne'er succeed.

EMILY DICKINSON

The pungent smell of bleach rips through my nostrils, and the familiar beep of a heart-rate monitor beats out a steady tattoo on my right. My stomach turns in on itself, suffocating any hopeful butterflies or birdies that might still be holding on from earlier in the evening.

Without opening my eyes, I recognize the sounds and smells of Outer Banks Hospital. Balling my left hand in a fist under the stiff white sheet, I press my fingernails into my palm, and pray for a few minutes alone before I have to deal with Mom or any other intruders.

I don't want to think about how I got here or the horrific scene I must've caused in the gym. Hot tears sting the backs of my eyes as my brain replays those last minutes at the game—Chatham's dad seated behind me, Maddie hassling me about plans for the night, the arc of the perfectly executed three-pointer that very possibly could've given the War Eagles their first lead of the night.

"Sweetie?" Mom whispers.

I freeze, holding my breath, desperately needing a minute to organize my thoughts before dealing with her.

"Sweetie?" She rubs my arm. "I know you're awake. Talk to me. Please."

I shake my head.

She brushes the hair back off my forehead. "You seized at the game."

I turn away.

"The medics brought you to the hospital." Her hand falls from my face.

I grit my teeth—annoyed that she's hovering and annoyed by the sudden absence of her hand. I want her to comfort me, to take care of me the way Dad would've. But at the same time I know she can't.

A pent-up sob rushes from my mouth. Hot tears escape my tightly closed lids, burning my cheeks. I swipe at my face, opening my eyes to a dimly lit, curtained-off corner of a room. From the sound of the drunken cursing on the other side of the screen, I must be stuck in the emergency room with the Friday night party crowd. That means my vital signs weren't bad enough to warrant being admitted to the hospital. I'll be going home tonight.

I know this drill—IV anti-seizure meds, observation, and then back to my crappy life. Except now my life's the crappiest it's ever been because I tried to live a lie and got busted. It's like I accidentally hit Send on a group message to everyone at North Ridge High School, delivering a viral video of myself seizing and doing God knows what else in front of a packed gym.

I bet it was the highlight of Maddie's semester—probably

the entire school year, maybe her life—if she wasn't too trauma-tized by the bodily fluids and the messiness of the whole ordeal.

Mom sits down in the chair beside the bed, reaching through the bedrail to touch my arm. "Emilie, there are people who want to see you."

I clutch my head in my hands, tugging on my hair, in an effort to compose myself. "No. No way."

"I sent everyone away but Chatham and Ayla." She pulls my hands away from my face, squeezing them in her palms. "I thought you might want to see them."

I yank my hands free, covering my mouth. "I'm . . . going to . . ."

She grabs a pink, kidney-shaped barf bucket from the nightstand, pressing it under my chin as I heave. After several gut-wrenching spasms, I regurgitate a dribble of yellow bile from the depths of my stomach.

Mom wipes my chin with a rough white washcloth. I don't fight her. What's the point? I may as well let her take care of me. I'm probably never going to be able to do it myself.

"Take a sip." She lifts a Styrofoam cup with a Flexi-Straw to my lips. "In a minute, I'll go tell them you don't want to see anyone tonight."

"Ever," I mutter, my tongue thick from the seizure meds and the cold water.

She raises a skeptical brow.

"Ever," I repeat, fighting off a sudden, overwhelming urge to sleep. "I'm not going back to school, and I'm not going to see them again. Ever."

Later, I wake to the sound of hushed voices outside the drawn curtain.

"She's not feeling too good about herself right now," Mom whispers, the high-pitched tone giving away her near panic.

Good. She should be stressed. If it weren't for her, none of this would've happened. Well, I still might've seized, but it would've been in the privacy of my own home with Hitch at my side, not in front of a crowd of strangers. It's payback for her making me go to the Ridge.

"It's really not that big a deal," Roger soothes.

He just dropped about seventy-five more flights in my book. Not a big deal? The guy isn't just a nerd. He's an idiot.

Mom sniffles.

"She's a beautiful girl. And smart. She's got so much going for her." He pauses, probably massaging her back or something.

Hmm. If he knew I was awake, I'd think he was trying to flatter me. Yuck.

"Everyone has flaws, Connie. Some of us hide them on the inside," he says. "Some can't be camouflaged so easily. But we're all flawed. We're all human."

"You're right. It's just—" She breaks off, sobbing.

I grit my teeth. I know it's hard on her being a single mom, especially with my epilepsy. But I want to scream. She's not the victim. She's not the one who deserves to be comforted. It's me. I'm the victim. I'm the one trapped in this nightmare.

I want to stomp my feet, punch my pillow, bang my head against the wall. But I can't. I can't do anything but lay here. The high doses of Phenobarbital or whatever they injected me with slow everything down—my speech, my breathing, and the muscle contractions required to stomp, punch, and bang. I bite back the scream rising in my throat and taste hot, coppery blood on the back of my tongue. When I gag, their conversation screeches to an abrupt halt.

Mom peeks around the curtain. She sees me awake and steps into my white cubicle. Her posture is ramrod straight, her face dry. But she can't hide the swollen eyes.

"Hey, sleepyhead." She stands over me, running the fingers of her left hand through my tangled hair. Our eyes meet for a second before I look away. A clean pair of jeans and the Cape Hatteras National Seashore sweatshirt lay on the chair beside the bed. The dark green hoodie reminds me of Chatham and the other people I lied to. I won't be able to hide from the wreckage forever.

I shake my head.

"What's wrong, baby?" Mom glances from my face to the chair, obviously trying to read my thoughts.

Hmm. Let's see. "Nothing," I lie, already falling back into the deception routine. It's like riding a bike. Once you master the technique, you never lose it. You might be a little wobbly at first, but you never forget. "Nothing. I just . . . I just want to go home." I fiddle with the IV taped to the back of my left hand, wincing at the pressure when I jar the needle.

Mom pulls my hands apart, gripping each of mine in her own. "The nurse said she should have your discharge orders after the next vitals check."

I know this drill too. Mom will be comforting and nurturing for a few hours, maybe a day, but eventually she'll get tired of me feeling sorry for myself. Then we'll go back to the merry-go-round of our life. But instead of ponies and gold rings, our carousel sports ghosts of dead dads and epileptic demons.

I shake my head, trying to rid myself of such morbid thoughts, but what's the use? This is my life—real life. I tried public school. I tried making friends. I did everything Mom and Dr. Wellesley wanted me to do and then some. I climbed a *lighthouse* with the cutest boy in school and kissed him, and look where that got me.

Right back where I started.

CHAPTER THIRTY-ONE

I'll tell you how the Sun rose—
A Ribbon at a time—

EMILY DICKINSON

Mom lets me stay home Friday. Even she isn't crazy enough to try to send me to school after a grand mal seizure and a sleepless night in the emergency room. She's pretty cool Saturday. Sunday morning, she reaches her limit on my wallowing. I hear my bedroom door creak open. Hitch lifts his head, ready to greet the day. I stay frozen in my fetal position with my back to the door, hoping she'll go away. I'm pretty sure it's her Sunday to work at the library.

If I stay in bed long enough, she'll have to leave, and I won't have to deal with her. I wait for the door to close again, but it doesn't. Instead, soft feet pad across the rough floor to the side of my bed. I bite the inside of my cheek and count silently. *One one thousand. Two one thousand. Three one thousand.*

She sits down on the edge of the bed. Hitch lays his heavy head gently on my hip. The bed shifts when she pets him.

Four one thousand. Five one thousand. Six one thousand.

"Sweetie, I know you're awake."

Crap.

"Listen . . ." She rubs the back of my arm. "I've been thinking."

Not good.

"I'm not going to force you to go back to school against your will."

I open my right eye a fraction of an inch. If I've heard Granddaddy Day say it once, I've heard him say it a hundred times: "If something sounds too good to be true, it is." Lying perfectly still, I wait. I know Mom well enough to know there has to be a catch. There's always a catch.

"Really, though." Her hand freezes on my bicep. "I don't think you should stay home. You've made huge accomplishments—come a long way. I think you should go back to school and finish what you started."

Umm, not in this lifetime. Or the next, for that matter.

"Your friend Ayla and several others left the game and followed the ambulance to the hospital." She pauses when I stiffen. "They were worried about you. It wouldn't have been so terrifying for them if you'd been honest about the seizures."

Well, imagine that—me, wrong again. Seems like my secret's out and Mom knows I didn't tell people the truth about my epilepsy. Biting my lip, I refuse to submit to the tears welling behind my closed eyes.

She squeezes my arm when I still don't respond. "But no matter what—" Her voice cracks. "No matter what I think . . . I'm not going to force you to go back against your will."

Now a twinge of guilt nibbles my insides. She loves me. And I love her too. But I don't know how to show it anymore.

"You're practically an adult. I'm going to trust you to start making some of your own decisions. I'm not going to pressure you to go back." She lifts her hand to Hitch's head, wiggling the thick fur and loose skin on the top of his skull. "But I'm not going to let you lay here and feel sorry for yourself either. So get up. We have breakfast to eat and errands to run."

I'd rather take an ice bath than tag along on her errands, but I bite my tongue. "Give me a second, okay?" Squeezing my eyes shut, I swallow the victory chant rising in my throat. There's no way I'm arguing a minor technicality like weekend duties when I just won the whole freaking enchilada, the golden ticket, the *war*.

Woo-hoo. Yippee. Yee-haw. No more risk of humiliation—at least not in a public high school. I'm not going back, not going back, not going back.

"Come on, Hitch." She pats her thigh as she pads out of the room barefooted. "I'll take him out so you can get ready."

Hitch leaps off the bed. Normally, I'd disagree. He's my dog, my responsibility—my best friend. But there's no way I'm risking opening my mouth and inserting my foot.

The door clicks shut, and they're gone. I sit up, looking around my silent room, frozen in time exactly the way it was when Dad died. My sails deflate a little. Not going back to school means staying cooped up in my sad little shell and watching from the shore as everyone else, including my mom, ventures out into new territory, spins the wheel of fate, and takes a chance on life. Staying home means no Chatham, no Ayla, no life. No Ms. Ringgold, no lit mag, no nothing.

Am I seriously contemplating going back to school? No. Avoiding the mirror above the dresser, I drag myself across the room and into a pair of sweatpants and a long-sleeved gray T-shirt.

Less than an hour later, a waiter at the Crow's Nest seats us in a corner near the back door, away from the Sunday-morning breakfast rush. Unlike most of the restaurants on the beach that close in the off-season, the Nest stays open year-round. And it's always crowded. They serve the best pancakes and sausage east of Raleigh.

But I'm not ready for pancakes yet. I'm still a little groggy, and my stomach's weak from the extra meds and the missed sleep Thursday night. A dull headache pulses behind my left eye. I imagine this is what a hangover would feel like. Not that I'll ever know. There are so many firsts I'll never experience now that the seizures are back: driving a car, drinking champagne at my wedding, skinny-dipping in the Atlantic.

"What can I get you?" a twenty-something waiter with ash-blond hair and a nice smile asks, interrupting my mopey thoughts.

Mom orders without opening the menu. "I'll have the Captain's Special."

The guy looks up from his notepad, eyes wide. "With all the fixings?"

"Yep." She beams, her cheeks flushed. "I'm starving." And she must be if she's going to eat eggs, sausage, grits, hash browns, *and* pancakes.

Charming Waiter Boy turns on me. "And for you?"

"An English muffin and apple juice."

His face drops. "How 'bout some ham or a side of grits?" He winks. "Something that'll stick to your ribs."

"No, thanks." I fidget with my fork as he scribbles down our order. Swallowing a sip of lukewarm water, I wish he'd head back to the kitchen. When I look at Mom, she raises an inquisitive brow.

"What about some orange marmalade or honey for the muffin?" He grins hopefully.

So much for him leaving. It's like he's vying for some Server of the Year award or something. "Okay." I compromise. What's the point in arguing? "The marmalade sounds good."

He nods, satisfied, and tucks his pencil behind his ear, then finally turns on his heel and scoots around a group of old men seated in the noisy dining area.

Mom excuses herself to go to the bathroom, and I reach for a folded newspaper left wedged between the condiments and the wall. When I pull it toward me, it flops open to the sports page. The large-font headline reads "Buzzer Beater Decides Match between Local Rivals." I skim the first few lines. "North Ridge loses to the War Eagles by two." My stomach turns. "After a medical emergency in the stands interrupted the game at the halftime buzzer, starting point guard Chatham York walked off the court, leaving teammates in a lurch. The Ridge managed to hang on till the final seconds of the game with Seth Ross filling in."

My eyes race to the end of the article, but my brain fails to comprehend the words. Chatham walked off the court in the middle of a tied game with everyone watching, including his dad, to follow me to the hospital—where I refused to see him.

My eyes pause on the last sentence. "War Eagles center Matthew Thomas fired off a half-court shot for the win at the buzzer."

I'm glad I've already decided not to return. Facing the student body, who surely blames me for the loss to their major rival, would be too much even if I wanted to go back.

I cringe at the sidebar image of a crying North Ridge

cheerleader wrapped in the arms of another face-painted member of the squad. A second photo shows the War Eagle bench charging the court, ready to dog pile the teammate who sank the winning shot.

I shrink down in my seat and undo my ponytail in an effort to camouflage my face. Folding the paper inside out, I shove it back where I found it and hope nobody recognizes me.

"Why so glum?" Mom slides into her seat. "I thought you'd be in a better mood after our discussion."

I shrug. What is there to say? She's right. I should be happy now that I got my way on the school thing.

Chipper Surfer Waiter Guy appears, grinning from ear to ear, and slides four plates heaped with food in front of Mom. He turns to me empty handed. "Your food will be out in a second."

The muscles in my face twist into a stiff smile. "Thanks."

He scurries off in the direction of the kitchen as Mom digs into a pile of hash browns smothered in fried onions, cubed ham, and shredded cheddar. "Want some?" she asks around a mouthful of potatoes.

"No, thanks." I try to relax my rock-hard face. Nothing happens. I think I'm fossilizing.

When Chatham and I first started researching Emily Dickinson, I couldn't understand how such a gifted writer could become a recluse. But I get it now, because all I want to do is go home and crawl under the covers. I glance across the crowded dining room, contemplating an escape to the bathroom.

Our waiter weaves his way toward our table with my sad little English muffin and a ramekin of marmalade. "Here we go." He slides the white bread plate in front of me. "Can I get y'all anything else?"

Um, yeah. Some camouflage and a good hiding place. "No, I'm fine."

Mom lifts her shoulders, her mouth too full to do anything but shrug.

Waiter Dude turns to check the table behind us. "Do we have many errands?" I ask, ripping my muffin into tiny pieces and nibbling at the rabbit-sized tidbits.

"No. I need to drop a birthday card for your grandmother at the post office and grab a few things at the grocery store." She swallows a cheekful of pancakes. "Oh, and . . . I have a couple of boxes to drop off at The Potter's House. A few of Dad's things." Her hand shakes a little when she dabs the corner of her mouth with her napkin. "It's time, sweetie." She reaches her free hand across the table.

I stare at it like its grown a sixth finger. The toasted muffin scratches the back of my throat. I chase the dry crust down with a swig of water. "The, uh . . . Potter's House?" A few of Dad's things?

She nods.

The slick glass slips against my wet palm, and water swishes over the rim. I mop the spill with my napkin, bumping the glass with my shaky hand and splashing more liquid on the table.

I'm not sure what freaks me out more: the possibility of running into Chatham volunteering at the thrift store or Mom's decision to get rid of Dad's stuff without consulting me.

All I know for sure is I've got a problem—a big problem.

CHAPTER THIRTY-TWO

Each that we lose takes part of us . . .

EMILY DICKINSON

E arth to Emilie. Come in." Mom hip bumps me in front of the avocados.

I look up from my white-knuckled hands on the grocery cart handle. "Um, yeah?"

"Do you want taco salads for dinner?" She digs around in a bin of tomatoes.

I shrug, propping a foot on the metal basket beneath the cart. "Sure."

She drops two almost-ripe tomatoes into a plastic produce bag and heads over to the lettuce. I follow, racking my brain for an escape plan. I cannot—repeat cannot—enter The Potter's House. Personally, I'd rather not enter the parking lot, but I know my mom. Nothing short of a natural disaster will keep the woman from her to-do list. So I'd better come up with a good reason why I need to stay in the car.

We're heading up aisle three when I start laying the groundwork for my master plan. "Is it hot in here?" I ask, pausing behind her when she stops to compare prices on the black olives.

"Not really." She counts on her fingers, calculating the cost per ounce, her eyes narrowing. When she doesn't look at me, I clear my throat. She glances in my direction and adds two cans of chopped olives to our cart.

I massage my temple, wincing for added effect. "I'm not feeling so great."

"We're almost finished," she says, sashaying around the endcap and up the next aisle. "You're probably just tired."

I sigh through parted lips, trying to gain her sympathy without going overboard. But she's not biting. She's totally oblivious as she triple checks her list.

I pray for divine intervention as we navigate the frozen food section. When we approach the register, I'm still praying. The tightness in my gut tells me I'm wasting my time, and my gut is always right. God knows I should've listened to it at the game on Thursday.

A few minutes later, we pile groceries in the backseat. As Mom's butt hits the driver's seat, her phone rings. "Hey, Rog." She smiles, clicking her seat belt into place.

Rog? Seriously? Rog? Is that like a nickname or a term of endearment or what?

While I was occupied with Chatham, their relationship moved to a new level, and I blame myself. I should've been home with Hitch and Mom instead of spending all my free time in the media center and going on dates. Maybe then I could have stopped this. Or at least understood why Mom was suddenly ready to move on when I wasn't.

Pressing my forehead on the cold window, I grip the door handle and try to block out Mom chuckling at something *Rog* said. The woman driving the car is a complete stranger. She doesn't brake as we cruise through a yellow light. She turns in to The Potter's House without signaling.

At least the place looks deserted—no black SUVs with bicycle racks or winches anywhere to be seen. I relax until Mom gestures toward the trunk with her free hand.

Uh-uh. No way. Not going to do it. I shake my head. This was her idea. She should suffer the physical loss of tossing Dad's stuff, not me. When I don't move, she pinches her lips together. Her brow furrows. I freeze, making no effort to move.

"Let me call you back," she says to Rog, ending the call and turning toward me. "Emilie, we've discussed this. Dad will always be with us. Getting rid of his old clothes isn't going to change that. He didn't even care about clothes. How about we do it together—"

Her phone vibrates, interrupting her little pep talk. I recognize the library name and number when it flashes on the screen.

"Just take your call, Mom." I gesture for her to pop the trunk and step out of the car. My ribs close in against my lungs and heart as I round the back. Her moral support isn't going to make this any easier. I may as well do something on my own.

I peek into the trunk. Staring up at me are the cardboard boxes of Dad's clothes I found in their closet a few weeks ago. My blood pressure kicks into Mach speed when it hits me. I could be walking on the beach tomorrow and see some kid who's into the whole vintage thing wearing one of Dad's R.E.M. or U2 T-shirts.

I brace myself on the trunk, inhaling through my nose to the count of three like Dr. Wellesley instructed, and contemplate my options: refuse to drop the clothes and risk a scene with Mom right here in the parking lot, or do what she wants and let another little piece of my father slip out to sea.

Reaching into the trunk, I stack one box on top of the other and lift them toward my chest. Tears prick the backs of my eyes.

Daddy, I'm so sorry—so very, very sorry.

Trudging toward the front door, I shift the boxes to my left hip and reach for the metal handle. The door swings open before I make contact. A younger girl with a head full of blonde curls props the door open with her foot. When my eyes adjust to the light, I blink in disbelief. It's Cindy. I'd recognize that hair anywhere. What I don't recognize is the glow on her cheeks and the roundness of her face.

"Oh my gosh. Cindy?" I bend down, place the boxes on the ground, and pull her into my arms.

She squeezes me back. "Emilie, hi!"

I hold her at arm's length to study her face. She looks . . . happy. Younger, somehow.

I pull her in for a second hug. "I've been so worried about you."

An older lady with gray hair and deep lines around her mouth steps out from behind the register toward us.

"Do you know this girl?" she asks Cindy, looking down at us over horn-rimmed glasses.

"Yes, Ms. White." Cindy clasps my hand like I might float away. "Before I was a hero, she was my neighbor."

The woman whips off her glasses, her eyes narrowing on me. I stand, smiling and holding out a hand to greet her.

She looks at my hand but makes no effort to shake it. Instead, she folds in the stems of her glasses and hangs them on the long chain around her neck. "Cindy, you know the rule about visitors." She gestures to a door in back, behind the wall-to-wall clothes organized on racks by color.

Cindy's face falls.

My outstretched hand drops to my side. "What's going on?" I ask, placing my other hand on Cindy's shoulder and forcing myself to meet Ms. White's penetrating stare. "I'm not a visitor. I'm here to donate clothes."

"In that case, let me help you." She steps forward, bending down for the smaller of the two boxes. "Cindy, you know you're supposed to be helping your mom in the storeroom."

"Please . . ." I swallow, trying to cover the squeak in my voice. Now that I've found Cindy and her mom, I have to know what's going on. "I was at the house the night the police came." I drape an arm over Cindy's shoulder.

Ms. White's tight lips relax. The right corner of her mouth turns up a fraction of an inch like she's about to smile, but she catches herself. "You have five minutes." She shakes a gnarled finger back and forth between the two of us. "No contact information, Cindy. I mean it."

I pull Cindy toward a sagging hand-me-down couch beside a shelf of gently used shoes. We sit face to face. I tuck a blonde curl behind her ear while Ms. White wrestles the boxes of Dad's clothes to an already crowded area behind the register.

"I'm a hero." Cindy squirms on the worn corduroy uphol-stery. Her eyes twinkle. She's lost the wide-eyed, ready-to-flee expression I'd become used to.

I place my hand on hers and smile, trying not to rush her but freaking out that Ms. White might run me off before I get the details. "Tell me about it."

"You know Daddy can be . . ." She lifts her shoulders, pausing for the right word and studying her hands. I don't speak, careful not to interrupt her train of thought. ". . . mean." She meets my eyes.

Nodding, I hold her gaze. I don't actually know much of anything about her dad except what I've seen or overheard from next door, but that's irrelevant. Right now, I just want to hear what happened before Ms. White checks her watch.

Cindy squares her shoulders, puffing out her chest. "My teacher said to call the police if someone's in danger. I never called when Dad spanked me, even when it really hurt, but Mommy was bleeding. Bad. So I called nine-one-one."

Her words hit me in the gut, knocking the wind out of me. I blink back tears, berating myself for not doing something to help Cindy and her mom. I saw the bruises, overheard the arguments, and did nothing. That's what I always do— nothing. Well, that and make excuses for why it's okay to do nothing. But this time doing nothing caused both Cindy and her mother harm.

"All the policemen said I'm a hero. Mommy too." She glances over in Ms. White's direction and lowers her voice. "Now we live in a big house with other women and lots of kids. But I'm not supposed to tell anyone where it is."

I shake my head. Here's this little girl defending her mother and standing up to an abusive father, and I'm too much of a wuss to stand up to Maddie or even to face my peers.

Pulling her against my chest, I rest my chin on her head and smooth her hair. "Oh, sweetie, you are a hero." And she is. If I had just one ounce of her courage, I'd be hanging out with Ayla or Chatham right now and taking my best friend with me to school on Monday. I'd be facing life head on like . . . my mom, instead of hiding from the world.

A flurry of activity near the register catches my eye. It's Ms. White waving at someone entering the store from the back. "Yoo-hoo, Chatham, over here."

I freeze, every muscle in my body contracting. Cindy squirms in my boa constrictor embrace. I can't look. I can't look. His SUV wasn't parked out front, right? There could be more than one Chatham. At least two, right? Please, please, please, let there be at least two Chathams on the Outer Banks of North Carolina.

One one thousand. Two one thousand. Three one thousand.

I can't *not* look.

I open my right eye a crack and lock eyes—well, one eye, anyway—with Chatham. *The* Chatham. The one and only Chatham who will ever mean anything to me. I want to run, but I'm trapped on the couch as Cindy slips from my arms.

He pauses halfway up the blue aisle, his jaw firm.

"Chatham." Cindy charges him, wrapping his legs in a bear hug. He pats her on the head and smiles, but the dimples I've come to adore are nowhere to be found.

CHAPTER THIRTY-THREE

Drowning is not so pitiful
As the attempt to rise.

EMILY DICKINSON

I push myself up off the couch. Every cell in my body wants to run. But I force myself to stand my ground. It's not Chatham's fault my life is such a mess.

He's a nice guy. But his jaw clenches as he approaches. I know what he's going to say—that this isn't working, that I lied to him, that he can't take care of someone like me. And I get it. I really do. I just don't want to hear the words.

Cindy smiles. When he bends down and whispers something in her ear, she skips toward the back of the store. Halfway up the aisle, she turns to me. "Come back and see me. Okay?"

I smile and wave, not sure whether I'm trying to reassure her or myself.

Chatham steps forward. "Emilie, we need to—"

"You don't have to say anything." Without my permission, my feet step toward the door. I clutch the handle but force my eyes to his face. He deserves at least that much.

Ms. White clears her throat. Chatham's head jerks toward

her, eyes widening as he obviously remembers we're not alone. I bite the inside of my cheek.

"Please, not here." I flick my eyes in the older woman's direction, hoping he understands how difficult this is for me. If I'm going to get dumped, I'd rather do it in private.

"Then outside." He places a hand on my upper arm. Citrus shampoo mixed with salty air and a hint of chlorine teases my nose.

"My mom's out there." I shake my head, looking away.

"Then where? When?" His grip on my bicep tightens. "You disappear. You won't answer your phone. How are we supposed to talk?"

I shake free, pushing the door open an inch. "What's the point in talking?" I peek out at Mom. She's still on the phone. "Are you really interested in me after what you saw Thursday?"

His lips part, but he doesn't speak for several long seconds. "I don't know."

His words cut like broken glass, but at least he's honest. I've known from the beginning I'm too much work. I never would've expected him to say yes.

I push the door forward a few more inches. Cool, moist air brushes my ankles, and I shudder.

"I might want to be with you if I knew you." He places a hand on the door, blocking my escape. "But you lied to me."

How convenient. Now he can blame the downfall of whatever was happening between us on me. He can kill it with the "You lied to me" line and avoid the guilt of breaking up with the disabled girl.

I sigh. I'm not being fair. That's not why he's doing this. It's because I don't deserve him—not after all that I kept from him and all that I put him through.

"I understand," I whisper. I press my shoulder against the glass door, pushing it from his hands, and trudge toward the Civic. I drop into the passenger seat, and Mom reverses without ending her conversation. Chatham watches as she executes a perfect three-point turn, his shoulders slumped, his lips compressed into a thin, firm line.

I stare out the window and fume—at God for dealing me this crappy hand, at Dad for abandoning me, at Mom for . . . well, for being Mom. And at Chatham—most of all at Chatham—for being too good to be true.

I press my knuckles into my thighs in an effort to refrain from banging my head against the glass.

Mom finally ends her call. "You okay?" she asks, turning toward me.

For a second I want to tell her. "No—yes—I'm fine." I fold my hands together. "I'm just tired."

"You've been through a lot these past couple days. You should probably take a nap when we get home. I've invited Roger to come over for dinner."

The nonchalant way she says it irritates me, like it's assumed I'll be glad to see him. "I don't feel like company."

She presses the power button on the radio with her red nails. "He's not company."

He's not family either, I want to say, but I keep my mouth shut. She's trying really hard—calling a truce on the whole school thing, taking me to breakfast. "Fine. You're right," I mumble.

My insides remain tense, but her hands relax a bit on the

steering wheel. And it feels kind of nice to not be adding to her worries for once. I have no idea how I'll accomplish it, but I'm going to try really hard to be civil when *Rog* arrives.

When we get home, I drag myself to my room. Lost in thought, I fail to acknowledge Hitch. He follows me anyway, sitting beside the bed. Tears sting my eyes. I want to hold them back, but the lack of sleep and the side effects of the extra meds are wearing on me. I'm sick of this life. I'm sick of life. Period.

Hitch whines and paws at the bed when the tears spill down my face.

"I'm sorry, buddy. You deserve better." I pat the quilt, inviting him to join me, and dry my face on the bottom of my shirt.

He grins and leaps onto the bed. When he does, his bushy tail swishes the half-full glass of water I left on the bedside table last night before bed. Water runs into the partially open drawer and trickles to the floor.

I jump off the bed and grab a hand towel out of the dirty-clothes basket as Hitch drops into a down-stay on top of the covers and watches me with remorseful eyes.

"It's okay, love." I mop the water off the tabletop and floor and contemplate ignoring the water pooling in the drawer. Who cares if the seizure journal's ruined? I have to start over now anyway. I pluck it from the soggy mess, carry it across the room, and chunk it in the trashcan beside my desk.

Back at the nightstand, I push the drawer with my hip, but it sticks. Ms. Ringgold would love the symbolism: the drawer that won't budge is a perfect analogy for my clogged-up life. I dig around for whatever's causing the jam. Several thick pieces of paper are wedged in the small space between the back of the table and the back of the drawer.

I draw them out for closer inspection. My breathing catches. Even with the ink smearing around the edges from the spill, I recognize the handwriting. I thought I'd put all the cards and letters from Dad in a shoebox under the bed. But somehow I missed these.

I open the first one. On the cover, a little girl sits on her father's lap. The inside says something about a daughter outgrowing her father's lap but never his heart. My chest hurts like my ribs are pressing in on my lungs. The second—or is it third—round of tears forms in my eyes, and I'm not sure whether I'm crying because I miss Dad so much or because it feels so good to read his scratchy handwriting.

I carefully tuck the card back into its envelope and move on to the next. There's no text on the front, only a picture of early-morning pink skies over Nag's Head Pier. The inside's also blank except for Dad's scribbled note.

He left this one on my pillow one night before bed, shortly after he was diagnosed with cancer. I'd been having nightmares about him dying. He'd tried to encourage me to count my blessings, to be grateful. He'd said his cancer wasn't all bad, that it was a reminder of how short life is and an opportunity for us to celebrate our love and each other. And that's what we did until he was too sick to do anything but lay in bed. The three of us read poetry at night and went for long walks on the beach looking for sea glass. We ate dessert for breakfast and splurged on soft-shell crabs and lobster tails for dinner. I smile at a memory of him and Mom shoving Cool Whip-covered blueberry pancakes into each other's mouths.

By the time I reach the last line, I'm laughing and crying. I reread the last two sentences. *Emilie, when the water gets deep and the current strong, you have to swim. Promise me, you'll swim.*

And God help me, I'd promised. The epileptic who can barely doggy paddle promised her dying father she'd swim. It was a metaphor, right? He didn't actually think I'd swim. Right?

But what Mom and I are doing isn't even doggy paddling. We're treading water in a hurricane, choking on choppy water. Mom's made a few tentative kicks and strokes, but I've been pulling her down. She can't swim because I've tied myself around her ankles like a cement block.

I drop the cards on the bed and shove my feet into the nearest pair of flip-flops.

"Come on, Hitch." He rises, eyes and ears perky, tail wagging.

We pass Mom deveining shrimp in the kitchen. I don't speak.

"Where are you going?" she asks, pinching off a tail and adding it to the massive pile of heads and shells and guts.

"For a walk." I hold the door open for Hitch.

She points at me with her black-plastic deveiner. "Don't be late for dinner."

Tromping down the boardwalk behind Hitch, I avoid Cindy's house looming over me on the right. Guilt nibbles at my guts. That little girl had a lot of horrible things going on in her life, but when the current got strong, she swam. I'm twice her age. It's time for me to suck it up, to take control, and quit rolling with the tide.

By the time I reach cold, hard-packed sand, Hitch is romping in the choppy surf. With the exception of the happy golden retriever, the scenery matches my mood: fifty shades of dreary. Charcoal sand melts into a slate ocean, which blends into a foggy horizon. A brisk breeze lifts my hair off my face, leaving me exposed. I survey the beach. Not a soul in sight.

Hitch seems to sense my dark mood, gives up on his game of chase with the receding waves, and stays mostly by my side. The wind picks up, spraying my cheeks with needle-like shards of seawater.

I clench my fists and look up at the sky. "What do you want me to do, Dad?" I shout.

Hitch's head swivels back and forth in search of danger.

"You want me to swim?" I ask, stepping into the icy water. "Is that it? You want me to swim?" I slog forward.

It's official. I've lost it. My sanity died when I started screaming at a ghost—the ghost of the person I loved more than anything on the face of the planet.

White breakers foam around my calves. For once Hitch doesn't bound into the water. He stands to my right, frozen on the beach, whining. I ignore him, hauling myself farther into the surf.

A large wave knocks me off my feet. I lose a flip-flop and scramble to regain my footing. The toes on my bare right foot dig into coarse sand and crushed shells. I swallow a mouthful of salty water. My eyes stinging, I stumble back toward shore, try to catch myself, but fall flat on my butt. The wave that barreled over me seconds earlier rushes out to sea, pulling me along with it.

And I realize: I could unclench my fists and heart and

go with the flow—let the ocean have its way with me. Mom and Roger could have their happily-ever-after. Chatham could move on to someone else. Someone right for him. Ayla could capture me in her art.

I loosen my grip on the sand, allowing myself to be pulled beyond the white foam and into deeper water. The frigid ocean numbs my pain. Hitch barks and charges into the water. He tugs on the sleeve of my drenched shirt, then retreats when I don't follow and repeats the rescue attempt—bark, charge, tug, retreat—several more times.

He loves me. He's always loved me just the way I am. And if I'm honest and quit being a snot-nosed brat, I'd admit Mom has too.

What if I quit worrying about what people think? What if I wasn't afraid all the time? I'd be happier. I could live my life—really, really live.

Hitch barks like he can read my thoughts.

I brace myself on my arms, hoisting myself out of the sand. The water lifts me. I'm momentarily weightless. I realize I'm floating away from Hitch, and I heave myself over onto my belly and scramble on all fours toward shore. He meets me halfway, pulling me along by my sleeve.

Free of the icy water, I collapse face-first in the hard-packed sand. Hitch crouches beside me, licking and nuzzling my face until I force myself to my knees, wrap my cold arms around his muscular neck, and bury my face in his wet fur.

I pull back till we're eye to eye. "Hitch, I want to live."

He lifts one brow, smiles, then lowers his snout. I'd swear he nodded.

"I love you, big guy," I whisper, glancing out to sea. A sliver of sun peeks through the fog, and I smile, my teeth chattering.

I want to live. And if I want to live, it's time to start making some serious changes.

CHAPTER THIRTY-FOUR

It was not Death, for I stood up . . .

EMILY DICKINSON

I slow from a jog to a walk as Hitch and I head toward home, way too out of breath for someone my age. If I'm going to start making changes, regular exercise probably wouldn't be a bad idea. Studying the sand as it squishes between my toes, I draft a mental to-do list. First, try to be nicer to Mom. Second, replace my favorite flip-flops.

A speck of orange catches my eye, and I blink. I pause, holding my breath. Hitch doubles back to check on me, nudging my thigh with his nose.

It can't be.

I squat, balancing on the balls of my feet, afraid to believe my eyes. A frosty shard of glass glistens against a dark-gray backdrop of wet sand. I reach for it, half expecting it to disappear. It's not a dream. It's sea glass.

Orange sea glass.

I pry it loose, turning it over for closer inspection. It's smooth, almost soft, in my cold palm, sanded and buffed to perfection from tumbling along the ocean floor. The delicate treasure looks more like a shard of orange sherbet than glass.

Finally.

I laugh, holding it up to the sky—to heaven. "Daddy, I found it. I found your orange."

We spent days, weeks, months before his death searching for orange sea glass. Dad so wanted to leave me with the color of hope. We searched and scoured. Mom and I suggested purchasing a piece from a collector. Dad refused, saying we'd find it when the universe wanted us to have it—when we needed it most.

He was right. It's like God or the universe or whoever has been waiting for me to open my eyes. Now that I have, I see beauty and possibility everywhere. I focus on these blessings and . . . *bam*. The universe offers up more beauty and possibility.

I press the cool glass to my lips and hold it up in the fading daylight. "Kisses, Daddy. I love you."

The breeze caresses my cheek like a gentle hand, and I break into a run. Hitch joins me. Minutes later we're rushing along the boardwalk, onto the deck, and through the back door. We cross the threshold into a spotless house. Candles glow on the bar and table. All traces of shrimp guts and shells have been cleared away. The smell of chocolate chip cookies hangs in the air.

"Mom, where are you?" I brace myself against a barstool, trying to catch my breath. "I'm home," I shout. She doesn't answer, so I head down the hall. Hitch pauses to shake, showering the backs of my legs and the floor with a gritty mixture of salt water and sand.

Mom barges out of her room. "Good Lord. What's—" She freezes when she sees us.

I open my mouth, but don't know where to begin. How do I explain to Mom I left an hour ago bitter and lifeless and returned crazy to live? How do I explain to her my out-of-body experience? I can't. I have to show her.

She steps forward, brushing wet, tangled hair off my face. "Emilie, are you okay?"

"Yes. Yes." I wrap her in a wet hug. "Great, actually."

She laughs but doesn't pull away. "What in the world is going on?"

"I just . . ." I let go of her, careful to hide the glass behind my back. "I love you." I meet her eyes. "I love you."

She smiles hesitantly, like I've been possessed by a friendly apparition. Or maybe she's thrown off by the saturated hair and wet T-shirt look in November.

"I have something to show you." I pull my closed fist from behind my back. Her brow creases.

Flipping my hand over, I present the orange treasure. Neither of us speaks for a long time. Then she pulls me in hard against her chest, our hearts separated from each other by only a thin layer of cloth and skin. We don't move or breathe until Hitch stands on his hind legs and weasels his way in for a group hug.

I look at her and chuckle. She belly laughs. Then we're both cracking up—snorting and holding our sides. Hitch smiles, hopping back and forth between the two of us. To an outsider, we'd look happy—normal. Like a family.

The laughing subsides, and I pull her up the hall to the kitchen. Her warm hand clings to mine. She watches as I gently add the final piece to Dad's collection. Tears stream down both our faces. We stand still, clinging to one another. All is silent, except for the ticking clock over the window and the occasional hiss of a flickering candle.

I turn toward her, smiling.

"Emilie?" Her voice cracks.

"Yes?" The single syllable hangs on the air.

"Do you want me to call Roger . . . to cancel?"

Yes. Yes. Yes, my instincts scream. I inhale, counting to ten. She's already given me permission to quit school. Now she's offering to ditch Roger for *me*—at least for one night.

I open my mouth. My breath catches, and I swallow. Candlelight dances across Dad's collection. The orange reflects a ray of ginger on Mom's cheek.

"No, Mom." My shoulders relax. My fists unclench at my sides. "No. Let me take a shower. Then I'll help you with dinner."

She's smiling, but a fat tear rolls down her cheek when she nods.

Someone's flipped Wonderland upside down and is shaking us out, sending us back to the real world—or at least something resembling normal.

"Give me like ten minutes. Okay?" I leave her in the soft candlelight, determined to ignore the nerves quivering in my gut when I think about sitting through a meal with her and Roger.

Dinner is a relative success. I don't roll my eyes at Roger when he holds out my chair or choke on the shrimp scampi when he tells a knock-knock joke that wouldn't entertain a four-year-old. The three of us clean up in the tiny kitchen. I wash. Roger dries. Hitch lays at our feet, and it's really not that horrible. We talk about the weather. Roger admires the beach glass in the windowsill above the sink.

And then he picks up the orange piece with his free hand.

Every muscle in my body tenses. I don't want him touching Dad's things. I turn, ready to pounce. Mom stands behind him, mouth ajar, eyes wide like a bystander at a plane crash.

Awkward silence invades the room. Roger glances from Mom to me and back. From the look on his face, he knows he's blundered, but he's not sure how.

My heart softens. Roger is an innocent victim. He can't know what he's done wrong. He's trying his best.

"The orange is my favorite too." I smile, willing Dad and the universe to take note of my tentative strokes and flutter kicks. I may not make the swim team, but I'm trying.

The tension in the air dissipates. I exhale. Roger and I wipe down the counters while Mom sweeps. They ask me to watch a movie. I decline—nicely. Leave 'em laughing. That's what Granny Day says. I don't want to press my luck on the first attempt, swim out too far, and drown. So I head to my room. Hitch peeks at Mom and Roger on the couch but follows me.

"I put your phone in your room," Mom calls as I close the door.

I haven't thought about it since the game Thursday. When I pick it up, it's almost dead. I check my missed calls—nineteen in less than seventy-two hours. Ten from Chatham. Seven from Ayla. And two numbers I don't recognize.

Chatham called me ten times. There are a bunch of texts too, mostly from Chatham and Ayla. But also one from Ms. Ringgold, wishing me well. And one from Katsu.

My palms sweat at the thought of returning these messages, much less dealing with these people in person. I'm about to tuck the phone into my desk drawer for safekeeping when the swimming promise pops in my head, followed by an image of orange sea glass glowing in cold, slick sand.

Before I can change my mind, I scroll to Chatham's last text and hit Reply.

Hey.

He responds a minute later. Hey.

Well, that went well. I sigh, wondering what I'm getting myself into.

Do you still want to talk? I ask.

Several long minutes pass. I pace the floor, the phone clutched in my right hand. Hitch's head follows me like a spectator at a tennis match. I examine the fingernails of my left hand, contemplate tearing at a hangnail, think better of it, and shove my free hand in my front pocket.

When the phone vibrates, I jump. It slips out of my moist palm. I scoop it off the floor.

Yes.

He said yes. He said yes. He said yes.

I pump my fist in the air while Hitch bounces around my knees. When I throw myself on the bed, phone clutched to my chest, he joins me.

Crap. Chatham said yes. What do I say? I have to respond. When and where? Short, sweet, and to the point. I pat myself on the back.

At school? Can you meet me at
the pool tomorrow morning after
practice? Seven twenty?

School? I collapse onto the pillows while the universe enjoys its sick little joke, then type my response.

Sure.

Here goes nothing. I'm sinking or swimming—literally or figuratively or both.

CHAPTER THIRTY-FIVE

A Wounded Deer— leaps highest—

EMILY DICKINSON

Mom and I both oversleep in the morning. We were up past midnight. I had to tell her my plans for returning to school. The way her eyes bulged out of her head, I thought she might be the one having a seizure. Then she had to email Principal Brown, the counselors, and all my teachers to explain I'd have Hitch with me and to tell them to call her with questions or concerns.

I see only two concerns: One, I'll stand out like a prep at a punk concert with an eighty-five-pound golden retriever at my side. Two, Hitch will lick somebody to death.

When we pull out of the driveway five minutes late, my heart beats in my throat. I texted Chatham to say I'd be a few minutes behind, but he didn't respond. Probably because he's in the pool. Possibly because he's tired of dealing with me and my mistakes. Hitch sits in the backseat on high alert, looking official in his red-and-green canine assistant vest.

"I'll walk you in," Mom offers when we enter the car-rider lane.

I don't want to hurt her feelings after the progress we made last night, but I have to do this alone. "I'll be fine. Promise."

Her jaw twitches. She brakes too quickly, and we both jerk forward against our seat belts. I take a deep breath, unbuckle, and swing my legs out onto the pavement.

"Wait." She places a gentle hand on my arm. "I have something for you."

She opens the console between our seats and pulls out two tiny boxes wrapped in shiny orange paper. They're tied one on top of the other with curly yellow ribbon.

"What's the occasion?"

"No occasion." She leans over to peck me on the cheek. "I just love you."

We both jump when a car behind us honks. I hesitate.

"Take it with you." She presses her hand against my shoulder, gently nudging me out of the car.

I slide the presents into my backpack and step out of the car. The woman behind us holds a massive coffee in one hand and a cell phone in the other. I open the back door for Hitch. Her stern expression softens when she sees his smiling face.

I should've brought him with me to begin with—well, that and been honest with people.

Mom doesn't move until I blow her a kiss and wave her on.

Just like that, I'm headed back to school. A wave of déjà vu rolls over me. The halls are mostly deserted like that first day. But today Hitch's toenails clack out a happy little melody on the tile floor as he accompanies me to the far end of the elective hallway. My pulse throbs in my neck. I try to swallow, but my mouth is dry as toast. Hitch glances up at me, smiling reassuringly, sensing my growing anxiety.

When we reach the pool, the place is abandoned, the fluorescent lights turned off. I'm a few minutes late, but I would've thought someone would still be here or that Chatham would've waited for me. Unless he's tired of waiting on me.

I'm not that late, and swim team did practice this morning, because the cement around the pool is wet. I sidestep the shallow puddles in an effort to keep my feet dry. Hitch wags his tail at the feel of cool water on his paws. Unlike me, the dog was born to swim.

"What am I doing, bud?" I ask, plopping down on the cold metal seat. He rests his head on my knee, whining sympathetically.

I unzip my backpack to check my phone. The overstuffed compartment is crushing Mom's pretty packages. I pull them out. Now is as good a time as any to open them.

Hitch watches as I rip open the paper, then pause before opening the tiny white box. I gasp when I see the silver charm resting on a bed of cotton. It's a lighthouse. I lift it out of the box, turning it over in my hand.

The inscription on the back stills my racing heart. The tiny font reads *He will always light our way.* I swallow, trying to hold back the tears.

The kind gesture, the reference to Dad—both bring me great joy. I'm smiling. But I'm also crying, and my chest is so tight I think my breastbone might snap.

I wad the paper and shove it into my bag before opening the second package. It's my charm bracelet. She must've snuck it out of my jewelry box and wrapped it during the night. There's a little note in her neat print: *I love you. Mom*

It hits me: she's the one responsible for all the charms. I

always assumed it was good-natured, affectionate Dad. If I'd paid attention, I would've known the anonymously delivered charms were more her quiet, reserved way of showing love. She might not be as touchy-feely as Dad, but she loves me.

And I'm going to start showing her I love her.

I hang the charm on the bracelet and clasp it around my wrist, then stow the trash and empty boxes in my backpack. Hitch stands, sensing we're on the move.

"Let's do this, boy." Pushing myself up off the bleachers, I square my shoulders, determined to give this day a shot.

I'm admiring the way the morning sun, shining through the floor-to-ceiling windows, reflects off the water and onto my charm bracelet when my flip-flop hits standing water. My right foot slips underneath me. I swing my arms, trying to regain my balance. I'm going down, and I know it. Hitch plants his feet, ready to break my fall the way he's been trained to do in case of a seizure. But the water messes with his footing too. I hit him at an angle and knock him into the pool.

My temple whacks the concrete, and I hear myself scream. I lay there dazed for a second. When Hitch barks, I push myself up onto all fours, shoving off my backpack. He's swimming in frenzied circles near the ladder. I know he's not afraid of the water. It's my cry and our separation that's freaking him out.

I survey the pool—no shallow end. This is no recreational pool. It's the real-deal Olympic kind and deep—really deep. Over six feet, if I have to guess. I crawl to the ladder.

"Easy, Hitch. Easy." I have to stay calm for him. If I panic, God only knows what he'll do to himself trying to drag himself out. I lay flat on my belly, arms outstretched toward him.

He makes a beeline for me, barking low and deep like he's

in pain. My head tells me he's fine. Goldens were bred for hundreds of years to retrieve ducks in the rough and icy waters of the Chesapeake Sound. An unexpected dip in an indoor pool isn't going to hurt him.

But the panic in his eyes and the way he's swimming with his mouth open causes my heart to race.

"It's okay. It's okay," I repeat, reaching for his front legs and trying to lift him up the ladder. Even if I could dead-lift eighty-five pounds out of the pool—which I can't—there's no way I could lift eighty-five pounds of wet, flailing golden retriever.

I have a good grip on his left forearm, not his right. But I dig down deep, grunt, and heave. He shrieks when I yank on the left leg.

Crap. Crap. Crap. I hurt him.

"Hitch, I'm sorry."

He leans to the left on the next circle.

A scream rises in my throat, but I hold it in. He'll flip. And if I leave him, I don't know what he'll do. His eyes are bugging, and every time he barks, he swallows pool water.

Can't someone hear him barking?

I have to do something, so I kick off my shoes, suck in a deep lungful of air, and slip into the pool. The cool water takes away my one good breath. I gasp, moving my arms and legs instinctively, doggy-paddle style like I did in first grade. For the millisecond it takes Hitch to reach me, I think my rescue attempt might work. I might be able to swim.

He's leaning to the left but smiling as he closes the short gap between us. When he reaches for me with his good paw, his claws tangle in my wet shirt, pulling me under.

I choke on the chlorinated water but somehow drag myself

to the surface. We inch forward. The six feet to the ladder shouldn't be a big deal, but it feels more like six miles. My arms and legs scream. I tread water and cough, trying to expel the pool water from my lungs, and form a plan. Hitch turns on me, concern etched in his face. If I don't do something fast, he's going to reach for me again.

And that is not an option.

It's a recipe for disaster.

CHAPTER THIRTY-SIX

A charm invests a face—

EMILY DICKINSON

Hitch, freeze!" It's not a command I've used often, because he's so well behaved. We've certainly never practiced it in the water. But it is a command the canine assistant trainers teach for emergencies like this when a dog is in danger. He looks skeptical, but he does what he's told, struggling to tread water despite his injured leg.

I'm not used to being on this side of the rescue team, but it's my turn. I have to do something. So I kick like I've never kicked before and pull with my arms the way Dad instructed when I was little. Hitch whines when I pull away from him but stays in place. My fingers brush cold steel and I latch on for dear life.

Without releasing my death grip on the ladder, I turn back to Hitch. "Hitch, come," I say, trying to control the panic in my voice. As he approaches, I wrap one arm around the side rail and brace my foot on the bottom rung. With my free hand, I tap the top step the way I tap the couch or the car seat or wherever I want him to jump. Of course he can't jump, but he is able to snag the rung with his good paw.

My teeth chatter as I contemplate my limited options.

Dragging him out was an epic disaster. I can't imagine how my releasing the ladder and pushing him upward will go any better, but it's the best I've got.

"Watch me, Hitch," I say, my chest aching from the water I swallowed or fear or both.

As I loosen my grip on the side rail, one of the heavy metal doors whooshes open. "Anyone in here?" Chatham calls.

I open my mouth to scream but break into another fit of coughing. Hitch barks frantically.

Flip-flops slap the wet concrete. "Emilie? What the—" Chatham reaches down to help me.

"No." I shake my head. "Hitch is hurt. Help him. Don't pull on his leg."

Without hesitation, he drops to the wet cement. Lying on his stomach with his cheek pressed to the ground, he reaches his long arms beneath the water and grabs Hitch under the arms like a child.

"Look at me," he says, determination etched on his face. "You're going to have to help me get him up." He nods at the silver rail. "But keep one hand on the ladder."

He doesn't have to worry. I'd rather walk across a flaming bed of knives than risk going under again.

Somehow, we hoist Hitch up the ladder and onto the concrete pool deck. He flops on his side, one eye closed, sides heaving, but manages a weak thump of his tail.

I breathe a sigh of relief. "Thank you, Chatham," I whisper, looking up at him without releasing my death grip on the ladder.

"Y'all scared the crap out of me." He gestures to the ladder. "Now, let's get you out of there."

I place my other foot on the bottom rung and reach for his

outstretched hand. My legs shake as I climb. When I reach the top, I crawl over to Hitch.

"Oh, baby, are you okay?" His tail thumps the wet cement for a second before he raises his head to kiss my cheek.

Chatham squats beside us, resting a hand on my back. "He's okay. Are you?"

"Yes."

"Then come here." He pulls me to my feet, then to his chest for a hug. When he squeezes me, my wet body melts against his. I tilt my head to look up at him. His lips part. A bead of water hangs on his angular jaw.

Hitch sighs, dragging himself up on his three good legs. Once there, he shakes, showering us with gallons of wet-doggy water.

Chatham laughs and pulls me to the metal bleachers, where we sit more on Hitch's level. Hitch rests his tender front leg on Chatham's lap and delivers a nice, big kiss on the lips. Chatham chuckles, wiping his mouth with the back of his hand.

I grab him by the collar of his wet T-shirt. "My turn." I smile, pressing my lips to his quickly, then pull back. I'm a changed person after my near drowning in the pool and my icy dip in the Atlantic yesterday.

But we still haven't had a chance to talk. After the fiasco at The Potter's House, Chatham probably wants nothing to do with me. I hang my head, shivering now that the adrenaline's wearing off.

"Hey, I helped saved your life." He grins, hauling me closer. "I'd think you'd be a little more appreciative."

He traces the outline of my lips with his pointer finger, then leans in to brush the corner of my mouth with his own, his breath warming my cheek. My hands reach for the back of his neck, tangling in his wet hair.

He pulls back, studying my face. "Are you sure you want this?"

"Yes." I've never been so sure of anything in my life. "Yes. Are you sure *you* want this?"

"Yeah. I'm sure," he says, his mouth centimeters from my lips.

"How do you know?"

"I've known since the second day I saw you."

I study his face, wondering for a moment if he's teasing me. Since the second day? I don't even remember what we said or did the second day I knew him.

"Yep." He pulls me farther into his lap. "You had me with the *Ferris Bueller* quote. I knew then you were smart and funny. Somebody I wanted to get to know better."

I try to maintain eye contact, but my gaze keep dropping to his lips. If he doesn't kiss me—really kiss me—I'm going to self-combust. I pull his mouth to mine, greedy. I tell myself to keep my eyes open, to memorize every detail of his face, but reason disappears when he kisses me long and slow.

Hitch barks. Our eyes pop open, and we disintegrate into a fit of laughter. I've laughed more in the last forty-eight hours than I have in the last four years.

When the bell rings, we scramble into high gear—gathering shoes, finger-combing our hair, wringing water from our clothes.

Chatham's eyes travel the length of my body. "We're going to have a lot of explaining to do."

I shrug. For once in my life, I don't care what anyone else thinks.

CHAPTER THIRTY-SEVEN

Triumph—may be of several kinds—

EMILY DICKINSON

We wait near the double doors for the hall to clear. As we rush to Ms. Younghouse in the clinic, Hitch barely favors his left leg. It seems like he just needed a few minutes to recover from the panic caused by my fall and the shock of me almost ripping his leg out of its socket.

Nurse Younghouse clucks like a mother hen when she sees our wet clothes and forces us into spare PE uniforms she keeps for dress-code violations and emergencies. While our things tumble in a dryer in the back room, she swaddles us together in a cotton blanket. We're two shivering caterpillars crammed in one cocoon, and I must admit it's pretty cozy.

Ms. Younghouse rubs Hitch with a thick white towel, paying special attention to his ears and tail. Just to be safe, she tapes a couple of ice-filled sandwich bags around his leg. "How long were you under?"

"It couldn't have been more than a few seconds." I concentrate on her eyes, willing myself not to blink. "I promise."

"She was above water when I came in." Chatham crosses his heart with his finger. "Scout's honor."

"Okay, Emilie. But I still have to call your mom." She reaches for the cordless phone on the desk behind her.

Chatham squeezes my shoulder while I fiddle with the charm bracelet dangling from my wrist. Ms. Younghouse delivers a quick recap of what happened, reassures Mom I'm in good condition, then hands me the phone.

"Are you okay?" Mom asks, her voice squeaking on the last word.

"I'm fine, Mom," I promise. And I am.

"I'll be there in fifteen minutes." Her voice is muffled like she's holding the phone to her ear with her shoulder and digging in her pocketbook. Keys jingle in the background.

"No, really, I want to stay."

Ms. Younghouse and Chatham watch my face expectantly.

"Okay . . ." Mom doesn't sound confident. "If you're sure."

"I'm sure." I glance down at the lighthouse charm hanging from my wrist. "And Mom—"

"Yes?" she answers before I finish.

"I love you."

"I love you too." The smile in her voice reminds me of that Dickinson quote Chatham and I annotated what feels like ages ago—the one about not living in vain if you can stop one heart from breaking. It feels good to be mending Mom's heart for once instead of breaking it.

I agree to meet her in the pickup line after school and hang up.

Ms. Younghouse leaves to collect our clothes. Hitch pads along behind her, completely recovered from our ordeal. Chatham rests his head on top of mine.

"I thought you weren't coming this morning." I break the silence.

"I waited." He pulls the blanket tighter around my waist. "You didn't show and Coach Carnes wanted to see me."

I deflate a little, my shoulders hunching. "Are you in trouble with the team because of Thursday?"

He waits several seconds before responding. "I'm not on the team."

What? How? "This is my fault."

"No." He hooks my chin with his finger, turning my face toward his. "I told Coach I was finished."

"You can't quit. Your dad will flip."

"I'm *not* a quitter." A two-dimple, full-on smile lights his face. "I made a choice. I chose to focus on what I want: to focus on swimming." He kisses the tip of my nose. "My dad can deal with it. Besides, this way we might actually get to see each other once in a while."

The hummingbirds are back, swarming in my belly. "But you said everything between us was built on lies." My voice catches.

"You wouldn't answer my calls or texts." His smile falters. "I was mad. And confused."

"What about my seizures?" I whisper, unable to meet his eyes, picking at a loose thread on the blanket.

"Let's focus on what we can control and worry about the other stuff later." He squeezes my hand.

"You're right." I rest my head in the hollow beneath his chin and close my eyes.

Ms. Younghouse breezes in with our clothes. "Okay, love-birds. It's time to get y'all to your next class. The bell's going to ring in ten minutes."

She releases us and we head toward Ms. Ringgold's class. The room looks empty, but the lights are on. It's her planning period. Chatham knocks.

"Come in," Ms. Ringgold calls.

Chatham eases open the door. She's at the back of the room, rotating potted plants near the window. As soon as she spots us, she rushes over, dropping to the floor in front of Hitch, scratching him under the chin.

"Well, aren't you handsome?" She makes kissy faces at him. Hitch eats it up, smiling from ear to ear. "Hi, to you too, Emilie." She pushes herself off the floor and hugs me. "Welcome back."

"I'm glad to be back." I lean into her hug. "Is it okay if we hang out in here till the bell rings?"

"Absolutely. I'm just debudding the violets." She points to a ceramic pot at the end of the row. I'm pretty sure it's the plant I noticed drooping a week ago. She pinches a purple bloom near the green leaves, snips it off in one quick motion, then tosses it into an empty coffee cup. "So, Chatham, your grades have improved recently," she says, beaming and plucking another bloom from the plant.

"Thanks to my new tutor." He drapes an arm across my shoulders. It feels natural, like the indentation under his arm was carved out and custom sized to fit me. My spine straightens.

Ms. Ringgold nods, shifting plump leaves out of the way to reach another bloom. She glances up and catches me staring.

I point to the flower. "You're ripping off the blooms."

She smiles, her eyes twinkling. "No. I'm pruning back old growth to make room for the new. It'll come back even healthier with more blooms in a couple of weeks. Watch and see."

The bell rings. Maddie and a few chatty girls stumble into the room. When they see us, their voices drop several notches. My stomach drops even further.

"Y'all see me after school if you need me. Okay?" Ms. Ringgold says, heading to her desk, ready to start class.

Chatham and I slip into our seats in the back. A few people glance at me and Hitch but look away. Their eyes dart around the room, looking at the floor, the whiteboard, out the window—anywhere but at us. No one acknowledges me until Ayla walks in. She sees me and stops, her face expressionless. I smile and wave, praying she doesn't pretend I'm invisible like the rest of the class.

She hesitates. For a second, I think she's going to ignore me, and I wouldn't blame her. Then she blinks and smiles. I can't explain it, but I just know things are going to be okay with us.

She hurries over. "I've been trying to call you." She bends down to hug me and Hitch.

"I know. I'm sorry . . ." What can I say that won't sound like an excuse? "There's been a lot going on."

Ms. Ringgold claps her hands and clears her throat. "It's going to be a great day, guys. We have a new student." She smiles at Hitch. He beams, his tail thumping the tile floor.

Derek laughs and tilts his chin at me and Hitch in greeting. Nobody else moves or makes a sound.

"I'll save you a seat at lunch," Ayla whispers, turning toward her desk.

Chatham tugs on her paint-splattered sleeve. "Save two."

Ayla steals a glance at me. I nod.

"Okay." She smiles, then heads to her desk. "See y'all at lunch."

Ms. Ringgold points at the board. Wild red hair bounces around her face. "We're going to try to get through a few more American-author presentations today." She surveys the room. "Any volunteers?"

No one breathes. There's enough nervous energy in the room to ignite an electrical storm.

I peek over at Chatham. He raises an eyebrow. A mischievous smirk dances at the corners of his mouth as I raise my hand.

CHAPTER THIRTY-EIGHT

I read my sentence—steadily—

EMILY DICKINSON

"Excellent." Ms. Ringgold waves me and Chatham to the front. She scurries to her desk, turning on the projector and pulling up the slideshow we emailed her last week.

Chatham waits for Hitch and me to make our way up the tight row before following us. We take our places—front and center, Hitch on my left, Chatham on my right. I try to swallow, but my dry throat constricts. Hitch sits beside me, his leash slippery in my palm.

I'm supposed to start with Dickinson's biography. Chatham's going to analyze a poem. We're supposed to close with a famous quotation or short reading.

The clock above the board behind us ticks. Hitch nudges my trembling thigh, shaking me out of my deep freeze. My mouth opens. "Emily Dickinson is probably America's most famous female poet. Partially because of her unique voice and style. Partially because of the mystery surrounding her reclusive nature."

Ayla perches on the edge of her chair. Ms. Ringgold clicks her keyboard, and a grainy black-and-white photo of a plain woman appears on the screen, accompanied by a bulleted list of biographical information. *Date of birth—1830. Date of death—1886. Education—Mount Holyoke and Amherst Colleges.*

The knots in my throat and stomach loosen as I talk. A girl I don't know in the middle row smiles. I'm pretty sure I make eye contact with a guy in the back.

Ms. Ringgold forwards to the next slide. I'm supposed to be talking about Dickinson's personal life—how she was called "The Myth" by her neighbors because she chose to stay secluded in her father's home and entertained very few visitors. But I go rebel. Before I can stop myself, I'm digging into rumors surrounding her health.

"A popular biography published in two thousand and ten suggested she might have suffered from epilepsy." I pause, waiting for my peers to acknowledge me. The second hand ticks. Maddie makes eye contact. The girls, who have been following her lead, look up. "Some of you might have seen what epilepsy looks like if you were at the game Thursday."

No one moves. Even Ms. Ringgold is frozen—speechless.

"I have seizures." There, I said it. I inhale, pausing to choose each work carefully. "I'm not mentally disabled. I'm not possessed by demons." My voice rises. "And, no, I'm not contagious.

"It's like an electrical disturbance in the wiring of my brain. That's it. Otherwise, I'm normal. And I don't want to lock myself away from the world like Emily Dickinson because my epilepsy makes me and other people feel uncomfortable. Not anymore."

Chatham reaches for my hand, lacing his fingers with mine. I square my shoulders.

"I want to be in control." My voice shakes. Hitch nuzzles his head under my free hand, encouraging me. "I want to be a part of this school. If you're interested, I'll tell you anything you want to know, so you don't have to be afraid of me or anyone else who has epilepsy."

I've laid my heart on the line, and all it's earned me is a bunch of blank stares.

Chatham releases my hand. "I don't know about y'all, but I don't feel like talking about meter or syntax after that." He chuckles, but his weak attempt at humor sails over the heads of the audience.

Everyone looks to Ms. Ringgold. She blinks several times, presses her lips into a thin line, and shakes her head. I'm pretty sure it's not the fluorescent lighting that's making her eyes water.

"Then let's close with an excerpt from our favorite poem." Chatham steps toward the class, sweeping an open arm in my direction. The boy knows how to work a room.

All eyes are on me. My lips part. "'Hope' is the thing with feathers—" My voice shakes. I start over.

> "'Hope' is the thing with feathers—
> That perches in the soul—
> And sings the tune without the words—
> And never stops—at all."

I finish loud and strong, hoping for some positive reinforcement—maybe a few smiles or a thumbs-up. But my classmates just stare.

Tears sting my eyes. My vision blurs. I bite my lip. I absolutely refuse to cry in front of these people. The old Emilie would bolt right about now. The new Emilie stands her ground, glancing around the room. Ayla and I lock eyes, and she smiles.

A slow, methodical, *clap*-pause-*clap* sounds to my left. I survey the group for the random applause giver.

It's Maddie.

Our eyes meet, and she stands, clapping louder and faster. Ayla stands to join her. The rest of the class follows. Chatham wraps his arms around me, his heart beating against mine in an iambic tetrameter that would make Emily Dickinson proud. Hitch barks, and the room erupts in laughter.

Dickinson was a genius. I totally get what she meant. Hope *is* a thing with feathers. It's fluttering inside of me right now like hummingbird wings. Maybe that's what's been there inside of me all along: hope.

As Chatham, Hitch, and I return to our seats, people pat my back. Someone ruffles Hitch's fur and congratulates us as we weave our way to the back of the crowded room.

I wish Mom could see this.

Or Dad.

I slide into my seat. The charm bracelet jingles on my wrist. I remember the inscription on the back of the lighthouse.

He will always light our way.

And he did today. He lit my way with industrial strength, thousand-watt bulbs, and I love him.

The class finally settles down, and Ms. Ringgold spends the rest of the period talking about the significance of poetry and prose to enlighten audiences. She keeps referring to how I was able to use Dickinson's theme of hope to deliver my message today.

With the exception of the near drowning this morning, today has been amazing. In World History, Maddie tells me her cousin has epilepsy. She thought I did a really great thing explaining my seizures to our peers. It's one more reminder of how self-absorbed I've been. Thank God I've learned my lesson.

Chatham sits with the lit-mag crew at lunch. Ayla and I make plans to hang out this weekend.

But the highlight of the day is walking out of seventh period with my best friend leading the way in his green-and-red vest and Chatham waiting outside the door to walk me to the car-rider line.

"I could take you home." He slings my backpack over his right shoulder, pulling me into his side with his left.

I smile. "I know. How 'bout tomorrow? I need to talk to my mom today."

We push through the front doors. She's first in line.

Chatham kisses me on the cheek in front of God and everyone. My heart beats out a little happy dance inside my chest. I could still seize at school or with Chatham, but somehow I feel like now that my secret's out in the open, I can handle it if I do.

He opens both passenger-side doors for me and Hitch and greets Mom.

"Thanks, Chatham." She leans across the console to speak to him.

"Any time." He shuts the door.

I roll down the window. "Call me later. Okay?"

"Okay." He waves as we're pulling away.

"How was your day?" Mom asks, turning left onto the bypass.

Hitch lays down on the backseat, exhausted from watching over me all day.

"Great." I turn toward her in my seat. "The bracelet helped."

She keeps her eyes on the road but takes one hand off the steering wheel to squeeze my arm. "Good."

The sun gleams on the hood of the car. I inhale, basking in the moment. The world is full of opportunity, like the open sea. My heart is light—lighter than it's been in ages—floating on a wave of possibility.

Mom and I needed to reset our course. Now that we have, we're ready to buoy one another, ready to dive back into life—ready to swim.

Acknowledgments

This book has been a lot like a team sport. It never would have made it to the big game without coaches, cheerleaders, trainers, equipment managers, teammates, and of course a few fans.

First, thank you, editor extraordinaire Jillian Manning. You had a vision for Emilie. Her story is a thousand times stronger because of you. I am forever grateful to everyone on the Blink/HarperCollins team.

Also, thank you to my dream agent, Amanda Leuck. Without you, this manuscript would be collecting dust under a bed or wasting space on a hard drive.

Thanks also to my lovely critique partners, Kim MacCarron, Holly Bodger, and especially Amy DeLuca, who has been with me since day one. I'm forever grateful to Alan Arena, who gave up coveted video game time to read for me, and to Nancy Jackson and her red pen. And thanks to Laura Baker and her Discovering Story Magic classes.

This book would not have been possible without my Georgia Romance Writers and Romance Writers of America tribes. Thanks especially to Sia Huff, Tammy Schubert, and of course my 2014 Dreamweaver and 2016 Mermaid sisters.

Then there are students past and present who cheered for me and loved me as much as I loved them. Wildcats, Raiders, Mustangs, and War Eagles, look at my face. Thanks for making me want to come to school every day and for not complaining when I dinged you with the occasional flying Starburst.

Finally, thanks to my supportive family. I have the best mother-in-law and father-in-law a girl could dream of and a stepfather who is also a friend. My brother, Mickey, and sister, Nicole, always believed in me. My parents, Emilie and Roger, loved me unconditionally. My children, Beattie and Trey, loved me and didn't complain too much when I sat hunched over the computer for hours on end.

And of course, every strong team needs an even stronger head coach. My husband, Dusty, is the real thing at work and home. He teaches middle school and coaches basketball and deserves all the credit for keeping the crazy team that is our family together as I write.

Thank you all from the bottom of my heart and God bless.

The Thing with Feathers
Discussion Questions

1. Emilie is set on keeping her epilepsy secret. Why do you think she fights so hard to keep her friends from knowing about her condition? If you were her, would you do the same? Why or why not?

2. When Emilie first meets Chatham and Ayla, she stereotypes them based on their appearances and her first impressions. Discuss a time when you stereotyped someone, or a time that someone judged you before they got to know you.

3. Hitch and Emilie share a special bond. Consider your own relationship with animals. Have you ever experienced this kind of connection? If so, when?

4. Chatham tells Emilie that people should share their gifts with the world. Do you have any gifts that you choose to keep to yourself? Do you know anyone who does? Why do you think someone would keep a gift worth sharing to herself?

5. Each chapter of the book opens with an Emily Dickinson quotation. Choose your favorite chapter and discuss how the quotation relates to the story and to Emilie's character.

6. Relationships are often tricky. How do Emilie's relationships with Ayla, Chatham, and her mom create internal and external conflicts?

7. To protect her secrets, Emilie sometimes finds herself lying to those closest to her. Have you ever told a lie to protect yourself? What happened as a result?

8. Emilie overcomes her fear of heights when she climbs Bodie Lighthouse. When was a time you pushed beyond your limits and experienced success?

9. Emilie is a changed person by the end of the story. Consider how the tone of her body language and words changes from the first to the last chapter of the book. What physical and emotional evidence do you see to prove this change in Emilie?

10. Emilie eventually learns to believe in hope, and even embraces it as a theme for her life. If you could write a theme for your own life, what would it be?

If you loved reading
The Thing with Feathers,
turn the page for a sample from
McCall Hoyle's next book,
Meet the Sky!

CHAPTER ONE

So many worlds, so much to do,
so little done, such things to be.

ALFRED, LORD TENNYSON

Once upon a time, I believed in fairy tales. Not anymore. If Prince Charmings and happily-ever-afters were real, I'd have a godmother and a fancy dress. Instead, I've got a pitchfork and a pile of horse manure.

Don't get me wrong. I'm thankful for what I have. I'm thankful for the rumble of the incoming tide in the distance. I'm thankful to live on the barrier islands of North Carolina, which might be as close to heaven as anyone on earth will ever get. But I'm also realistic. I overslept this morning and have a tight schedule and five more stalls to clean before school. The smallest complication can knock my entire day out of whack, and when that happens, it affects the horses and what's left of my family. That's why I'm sprinting behind the bouncy wheelbarrow like I'm competing in some kind of *American Ninja* manure challenge.

"You okay, Mere?" I call over my shoulder as I dump the wheelbarrow full of dirty wood shavings on the manure pile.

"Yes," she answers from inside the barn. Her voice sounds the same as it always has. It's about the only thing in our lives that's still the same, though. This time last year, Meredith was applying to Ivy League colleges, helping me with the barn, and dancing her heart out. Since the accident, she's content binge watching *Full House* episodes and sitting alone in her room. Whether or not she believes it, she needs me. Mom needs me too.

And I will not complain. Ever.

Pushing my shoulders back, I drop the pitchfork into the empty wheelbarrow and march back up the little hill to the barn. Jack, the old sorrel gelding in the first stall, whinnies when I reach the concrete pad in front of the double doors. I need to keep moving. Any minute now Mere will have had enough. She'll be too hot or too tired and need to head back to the house. But I can't resist the old guy. He's been part of this family longer than I have.

Leaving the wheelbarrow in the middle of the aisle, I head to his stall. His ears perk up as I pull two carrots from the back pocket of my faded jeans. For just a second, his whiskered muzzle tickles my palm, and I forget the chores I need to finish before school. But not for long. When I glance out the opening at the back of his stall, the morning sun reflects off the dunes. It's going to be brutally hot in another hour. With a sigh, I give Jack a quick scratch under his forelock and return to the wheelbarrow.

I peek in at Mere each time I pass the tack room. She sits in a straight-back chair in front of a row of saddles and bridles. Her hands lie motionless in her lap as she stares at the blank wall in front of her. When I finish the fifth stall, I stand the wheelbarrow beside the pile of wood shavings at the back of the barn, then hang the pitchfork on the wall. Brushing my hands on my jeans, I head to Mere in the tack room and run through my mental checklist of assignments due today at school—an illustrated timeline for US History, annotations for English, and a translated paragraph for Spanish.

When my boots hit the hardwood floor, Mere blinks but doesn't move. "You okay?" I ask.

She shrugs.

I reach for her blonde braid to give it a gentle tug, but she slouches lower in her chair. I let my hand fall back to my side. Her thick hair reminds me of Dad's. She got his movie star good looks, complete with square white teeth and defined cheekbones. I, on the other hand, inherited more of Mom's girl-next-door vibe—pretty on a good day, but not startlingly so like Mere.

"Who colored that?" She points to a page torn from a coloring book that's pinned to the corkboard on the wall above the saddles.

"You did, with one of the tourist kids last year. Remember?" I shouldn't have said the *remember* part. She's sensitive about being forgetful.

Shaking my head, I try not to stare at the colorful picture. A little over a year ago, Mere colored every speck of the princess's skin neon green and her long hair violet. Pinned up beside the princess is a coloring page of a castle. I colored that one with the same little girl.

It had been raining that day, and Mere and I were supposed to entertain the kids of the family waiting to ride horses on the beach. The girl had painted the sky above the castle rosy pink. I'd colored the individual stones a bland gray and had never once gone outside the lines.

"I don't remember," Mere says, closing her eyes and resting her head against the back of the chair.

It's best just to let it go, so I don't say anything. I reach for her Pop-Tarts wrapper. "Let's pick up, okay?"

Mere nods and brushes a few crumbs from the table at her side to the floor. I double-check the latch on the feed cabinet before we head out. We can't afford a repeat of the mutant-mouse infiltration we experienced a few months ago—not with Mere's physical and occupational therapy bills stacking up on the kitchen counter. As I turn back to Mere, a cat brushes my leg and meows.

"Oh, Jim—" He stares up at me with pitiful eyes, balancing on his three good legs. His fourth leg hangs awkwardly above the floor. I doubt we'll ever figure out what took his paw. He waves the knobby leg at me when I don't move, clearly hoping I'll acknowledge his cuteness and whip out the cat treats.

Meow. "Come on, sweet boy." I lift the lightweight cat into the crook of one arm and scratch him under his orange chin. Mere finally gets up and walks over to nuzzle her cheek against Jim's. When he purrs, his whole body vibrates. He reaches toward Mere with his nub of an arm, and she and I both giggle.

I set him on the counter, then grab an empty bowl and the plastic tub of cat food from the overhead cabinet. When the first bit clinks the bottom of the metal bowl, he digs in.

"Okay, Mere, let's get you back to the house." I squeeze her hand and lead her toward the sandy hill that separates our house from the barn.

As we climb the steps to our cottage on stilts, I'm careful to position myself behind her in case she misses a step. She holds on to the stair rail, carefully planting one foot and then the other on each step. It's hard to believe this is the same girl who literally pirouetted and plié-ed her way through life, that all that muscle coordination and grace could be ripped away in an instant.

I sigh as the sun rises off to the east over the Atlantic. Swirls of pink and orange mingle with the occasional wispy cloud, kissing the gray-blue water where they meet on the horizon. The brushstrokes of color take my breath away. They're almost beautiful enough to make me believe in fairy tales again.

Almost.

I wipe a bead of sweat from my forehead as I reach for the doorknob. Despite the colors whirling in the sky and the grumble of the distant surf, the air has been oddly still the last couple of days. There is no rustling of sea oats today, not even a hint of a breeze. And it's hot. And humid—unnaturally so, more like July than October.

"That was quick," Mom says as we enter the kitchen. She turns down the volume on the weather radio she's been listening to 24/7 since a tropical depression formed out in the Atlantic three days ago. As the screen door bangs shut behind us, I realize a wave of bacon-y goodness fills the kitchen.

"I used my super manure powers." I swoosh my arms back and forth, ninja style.

A faint smile lights her face as she stands perfectly still, her metal tongs hovering above the frying pan. Her small frame and light-brown ponytail are identical to mine. In fact, people used to confuse us for sisters. But now her skin has lost its healthy and youthful glow. My chest tightens at the sight of the furrows in her forehead, deep enough to grip a pencil.

"You're working too hard, Sophie. I wish we could afford to hire someone."

If Dad hadn't left, she wouldn't have to worry about me. Before the accident, Mom ran the business side of things—answered the phone, paid the pills, advertised on social media, even dealt with finicky customers looking to purchase once-in-a-lifetime memories for themselves and their children. With Dad gone, the place was going downhill—fast. I might be a manure master, even a veterinary technician in a pinch, but I wasn't that great with hammers or handiwork. Last year, we had tourists lined up months in advance. Now, people could show up unannounced and pretty much be guaranteed a ride.

When the grease in the pan pops, Mom and I both jump.

"I told you it's not a big deal. I've got it." Mere and I wash our hands at the sink, then I hand Mere a pillow from the nearby couch as I guide her toward the breakfast table. She grips it against her chest. Somehow squeezing an object against her core improves Mere's balance—something to do with centering or activating one side of her frontal lobe. Plus I think the velvety texture soothes her somehow.

Mom has good intentions with the whole let's-find-someone-to-help-around-the-barn project, but she's living in a dream world if she thinks anyone would shovel horse poop and haul hay bales for what we could afford to pay anytime in the near future.

"Someone moved into the cottage near the dunes," she says as she flips a piece of bacon.

"Mmm hmmm." I grab three plastic cups and a carton of OJ from the fridge and head back to the table.

Mere smiles when I approach. I unfold the cardboard spout and fill her cup.

"I'm pretty sure it's the same family that used to live there. What was their name?"

My hand jerks. Juice splashes Mere's arm, and she gasps. Mom turns around to see what happened.

"You okay?" she asks.

"Uh, yeah."

I scurry toward the sink for a towel. I'm being silly. First, it's probably not the same family. Second, even if it is, it's not a big deal. So what if I had the crush-to-end-all-crushes on Finn Sanders. So what if he said he'd meet me at homecoming and didn't show. It was freshman year. It was a crush. It wasn't like we were together or anything. It wasn't even a real date. But it was still humiliating. Yesenia and a couple of other girls came over to my house ahead of time. Mere did our hair and makeup. They were as excited as I was. Then he didn't show, and I spent the night acting like I didn't care.

Even if it is Finn, he and I have no reason to interact or cross paths now. We became friends in middle school when we were dumped into the morning chess club together; the school had to do something with us since our moms dropped us off so early. Finn and I became obsessed with beating each other and with putting our heads together to beat Mr. Jackson and his Dutch Defense. It was surprisingly fun. But that was years ago. I can't even remember the last time I played chess or thought about Finn.

"I just drew a blank. What was the boy's name? Jeff?" Mom lays the last slice of bacon on a paper plate to drain.

"Finn. His name's Finn." I dab Mere's placemat and arm with the towel while she hums a piece of music she danced to a couple of years ago.

"That's right—Finn. Maybe he'd like to earn a few dollars helping around the barn." She brings the bacon and a plate of blackened toast to the table, and I do my best not to sigh.

"I've got it, Mom. I promise." I try not to sound concerned as I slide into my seat and reach for a piece of toast. I really don't want her asking me why I'm not eating, but suddenly a flock of seagulls is swarming in my belly.

"Something will work out. It has to. You can't keep going like this." She pushes the plate of bacon toward me.

She's the one who can't keep going like this. But instead of arguing with her, I bite into my dry toast and try to swallow my feelings.

"I bet you'll see Finn today. You could ask him about it."

Or not.

My throat tightens around the single bite of toast as I twist my lips into a smile and check the time on my phone. I have precisely twelve minutes if I'm going to leave on time.

I may not be able to leave home a year early for college like we'd planned. I may not be able to follow my dreams of veterinary medicine. But I can control one thing. I can control whether I talk to Finn Sanders.

And let me assure you, there won't be conversation or anything else going on between us.

Meet the Sky

McCall Hoyle

With nothing but pain in her past, all Sophie wants is to plan for the future — keep the family business running, get accepted to veterinary school, and protect her mom and sister from another disaster. But when a hurricane forms off the coast of North Carolina's Outer Banks and heads right toward their island, Sophie realizes nature is one thing she can't control.

After she gets separated from her family during the evacuation, Sophie finds herself trapped on the island with the last person she'd have chosen--the reckless and wild Finn Sanders, who broke her heart freshman year. As they struggle to find safety, Sophie learns that Finn has suffered his own heartbreak; but instead of playing it safe, Finn's become the kind of guy who goes surfing in the eye of the hurricane. He may be the perfect person to remind Sophie how to embrace life again, but only if their newfound friendship can survive the storm.

> "Meet the Sky *is an endearing story*
> *about how love can help us weather*
> *the storms of life.*"
>
> — Katie McGarry, acclaimed
> author of *Breathe*

Available in stores and online!

McCall Hoyle writes honest YA novels about friendship, first love, and girls finding the strength to overcome great challenges. She is also a high school English teacher. Her own less-than-perfect teenage experiences and those of the girls she teaches inspire many of the struggles in her books. When she's not reading or writing, she's spending time with her family and their odd assortment of pets—a food-obsessed beagle, a grumpy rescue cat, and a three-and-a-half-legged kitten. She has an English degree from Columbia College and a master's degree from Georgia State University. She lives in a cottage in the woods in North Georgia, where she reads and writes every day. Learn more at mcallhoyle.com.